RABBIT MOON

JAN D. PAYNE

Marin Sinclair: Book One

This project was made possible by a grant provided by the Five Wings Arts Council with funds from the McKnight Foundation.

FIVE WINGS
ARTS COUNCIL

MᶜKNIGHT FOUNDATION

First paperback edition July 2024

Book edited by The Story Laboratory
Book design & production by Domini Dragoone
Cover Image "Road to Jupiter" Courtesy Charles Ruscher

ISBN 979-8-9910625-9-6 (Paperback)
ISBN 979-8-9910625-0-3 (eBook)

RABBIT MOON

PROLOGUE

"They were killing dogs the day my father and I arrived on the Diné reservation," Marin said, and the woman in the leather armchair glanced up. "I was terrified my dog would be killed. Doesn't it seem to you, Doctor Lippmann, that I should be having nightmares about *that* rather than about something that never happened?"

Dr. Lippmann wrote a few words in a notebook and looked up at Marin. "Our subconscious doesn't always make sense in our waking life," she said and paused. "Killing dogs?"

"Stray dogs tend to run in packs, kill the sheep."

"These dogs are not part of your recurring dream then, Ms. Sinclair?" she said, looking at her notes.

"No, the dream is the attack by the eagle…forcing me to jump from the mesa cliff," Marin said. She kept her voice steady, but the doctor looked up.

"That must be terrifying," she said, and Marin swallowed. "And the eagle has the face of your friend—Vangie Tso—correct?" the doctor said, writing the name in her notebook.

"It's T-s-o," Marin corrected. "Vangie is Diné…Navajo, and yes, the eagle has her face," she said, rising from her armchair and crossing to the tall windows along one wall.

It was early summer outside, the strong Arizona sunshine streaming through the glass, and Marin put her hand on a warm windowpane. In a small park below, there were new leaves shining green on the cottonwood trees and a young boy and a big dog playing a game of fetch.

Marin longed to be outdoors herself. She'd spent most of the past six months inside, caring for Mark. A fresh stab of grief turned her away from the window and back to the room.

"Shooting dogs doesn't seem to fit with the picture of a government school," Dr. Lippmann was saying, and Marin let the silence lengthen before she spoke, not sure what she wanted to say. It was impossible to explain her life there in a way someone like this, in a place like this, would understand, but she'd promised Mark she would try. She returned to her armchair, resigned.

"I know Mark Winfield asked you to see me as a favor," Marin said, "and I promised him I'd come, but I'm just not sure that...that any therapy will help. "I do appreciate your seeing me, though."

"Give us a chance, Ms. Sinclair. It's your first visit. Mark was a wonderful man, and he spoke very highly of you. I was saddened to hear of his death. You made the final months of his life bearable in so many ways."

"Mark made my life bearable as well," Marin said.

"Let's begin again, Ms. Sinclair...a quick review of what Mark told me would be a good place for us to start, don't you think?"

"Please call me Marin," she said.

"And I am Elizabeth...Mark called me Lizzy," the doctor said and laughed.

"You don't seem much like a 'Lizzy'," Marin said, smiling.

"I'm not. It's probably why Mark did it. So...tell me, Marin, how long have you worked as a..." the doctor paused, looking at the notebook.

"Doula," Marin said. "I'm an end-of-life doula. I work through an agency here in Flagstaff."

"How long have you worked as a doula?"

"Almost five years," Marin said.

"Mark said you cared for your father?"

"Yes, until he died...Alzheimer's disease."

"And you're how old? Thirty? Thirty-one?" Dr. Lippmann asked.

"Thirty-one," she agreed.

"Mark said you're not married. What about family or other relationships?"

"Friends at work, and my clients," Marin said. "No relatives still living. I'm an only child...my parents married late in life."

Dr. Lippmann wrote another few lines in the notebook, and Marin rose, walked back to the windows.

"Things are much the same way here, in Flagstaff," Marin said, and Dr. Lippmann looked up.

"The dogs, I mean, animal control. The animals are put down here as well, we just don't see it."

"I can certainly see why you were afraid your dog would be killed..." Dr. Lippmann began.

"There weren't animal shelters," Marin said. "No vets or doctors—no dogcatchers, no trash pickup—no stores except a trading post several miles from the school."

"I've heard...disparaging things about the BIA schools," Dr. Lippmann said, and Marin met her eyes.

"Touchy subject?" Dr. Lippmann asked. "I understand almost all the boarding schools were closed years ago."

"It was for the better," Marin said.

"That sounds rather fatalistic. People of diverse cultures have lived together quite successfully throughout history."

"I guess that depends on who you talk to," Marin said.

"Were you happy there?" Dr. Lippmann asked.

"Happy enough...though I did accuse my father of moving me to Venus."

Dr. Lippmann raised an eyebrow.

"The surface temperatures and atmospheric pressure on Venus are so high that anything foreign is instantly melted and crushed," Marin said, turning back to the window. The boy and the dog were gone now, and the small park was empty.

Dr. Lippmann filled two teacups and gestured to Marin to come and sit. "Melted and crushed...strong words," she said. "Your father didn't help you adjust to your new life?"

"He tried...but I didn't want to be there any more than most of the boarding students did," Marin said, returning to the armchair and glancing at the porcelain clock on the small table. "Before you ask, I never heard of any abuse at the school—though enforced presence is an abuse in itself—and my relationship with my father was good."

"He loved you?" the doctor asked, lifting the pen.

"He did," Marin said. "But a part of him was just gone after my mother's death. It was a part that never really came back."

"Were you angry with him?" Dr. Lippmann asked. "About the move to the reservation?"

"I was at first. Leaving the home we'd had with Mom, moving because of his new job, a new life—it felt like losing Mom all over again."

"Did you tell your father how you felt?"

"I was eleven years old. We didn't talk about emotions. Dad told me to have faith, to carry on, and that things would work out for the best."

"And did they? Work out for the best?"

"I suppose..." Marin said. "I didn't speak the language or under-stand the taboos, the jokes, the way life was lived. If it hadn't been for Vangie Tso..."

Dr. Lippmann picked up a white envelope from the small table. "Mark told me the dream started after receiving this?" she asked, and Marin nodded.

"An invitation to my ten-year high-school reunion. It came about two weeks ago...from Vangie."

Dr. Lippmann opened the envelope and took out the embossed card, reading it while Marin swirled the contents of her teacup, will-ing the session to be over. She didn't need to be reminded of things that happened in the past; forgetting was hard enough.

"It seems straightforward," Dr. Lippmann said, "but Mark said there are inconsistencies?"

"Vangie and I haven't kept in touch, but our tenth graduation anniversary was almost four years ago. Vangie wouldn't make a mistake like that."

"Perhaps this was meant for someone else, a wrong address," Dr. Lippmann said, but Marin shook her head.

"It came to my house...not the agency apartment, but to my dad's house, my house now, here in Flagstaff. Very few people know that address, but it's the one Vangie would know." Marin pointed to a handwritten line following the signature: *Evangelina Tso.* "I recognize Vangie's handwriting...here, where she says 'Marin, please come' but Vangie never called me by my name."

"I understand the oddities, but I'm more concerned about your reaction to them—a recurring nightmare in which Vangie Tso plays an integral part. You said Vangie was a close friend...the two of you didn't keep in touch?"

"My father retired from teaching after my high-school graduation, and we moved here to Flagstaff."

"You chose not to stay in touch?"

"We didn't really choose one way or the other," Marin said. "I moved here, and she stayed there. There was college and grad school... then my dad's illness...we were from different worlds, like I said."

"The two of you were friends. You couldn't bring your worlds together?" Dr. Lippmann asked. "Combine the best ideas and beliefs from both?"

"That's probably the hardest choice of all," Marin said, "and one not often allowed by either side."

"Would Vangie agree?"

"Vangie tried to do exactly that, but death has a way of changing your viewpoint, and there was...a lot of death there."

"Anyone specific?" Dr. Lippmann asked. "You lost someone?"

Marin didn't answer, and the slanted shafts of afternoon sunlight advanced slowly across the carpet as the small clock ticked away the hour.

"I only want to help," Dr. Lippmann said. "Can't you lower your defenses and talk to me? Did something happen to Vangie? To someone else? Suicide perhaps?"

"There's more than one kind of suicide," Marin said, willing the session to be over and her promise to Mark fulfilled. "Drugs and alcohol for instance...they can create a world where you're powerful and in control...but you know this. I'm not saying anything new."

"You've obviously given this some thought," Dr. Lippmann said.

"I lived in a place where it mattered," Marin said.

"The mesa in your dream," Dr. Lippmann said. "Mark said it's a real place?"

"Yes," Marin said. "It's somewhere we didn't go. It's haunted."

"Crying Woman Mesa..." Dr. Lippmann said. "Mark told me the story. A woman who fell to her death."

"Or was pushed," Marin said. "No one knows for sure."

"A rather significant dream to have about a place you didn't go," Dr. Lippmann said, her voice quiet.

"Mark thinks it's a memory," Marin said. "One I've buried."

"Do you think that as well?"

"If it is, I don't know what it could be or why I'm remembering it now. It's been years."

"Mark's coming death may have triggered the dream—the memory," Dr. Lippmann said. "A feeling that things are beyond your control."

"If I felt I had control over anything, I probably wouldn't be here," Marin said.

"We're all emotionally invested in feeling we are in control of our lives," Dr. Lippmann said. "The effort used to try and maintain that control may have disrupted your inner harmony."

"*Hozho*," Marin said. "The way of harmony."

"Yes?" Dr. Lippmann said.

"The Diné belief system, the Beautiful Way," Marin said, "it's a way of living in harmony with yourself and the forces of nature, staying in harmony with the natural rhythms of the world."

"Caring for the dying may give you a feeling of control—you stare into the face of death, defying it, one could say—and that provides you an inurement against death."

Marin almost laughed at how far from the truth that was, but she was so tired...she'd been months with Mark, on call twenty-four hours a day, playing chess with him in the middle of the night or reading aloud to him when he couldn't sleep, coping with his erratic appetite, and regulating the medicines which proved useless in prolonging his life. Now Mark was gone, and she was here as she'd promised, listening to these words about defying death—about guilt, loss, regret—and she was just too tired to decipher them all. Vangie had always told her of the power of the spoken word, and Marin believed it to be true.

"I'm not God," Marin said at last. "There is no such thing as defying death. No matter what I do or don't do, they will die."

Dr. Lippmann nodded, and when she spoke her voice was gentle. "You've worked so hard to shield yourself from death—you lost your mother at a young age, and you grew up in a place where death is prevalent...a place where the suicide rate is eighteen times the national average."

Marin began a protest, and Dr. Lippmann held up her hand.

"No, wait...I just want you to think about your chosen work," she said. "Consider that your work with the dying can also be another shield—a way to resolve feelings of guilt, or even a way to punish yourself. The dying offer you a kind of refuge, a release from any continuing commitment on your part. There is no need for long-term trust, no need to develop or continue a lasting relationship. There's no unexpected loss, and no guilt on your part."

"Meaning I *want* them to die?" Marin said, her face hot. "You think I don't feel pain when they die? I hate the fact that they die, I hate knowing I can never bring them back..."

"Never," Dr. Lippmann agreed, her voice quiet. "Nothing you do—no atonement, no penance, no amount of regret or grief—will bring them back, no matter how hard you try or how many times you try," she said. "Perhaps it's time to forgive yourself for things you couldn't control."

Marin didn't speak, her lips tight, and for several minutes the quiet ticking of the clock was the only sound in the room.

"How many of those dying have you cared for, Marin?" Dr. Lippmann asked. "How many deaths?"

Tears filled Marin's eyes, and Dr. Lippmann spoke again. "You've made an enormous effort to bury your feelings about the past...your mother's death, your feelings about your father, the move to the reservation—those and other felt losses. Other than the clients you work with, are there any personal relationships in your life?"

Marin shook her head. "No. No relationships, Doctor."

"You said you were here because of a promise you made to Mark. What was it?"

Marin sat on the edge of the leather armchair; her fingernails curled into the cushion bindings. Mark had made her promise she would go back and find Vangie...go back and reclaim her life.

"I promised Mark...that I would choose to live," Marin said.

Dr. Lippmann picked up the invitation and handed it to Marin. "Will you go?" she asked.

Marin nodded. "I promised Mark I would try to resolve some things, and I keep my promises."

Dr. Lippmann drew breath as if she wanted to say more, but she paused. "I'd like to prescribe medication," she said. "Your job is demanding an emotional toll on your life, a heavy one."

Marin clinched the armchair bindings until her fingernail beds began to throb. "The pills will numb me to feeling anything," she said. "Feeling bad is at least feeling something."

"Your life should be more than bad feelings," Dr. Lippmann said. "The pills will give you the chance to even out a bit, to reach an emotional ground level. Then you can explore what living means to you and how to get there."

"I'll try," Marin said.

"I'd like to close with just one more thing...The eagle in your dream with Vangie's face—the attack—is it possible those are your feelings toward Vangie...and not hers toward you?"

"I don't understand," Marin said.

"It's *your* dream, Marin, and in it, Vangie attacks you and forces you to jump from the mesa's edge..."

"But—I'm not angry at Vangie...*she's* angry at me."

"Perhaps the anger is something *you're* feeling—an unexpected attack from a friend. An attack which came out of a 'clear blue sky'—the sort of sky one might see over a mesa, maybe?"

Marin was silent, and Dr. Lippmann reached out and touched her hand. "It's just something to think about," she said, taking a prescription pad from a drawer. "I know you are busy with the final arrangements for Mark's memorial service, but I want to encourage you to have this filled...and I'd like to continue these sessions, perhaps once a week? You *have* made progress today, even though you may not feel like that's true. Give yourself time. Give yourself the same grace you extend to those in your care...the same grace I know you extended to Mark."

"I'll call and reschedule later if that's okay..." Marin said.

"Of course," Dr. Lippmann agreed, standing at precisely the moment the small clock began to chime the hour. "Fill the prescription, Marin. I think you'll find it helps."

"Thank you again for seeing me," Marin said, standing and stuffing the script into a pocket.

Dr. Lippmann sighed and walked her to the door. "You said Vangie never called you by your name. What did she call you?"

Marin stepped into the hall and paused between two brass planters precisely positioned on either side of the doorway. She brushed her fingers across a silky palm frond.

"Nightmare," she said. "Vangie always called me Nightmare."

CHAPTER ONE

The eagle's cries and Marin's screams faded, and she opened her eyes to morning sunlight and the breeze moving the bedroom curtains. She listened for the sound of Mark's breathing, but this was her own bedroom and not the armchair at Mark's bedside—and she would never hear his breathing again.

With Mark's coaxing, she'd agreed to see Dr. Lippmann when the dreams had grown more frequent, agreeing to let Mark cover the cost. He'd been certain the doctor could help, and had wanted Marin to be, if not happy, then at least at peace with herself after his death.

"Your psyche is trying to tell you something," Mark had said, tapping her gently on the forehead. "The mesa memory is in there somewhere, trying to get out. My advice is to see Dr. Lippmann, let her help. Then, I think you need to go to this so-called reunion, talk a few things out with Vangie Tso. It's not rocket science to realize this dream-vision thing started after you got that invitation."

"But I don't think..."

"Do it," Mark had said, and tapped his chest. "I can afford it. Dying man here; death-bed request."

Mark hadn't realized Marin's true fear was she was losing her grip on reality, afraid of developing Alzheimer's disease as her father had.

Mark knew Marin had cared for her father at home until his death, but he didn't know everything...how isolated she'd been, unable to maintain relationships with former friends or have a life of her own. Mark came from a wealthy family; he didn't realize how out of reach the expense of a memory-care facility could be, didn't know how she'd depended on hospice visits to have even the free time to shop for food. After her father's death, she had closed the big, Victorian house and contracted with a local agency as an end-of-life doula to make enough money to pay the mortgage and her father's medical bills.

"Any relationships?" Dr. Lippmann had asked.

The doctor hadn't known the irony of her question.

She got up and wandered into the kitchen, standing undecided before moving to fill the coffeepot.

It was always like this afterward, the lassitude, the period when she didn't quite know what to do with herself, making the readjustment to living alone, to being in her own apartment and caring for herself instead of being fully given over to the care of someone else.

"It's *your* dream, Marin..."

"Just something to think about..."

So much for the visit to Dr. Lippmann.

"Nothing like your dream ever really happened?" Mark had asked in one of their last conversations...

"Standing on a mesa ledge and having an eagle dive at me...an eagle with Vangie's face?" she said and paused as if thinking. "I don't think so."

"No need for sarcasm," Mark said. "Obviously it's symbolism. Did Vangie blame you for something?"

"You'd have to know Vangie," she said. "That's not who she is. Vangie takes people as a whole—she doesn't try and change you; she just accepts you. Or she did when I knew her..."

"But the mesa itself, it's a real place?"

"Yes, it's behind the school compound, less than a mile away...but it's a place we didn't go—the mesa is haunted."

Mark leaned forward.

"The story is there was a stand-off on top of the mesa, a battle between the government authorities and a Diné man who had large holdings of land and sheep and horses...and two wives."

"That's allowed?"

"This happened around 1870," Marin said, "around the same time most all of the western tribes had been relegated to reservations...and to your point, the U.S. Supreme Court had only recently ruled polygamy illegal, a criminal offense."

"What a coincidence," Mark said.

"Yes, wasn't it? The Diné man was declared in violation of the new polygamy law...a ruse to get him out of the way to steal the property and animal herds from his wives."

She paused when Mark frowned.

"The Diné are a matrilineal society," she said. "It's the women who own the property and the herds, the women who inherit."

"Ahh...I see."

"So, rather than submit to arrest, and have their large holdings stolen—he took his wives and children to the top of the mesa and made his stand there when the authorities came to arrest him. There was a gun battle, and...'"

"He died there with his family," Mark said.

Marin shook her head. "No, he lived. According to the story, one of his wives jumped from the rim of the mesa to her death, and that ended the standoff."

"He wasn't prosecuted?" Mark asked.

"No, they returned home, kept their holdings."

"One of his wives jumped...voluntarily?"

"That's debatable. Her ghost, her *chindii*, has haunted the mesa ever since; you can hear her crying when the wind blows—which is always—so the mesa is called 'the woman who stands and cries' or, in English—"

"—Crying Woman Mesa," Mark said, and took a breath. "So...it's... haunted?"

"Haunted," Marin agreed. "I've heard her crying."

Mark frowned. "You said you didn't go there."

"We didn't," Marin said, her words slow. "I'm sure we didn't— *chindiis* are evil ghosts—no one went up there." She shook her head.

"I'm probably confusing it with some other mesa we climbed. No shortage of mesas on the rez."

"Except this mesa was close to the school, and you said you heard her crying," Mark said. "Sounds like the same one to me."

"You hear that moaning sound all the time…it's the wind blowing across the erosion cavities, the rock-pipes, in the sandstone. The holes have differing lengths, and they sound like organ pipes when the wind blows across them. Vangie and I used to crawl under the sandstone slabs to hide from Bailey, and we'd call or whistle up through them, but Bailey was a smart dog. She found us every time."

The coffee maker beeped, and Marin filled a cup. She missed Mark, her own apartment seemed lonely and stark after the months spent in Mark's home, where his own paintings on the walls reflected his artist's love of light and color.

She had one of Mark's paintings in the Victorian house, but there weren't many personal items here in the agency-provided apartment. A bookcase holding her father's books and the photograph of Bailey and Edison were almost the only signs the apartment wasn't for rent by the week. She was rarely here, so the decor hardly mattered.

No, Dr. Lippmann, no relationships.

Another stab of sorrow went through her at the thought of Mark, one more loss she had been helpless to prevent.

How long could she continue to do this?

She'd been caring for the dying for years now, and each loss added to the one before it, heaping another weight of sadness to a load she could barely carry. Despite what Dr. Lippmann had said, she had developed no inurement to death, her care for the dying hadn't made her tough; it had made her realize she was no more than a flag-bearer on a battlefield, watching the dying fall. How much insight had she gained over the years? About life? About herself? About God?

The God Mark had believed in so firmly.

Mark had tried to help, had tried to give her a part of his own faith, his assurance in the goodness of God, but Marin knew from years of experience that faith is necessary for the dying.

For the living, it comes harder.

She brushed at her tears. Dealing with death and dying was her job—had been for a long time now—and she had no use for maudlin sentimentality in herself or in others. Mark had certainly not had any for himself. Even near death, his faith had been strong, his concern not for himself but for others, for her.

The arrangements for Mark's memorial service were made, she needed only to make a phone call to put the preparations into motion. She would call Mark's family as well, give them her condolences, but not now.

"Do you keep in touch?" Mark had asked her toward the end. "You know, with the family?"

"Yes, I keep in touch. For a while anyway."

"Good," he'd answered. "You know my dad and I aren't close, but my mom will need you."

She'd smiled, but the reality was that after a death she was an unwelcome reminder of dark days, and no one had ever 'kept in touch' with her, or she with them.

She took her coffee to the bedroom and picked up the invitation on the nightstand. She'd promised Mark she would go, and she intended to be well on her way to Shiprock before the heat of the summer day set in, but she read the card again, whispering the words to herself and studying the formal signature—Evangelina Tso—underlined and in Vangie's remembered handwriting.

Vangie would know Marin would catch the significance of using her name, of using both their names, but that didn't explain why a woman as strong as Vangie Tso needed her help.

Please come, Marin. I need to see you.

The entire invitation was a mystery, for besides the fact that she and Vangie had not graduated in the year stamped on the invitation, and their tenth anniversary had passed several years ago, the address for the reception was odd as well—she'd looked it up and found it was the address for the county courthouse. Why hold a reception in a courthouse?

She and Vangie may not have seen or spoken to one another for years, but there was no reason to think Vangie wouldn't remember things from their shared past.

Things like Vangie never, ever, calling Marin by her given name, or addressing herself, ever, as 'Evangelina Tso.'

In Vangie's world, names were earned, and most everyone had more than one: names given in private naming ceremonies, names referring to birth clans, nicknames given to describe or to tease, but one name rarely used was the formal name listed on a birth certificate.

Those were kept in a drawer for legal purposes.

Marin replaced the invitation on the nightstand and again heard Dr. Lippmann's questions.

"You and Vangie Tso. Were you friends?"

"To live, Marin. What do those words mean to you?"

"What do you want from your life, Marin?"

She looked at the picture on the nightstand—Edison, sixteen years old and down on one knee, smiling beneath his red baseball cap, one arm around Bailey's ruff and the dog smiling a wide, doggy smile.

What did she want...

Family, home...a place to belong. All those things and one impossible thing more.

"I want things that have happened not to have happened," she whispered.

She replaced the photograph and pulled a canvas duffel bag from under the bed. No use feeling sorry for herself, and she began to pack for the weekend.

Nights were cold in the desert, and she pulled her old field jacket from the closet, running her hands through the pockets and finding a pair of gloves. It wouldn't be quite that cold in June—and she turned to toss them back in the closet before she saw it wasn't gloves she held, but a hat.

A baseball cap of soft red wool. Edison's cap.

When had she last seen this?

Not for ten years or more considering the hat was stored in a box in the back of her closet—certainly *not* in her jacket pocket.

Pushing aside winter sweaters and scarves she needed to pack away for the summer, she reached for the closet shelf, feeling for the box of keepsakes she kept there, things she didn't use but couldn't bear to throw away.

The box was there and seemed undisturbed.

She pulled it down and lifted the lid.

Nothing was missing as far as she remembered...nothing but Edison's ball cap.

She backed out of the closet and looked around the bedroom.

All appeared as it had moments before, but she walked around, looking under the bed and under the nightstand, alert for any differences she might not have noticed earlier.

She thought about the fact that she hadn't been in the apartment for anything more than to change one set of clothes for another since she began caring for Mark, and she hadn't worn the field jacket since... when? March?

There was no way to know when the cap had been put in the coat pocket.

Maybe she'd knocked the box onto the closet floor and didn't notice.

And then what? The cap jumped into the pocket?

Had she asked anyone to check or clean the apartment and forgotten?

No.

Maybe the landlord had come in, but he would have said he was coming, and certainly it wouldn't be to rummage through a box in the back of her closet.

Someone put that cap in her jacket pocket, a cap she hadn't worn for years—someone who had thought she wouldn't wear the coat again until cold weather.

She walked slowly around the apartment.

Nothing else seemed to be out of place, and suddenly she was scared.

What if she had put the cap in the coat pocket herself and didn't remember she'd done so?

Oh, God...

No, she told herself sternly. She hadn't done it herself.

A row of books on the hallway bookshelf caught her eye, and she picked up a slender volume of Shakespeare lying on its side.

Something out of place, after all, and her scalp tingled as she opened the book, letting the pages fall where they would, reading the familiar passages she'd read to her father almost daily during his long illness. Like music, Shakespeare's words had soothed him, calmed his constant agitation, the fear.

"There where I have garnered up my heart, where either I must live or bear no life..."

Othello's cry of anguish for a ruined faith, a lost love.

Edison's hat and now her father's treasured book, two items from lost loves of her own, two items she certainly would not have moved.

She snapped the book shut and replaced it on the shelf, suddenly in a hurry.

She should probably stay and call the landlord about changing the locks, but she'd promised Mark she would go to this reunion, and she kept her promises.

The faces of Edison and Bailey smiled up at her as she snatched up the duffel bag and the field jacket, and she gave the photo another glance, then stuffed both it and the baseball cap into the bag.

Her truck was parked in the garage at the Victorian house, and she'd intended to go over and pick it up, but she paused at the curb and decided to rent a car instead. Someone had searched her apartment, and they might or might not be aware of the Victorian house.

She preferred, suddenly, to be anonymous for this trip, and went back inside to cancel the cab. Instead, she called a nearby rental agency before calling the landlord and arranging to have the locks changed.

She closed and locked the apartment door behind her, not certain that locking it mattered, and walked the few blocks to the car rental agency.

In the bright sunlight of a summer day, it was easy to believe she was overreacting, easy to believe her doubts were the result of working long hours or her grief at Mark's death, except that now there was another piece to add to the odd reunion invitation.

Edison's red cap.

An overweight man stood behind the counter at the car rental agency, a half-smoked cigarette propped on the edge of a full ashtray.

"Can I help you?" he asked, glancing up.

"I called about a car," she said, and he looked closer at her face.

"Hey, I know you," he said. "You're the woman had your picture in the paper. You take care of that rich guy's son, the kid who's dying… Now, what is his name?" he said, looking at the ceiling.

"My picture was in the paper?" Marin said, surprised, but Mark was from a prominent family in the area.

"Yep. I saw it right here, couple of days ago."

He continued talking when she didn't answer.

"Great pic of you by the way, with your long blond hair and pretty face." He winked and brushed cigarette ash from his shirt.

"About the car…" Marin began.

"Winfield!" the man said, banging his hand on the counter, and Marin flinched. "I knew I'd think of it."

He paused, looked at Marin.

"Aren't you his nurse or something?"

"Or something," she answered. It might not have been such a good idea to rent a car after all.

"Paper says the kid's a goner but maybe he'll last long enough to throw some of daddy's money in your direction, right? He's sure got plenty," he added, and he laughed, his necktie knot bouncing below his florid face.

"Maybe I'd better just go..." Marin said, turning toward the door.

"Yeah, yeah...the car. I get it. Give me a minute. You only called five seconds ago...no need to get touchy."

Cigarette smoke curled toward her as the man reached into a wire basket and slapped a form on the counter.

"I need your license, and you gotta sign this insurance and liability form," he said, shaking out a fresh cigarette. He lit up as she read the agreement, and after a minute, he spoke around the cigarette. "It's your standard form...no hidden catches or anything."

Marin nodded and continued reading.

"It's a perfectly *standard* agreement," he said again, and she picked up the pen to sign.

"I like to read what I sign," she said and pushed the form across the counter.

"Poor kid, though," he said, taking the form and exhaling smoke in her direction." We all take our chances in this world...right? Win a few, lose a few."

Marin refrained from telling him the certainty of death was hardly a matter of taking one's chances, but she retrieved her driver's license as he consulted a list and tossed a set of keys with a numbered tag on the counter.

"I didn't mean nothing by what I said earlier," he said as she picked up the keys and turned to go. "About the kid and all, I mean. He a relative of yours?"

"He was family, yes," she said. "You might want to think about getting a checkup yourself," she added, looking pointedly at the ashtray before she turned to the door.

"Me? I'm healthy as a horse," he said.

"We all take our chances," she said. "Win a few, lose a few."

The rental car lot was almost full, and she walked along the rows slowly, looking for the parking spot matching the number on the tag, thinking about her name and picture in the paper and uncomfortable with the information. It wouldn't take much effort to come up with her apartment address, or to call Mark's family for the information after seeing her picture in the paper.

Another piece to add, but the big question was: why break into her apartment at all if theft wasn't the motive?

She found the parking space matching the number on the key tag, and she stopped and checked it again, walking around the car and debating whether to go back in and exchange it.

The red, low-slung sports car was brand-new and nowhere close to inconspicuous—she might as well spray-paint *TOURIST* on the hood and be done with it if she drove this across the reservation. She looked underneath—the car's clearance couldn't be more than a foot or so—it would never handle any dirt roads.

She'd have to go back in.

Her inner voice spoke up in protest, reminding her of her promise to Mark to rethink her old views, to start enjoying her life, and she reconsidered.

Like so many of her clients, Mark had walked fearlessly into death, leaving her with the stern admonition she was not to mourn his release from this life, or to feel regret about him in any way.

The rental was for the weekend only...and she didn't plan on driving unpaved roads, something which would void the insurance agreement.

Mark would have approved the red sports car for this trip, and she unlocked the door and slid behind the wheel.

CHAPTER TWO

THEN:
Sheldon and the Snake

The sky was a deep blue bowl tipped atop the browns and reds of the earth and Marin Sinclair, a resident at the BIA school compound as of three weeks ago, had never seen a sky so blue or earth browns so vivid.

A massive flat-topped mountain—a mesa, her father told her—rising to the south dominated the landscape, its red cliffs soaring into the sky with curls of white clouds floating above.

Birds—hawks or maybe eagles—circled the boulders around the mesa's base, riding the air currents to hang in the sky, floating there motionless for minutes at a time before catching another draft of wind and rising higher.

She sat on the steps of the stucco house she and her father had been assigned to and studied the mesa. Its heights called to her, presented a mystery, some secret of earth and sky she could only understand if she was on its top.

She had tried climbing it twice in the past two weeks, going over the stile across the compound's fence and setting off cross-country to the foothills of the mesa, but both times she was unable to discover a way to the top.

The boulders, heaped in tumbled piles around the base of the mesa, were stacked only about halfway up the sheer rock walls stretching into the sky, but she'd found no way to scale the wall itself. She was sure there must be a way up, a path leading to the top if only she could find it.

She sat with Bailey and considered the flat-topped mesa until she heard someone shuffling across the dirt that passed for their front yard.

Sheldon was coming.

Over the past two weeks, the staff houses had begun to fill as the teachers returned for the new year, and she and her father had met most of their new neighbors—but there was no one her own age until Sheldon Ellis arrived for a two-week visit with his aunt and uncle, teachers who lived next door.

Sheldon Ellis was from Kansas City, and he made it a point to say he was only visiting here. To Sheldon, this was just another summer vacation, and he would soon return to the *real* world, as he called it—which was Kansas City and nothing like here. Here the nearest town was miles away and entertainment was limited to a good imagination and hikes to the trading post—and even the post was four miles away.

Unlike Marin, Sheldon didn't have to learn how life was lived here, he could afford not to care one way or the other, and Marin envied him that; so far, her life here was scary and lonely.

And very real.

There was no one she could talk to about her fears, for though her father assured her that notices were sent out in advance when men were going to be shooting the stray dogs, she worried about Bailey and never let her go outside alone.

"Sheep are a cash crop on the reservation," her father had said. "Once a pack begins killing, they don't stop, Marin. It's done to prevent rabies outbreaks, as well."

Marin understood the possibility that the strays might form packs and kill the sheep, she even understood sheep were important here, like her father said, but it was hard not to get attached to the strays—most of them were friendly and wanted to be around people—but a dog was rarely lucky enough to be adopted by a family.

Sheldon was not someone she could talk to about any of this...as companions went, he was mostly just someone very trying to be around.

Marin did have to admit there wasn't much wrong with Sheldon's imagination. His first day here, he had gone snake-hunting outside the compound fence and caught a rattlesnake by means of a leather loop on the end of a long pole.

He'd even gone so far as to carry the hanging snake onto the school playground, holding the pole high so the kids on the playground could get the full effect of the long, writhing body.

It was a typical Sheldon thing to do, self-important and brash, and he'd only done it because he wanted to show off. Like now, strutting across the yard, whirling a lasso over his head...

"Look what I caught!" Sheldon called, twirling the snake. "I'm going to milk the fangs and sell the venom!"

She was on the swings, winding herself in circles until the chains were tight, and she let go and saw blurred snatches of Sheldon and a twisting snake whirling past.

"That snake is poisonous!" she shouted.

"Of course, it's poisonous!" Sheldon yelled back. "How else do you think I could get venom out of it!?"

Sheldon flashed past twice more, long enough for her to see the frantic contortions of the snake's body and Sheldon's expression as the snake managed to twist out of the leather thong cinched below its head.

She tried to stop the swing...

By the time she came full circle, the snake was wrapped around Sheldon's forearm, and he was shaking his arm frantically.

She pushed out of the swing, landing near Sheldon at the same instant the snake shot off Sheldon's arm and landed in the dust underneath the swings.

There was a wild scramble from the swings to the merry-go-round, and Marin pulled Sheldon onto it as well. All of them clustered tightly in the center while Marin waved her arms to get the attention of the other kids on the playground.

"Snake!" she yelled, pointing, and there was another scramble, this time for the street curb.

The snake coiled beneath the now empty swings and vibrated, the rattles shaking furiously and the triangular head weaving back and forth seeking something to strike.

Marin looked around for Bailey.

The dog was sitting on the curb, her tail wagging and nose sniffing with interest at all the bare feet suddenly nearby. Any second now Bailey would find Marin wasn't there and would come running over.

"Sheldon," she said, taking his arm, "you caught it once, you have to catch it again."

But Sheldon was staring at the snake, seemingly mesmerized by the weaving motions of the head and the vibrating rattles.

"Sheldon!" she cried. "Before it bites somebody!"

"No way," he muttered. "I'm out of here…"

"Use the stick, Sheldon," Marin urged, gripping his arm so he couldn't run. "The pole," she said into his blank stare, pointing.

The pole lay on the ground between the merry-go-round and the swings, and Marin stretched out on her stomach and tried to reach it.

The snake's head bobbed toward the movement of her hand, the forked tongue flicking to taste the air, the body so exactly blending into the color of the ground that the buzzing noise seemed to be coming from the dirt.

"I can't reach it," Marin said. "You'll have to try for it. You're taller."

"It's a tether pole, not a stick, and you can't make me," Sheldon said, pulling his arm from her hold, and this time the snake struck out at the movement before instantly returning to a coil.

Bailey barked and started across the playground.

"No, Bailey!" Marin ordered. "Stay there. Stay!"

She turned to Sheldon. "You can do it, Sheldon. You did it before."

Bailey took a few steps closer, slowly wagging her tail as if questioning this new game.

"Please Sheldon!" Marin said. "I'll help you. I'll help you get the stick!"

"I won't do it," he said, shaking his head.

"Sheldon, you are going to be in big trouble if that snake bites somebody. They'll...they'll probably arrest you. And you'll never see Kansas City again. You have to get that stick!"

Sheldon narrowed his eyes, but he lay down and stretched out one hand. Marin gripped the back of his shirt as he reached for the pole, his hand trembling. The snake trembled as well, searching for a target with its darting tongue, the rattlers one loud, continuous buzz.

"You can do it, Sheldon," Marin whispered.

Sheldon hooked the leather loop of the pole with the fingers of one hand and slowly drew it toward them.

"Good, Sheldon, good," Marin breathed, as he sat up, the stick in his hand. "Now for the snake. Hold the loop over its head..."

"I know that! Don't let go of me," Sheldon said, rolling back onto his stomach, and he took the pole in both hands and stretched it out, positioning the leather loop above the weaving head. The rattles vibrated, and the pole in Sheldon's hands shook as he eased the loop over the snake's head.

"Hurry, Sheldon," Marin breathed, her hand twisted in the back of Sheldon's shirt as the loop inched lower.

"Gotcha!" Sheldon crowed, yanking the loop tight and coming to his knees. Triumphantly he lifted the snake into the air, and Bailey ran toward the writhing body, barking.

Marin collapsed against the merry-go-round, one hand on Bailey's collar. "Hold onto it this time," she said faintly.

"It's just an old snake," Sheldon jeered, but Marin could see the color returning to his face.

The kids on the playground lost interest after the snake was caught, and they returned to pushing each other on the merry-go-round or spinning in the swings. A few came over to stare at the snake, but no one seemed especially disturbed, and no one had gone for help. Only Bailey still stood rigid, watching the snake's twisting body and barking until Marin hushed her.

"What'll you do with it?" one of the kids asked Sheldon.

"I'm going to milk it for the venom," Sheldon declared, but Marin figured it was more to save face than to have anything more to do with the snake.

As it turned out, when Sheldon's uncle found the snake, he put it into a glass jar and filled the jar with water. He also took away the pole with the leather loop.

Later Marin had studied the dead snake in the jar, examining the curved fangs with the small venom holes and the short, jagged teeth lining the inside of the jaws, and for a few nights, she'd dreamed about the snake, dreams where the snake bit Bailey and Marin was unable to save her.

Sheldon told her a few days later he didn't think a rattlesnake bite was all that poisonous but conceded that a bite could have serious consequences since they were so far from a hospital—which was not the case in Kansas City.

CHAPTER THREE

▲▲▲

T he car handled nicely, and the air smelled of mountain juniper as Marin left Flagstaff, the highway stretching ahead like a promise and the desert rolling on either side of the small red car in waves of brown, red, and purple.

The Painted Desert. It was incredible that such vivid color could be produced by such a mundane mineral compound as iron hematite.

The summer sun blazed from a sky of cobalt blue, and the air quality was so sharp she could see the San Francisco Peaks on the western horizon as if they stood no more than a stone's throw away.

During the years they'd dated, Edison had tried to teach her the Navajo names for all the sacred mountains that defined the boundaries of *Dinetah*, the homeland of the People, but she'd had trouble with the difficult pronunciations. The Diné name for them began with a "D," and she tried to coax the name from her memory. She knew the English names, knew the La Plata mountains of Colorado bordered Navajoland on the north with Mt. Hesperus, and she listed off the others in her head.

To the east, Blanca Peak, and to the south, Mount Taylor. The San Francisco Peaks of Arizona made up the western boundary.

"Doko'oosliid," she said out loud when the memory came, the phrase meaning 'the mountains fastened to the earth with a sunbeam.' She said the word again, pleased she had remembered, though the memory reminded her of Edison.

It was hard not to think of Edison Washburn on this drive into the past. Edison, who had left the reservation and lost his identity, and she herself, who had left to try and find one. She would do well to remember that, to keep in mind this trip was not an attempt to recapture something she'd never had.

The sun was strong, the glare reflecting off the bright hood of the car, and she pulled the red baseball cap from the duffel bag, assuring herself she needed it to shade her eyes and not because she wanted a part of Edison with her.

There was little traffic, the highway stretching ahead for as far as she could see, and the rolling pavement was visible all the way to the horizon. The sports car was fast and fun to drive, and she reveled in the forgotten joy of driving fast on the reservation's long highways.

She turned on the radio, and a voice shouted out that she was listening to the "station of the Navajo Nation" in Window Rock, Arizona, and she hummed along as she drove, listening to the local announcements in both Navajo and English, pleased to have found the remembered station.

The highway ahead disappeared into a sheen of watery vapor as she topped a steep hill, and she descended into the *Fata Morgana* mirage—common in the desert—made of temperature, sun, and steaming tar. Inside the mirage, the shimmering waves held the distorted outline of a large bird, its black wings spread wide, the long wingtips a wavering fringe of black.

She waited to see the reality emerge as she drew close—probably a hawk or an eagle with a kill—but as the heat waves resolved, the image became not a bird as she'd expected, but a man. A man walking along the shoulder of the highway, dressed in jeans, boots, and cowboy hat.

He probably wanted a ride, but the man made no effort to flag her down, and he couldn't miss seeing her. This deserted stretch of road seemed an unlikely place to hitchhike—she was miles out of Flagstaff—but the west, and especially the reservation, was ever deceptive in its apparent emptiness. He could be expecting someone.

He watched as she drew close, pushing his hat back from his face, and at last he put out a thumb.

He was an older man and Diné, his gray hair yarn-wrapped in the traditional *tsiiyeel* at the nape of his neck, and she passed him before she slowed and backed up. The practice of giving someone a ride, if you could, was one she'd grown up with, and she'd been on the receiving end more than once.

"I'm headed that-a-way..." the man said, jerking his thumb.

"Any place in particular?" she asked.

"*Tó Naneesdizí*," he answered.

"Tuba City is on my way," she said, and he smiled, his eyes cornered in a web of lines.

"You don't look like reservation," he said.

"I was once," she said, surprising herself. "This car's rented. I left my old *chidi* at home."

"Never hurts to have company on these roads," he said, his black eyes bright, his smile almost mischievous.

"I was planning to stop at the Trading Post in Cameron, get something to eat," she said. "Still interested?"

"Best green chili stew on the rez," he said as he opened the passenger door. "Their frybread's not bad either."

She drove on, listening to the radio as the miles passed, the man seeming content to ride without talking, until eventually she topped out on the long hill sloping down to the town of Cameron.

The view again claimed her attention, and seemed to claim her passenger's, too.

"Never gets old," he said, and Marin agreed.

She slowed to drink in the breathtaking panorama, the desert unfolding to the horizon in sheets of brown...to the west, the road to the Grand Canyon, and to the east, the Little Colorado River, its waters blinding bright and spanned by the old railroad bridge at the bottom of the hill.

Her passenger hadn't offered his name as they drove, and she didn't ask for one—names could be a tricky thing on the rez and not easily offered to strangers—but she told him hers and he offered his hand.

"Nice to meet you," he said, sliding his palm lightly across hers in the Diné way. "I'm Lewis George."

She was surprised at his ready offer of a name, and he smiled again. "You don't look much like a wolf-witch," he said.

"And you don't look like the skinwalker/hitchhiker in disguise," she said.

"Nope," he agreed. "I guess our names are both safe."

"You live in Tuba City?" she asked, and he shook his head.

"Just visiting," he said.

"I'm headed to Shiprock," she said. "Visiting a friend."

"Long way away," he said, and she laughed.

"I'm reservation, remember? I should be there for dinner."

"Kentucky Fried Chicken," he said, and she laughed again.

"Sounds like you've been there."

He nodded, patted the dashboard. "This baby should get you there fast," he said.

The old Cameron trading post, made of thick, weathered blocks of sandstone, was set back from the road near the river bridge, and its stone walls blended into the landscape as if part of the ground itself, shaded and partially hidden by a green cover of slender globe willows.

She parked near a sign advertising live rattlesnakes, and they headed for the roofed porch, pausing to look at the tangle of coiled snakes resting in a large glass terrarium and covered with a meshed screen lid.

Snakes...

"I wouldn't touch that if I were you," Lewis George said, tapping the back of her hand.

She blinked, her hand hovering just above the mesh lid, and she snatched it back, horrified. "I hate snakes," she said.

"Snakes can hypnotize you," Lewis said. "Make you sick in your spirit if you touch them."

"But... I've never wanted to touch them," she said.

He shrugged, making no comment, and they went inside, through the trading post and into the attached restaurant.

The stew and frybread was as good as she remembered, but she didn't eat much as the snake incident had unsettled her. She didn't remember reaching toward the snakes...didn't know why she would.

Lewis George's appetite made up for her own, and he finished Marin's meal as well.

"I wouldn't worry too much about it," he said.

Lewis George held the door open for her when they left, keeping his back to the glass case and hiding the snakes from her view, though she told him it wasn't necessary.

"Snakes can be sneaky, it's best not to give them any ideas," was his answer, and together they walked back to the car.

It was hard to leave the shining river behind as they left the Trading Post and crossed the bridge toward Tuba City, and she drove slowly, fixing the bright strip of water with the trestle bridge into her memory and keeping the view in her mirror as long as possible.

"Beautiful," she said. "I never get enough."

"The river has looked the same for hundreds of years," he said, looking out the window. "Or so they say," he added when she looked over.

"You're an interesting person, Lewis George," she said, and he raised his eyebrows and smiled.

She took a last look in the mirror, and instead of the river she saw the shiny chrome grill of a large truck almost on top of the small sports car.

Lewis George glanced over when she hissed an expletive, and he turned to look.

"This guy must want to pass real bad," he said, and Marin began to slow, though she hadn't yet been driving at road speed.

"What's stopping him?" she said, annoyed.

The truck stayed on her bumper, practically in her rear seat, and the driver didn't fall back or pass when Marin slowed, the truck looming over the smaller car. Her foot went to the brake before she thought better of it; a sudden stop on her part could put the truck into her rear seat.

"Think we should pull over?" she asked, but her passenger shook his head and gestured toward the empty road.

"Nobody out here but us," he said. "And I don't get the idea they want to talk..."

"Can you see anybody in the cab?"

He turned around. "Two white guys in sunglasses," he said. "Nice truck, too. A Chevy Silverado...looks new."

"Glad you're impressed," she said, and she sped up, hoping the driver was just annoyed with her for dawdling in the road looking at scenery.

"Got any suggestions?" she asked when the big Chevy didn't fall back but stayed tight against her bumper, the truck towering over the small sports car.

"Drive on to Tuba City, I guess," he said.

Several miles flashed by at road speed, and suddenly the driver gunned the blue Chevy and roared around, giving Marin a brief glimpse of the two men. She'd thought it more than likely it was local teens out for a drive, happy to have found a woman driving a sports car to help them pass a boring summer day, but these guys were not bored teenagers.

Apprehension took the place of annoyance when she topped a rise and saw the big Chevy stopped in the highway ahead.

"Road tag," she said, and Lewis George nodded.

"Looks like it," he said.

She'd been caught in this game before on empty stretches of reservation highways, a sort of leapfrog fueled by boredom or liquor or both, the game a matter of passing or slowing down or racing side by side, each trying to pass the other until the instigators tired of the game.

Edison had loved this game, especially in the nighttime—he liked the speed, the risk of meeting an oncoming car—he'd called it 'reservation chicken.'

Deliberately she took her foot off the gas pedal, indicating her unwillingness to play, but in response the other driver reversed the big truck to come alongside her, gunning the engine to surge up and back again, daring her to speed up, but she remained passive, not looking at the two men and doing little more than idling in the road.

The game became a battle of wills, both vehicles all but standing still in the hot sun while the minutes passed.

Marin's cotton shirt began to stick to the seat, and she hoped these two men wouldn't be content to sit in this heat for long and would give in. Lewis George seemed unaffected, unconcerned by either the heat or the Chevy truck.

She scanned the highway ahead and behind, hoping to spot on-coming traffic, but there was nothing.

"Any more suggestions?" she asked, and Lewis shrugged.

"I guess we could race them," he said. "We're probably faster than they are."

"Did I mention this car is a rental?" she asked. "I don't think drag-racing was covered in the insurance agreement. In fact, I'm sure it wasn't."

In the other lane, the two men seemed to be talking as well, arguing, the passenger shaking his head and removing his sunglasses as he pushed his hands repeatedly through his short blond hair.

Marin glanced at the driver.

As if he felt her gaze, the dark-haired man looked up and smiled— his teeth white and even below the dark glasses—and she willed herself to wait them out, gripping the steering wheel until her fingernails bit into her palms, close to giving in to the urge to run.

Beside her, Lewis George reached across and touched her arm.

"Don't worry," he said.

"Looks like we're going to be together longer than you planned," she told him.

"Much longer," he said, and smiled.

Marin glanced over and frowned, but before she could ask him to clarify, the Chevy truck came to life and roared around them, giving Marin another glimpse of the two men—the fair, sunburned face of the blond passenger, and the deeply tanned face of the driver, his eyes hidden behind the dark glasses.

She expelled the breath she'd been holding and wiped sweaty palms down her jeans. The truck disappeared into the highway's heat waves, and only then did she think about getting a plate number.

"I don't suppose you got their license number?" she asked, but Lewis George shook his head.

"Too far away for these old eyes," he said, and Marin frowned. His eyes looked sharp enough to her.

"I'm older than I look," he said.

"I'm glad you were here," she told him. "I think you scared them off when they saw I wasn't alone."

"I doubt they even saw me," he said, shaking his head. "People don't."

She shifted into gear and waited a minute on the shoulder of the road to give the two plenty of time to get ahead, thinking about their unexpected capitulation.

It wasn't long before she saw the reason. A large tour bus, which had certainly been visible to the two in the truck from their higher vantage point, motored alongside and passed without slowing, its seats filled with people in hats and sunglasses.

Marin waved as they passed, grateful for fellow travelers, and feeling more comfortable with the bus between her and the truck, she pulled onto the highway.

The distant hill over which first the truck, and then the tour bus, disappeared rose ahead, and she topped it in turn, descending into heat waves which this time dissolved into a roadrunner racing beside the highway.

Lewis George drew her attention to it, and she slowed to pace the bird for a stretch, hoping the tourists had seen the uniquely south-western sight.

She was resuming road speed when Lewis George reached for the passenger grab-handle and pointed. The Chevy truck was stopped dead ahead, turned crosswise in the center of the highway.

It took a moment for the scene to register and when it did, Marin stomped both the brake and the clutch and swerved to avoid broadsiding the truck.

Dust and gravel flew as she hit the shoulder of the road at speed, the rear of the car skewing wildly, but she didn't stop, knowing it was probably what the driver of the truck expected. She geared down, leveraged the car out of the skid, and stepped on the gas. The engine roared and she lifted her foot off the clutch, the tires spinning before they caught, and the small car surged forward with a swell of power that pushed her back into her seat.

The truck jerked forward, attempting to prevent her gaining the pavement, but she didn't hesitate or slow, and suddenly the truck was behind her in a thick cloud of dust.

She shifted gears, still accelerating, and the low-slung car seemed to settle lower to the road for a fraction of a second before shooting ahead.

"Yee-hah!" Lewis George cried, and Marin glanced over, widening her eyes.

"Yeah..." she said, impressed herself with the little car. "Yee-hah, indeed."

The road ahead was clear of traffic, the bus nowhere in sight, and she kept her foot hard on the gas.

A highway sign flashed past—the Tuba City junction—and she braked hard and reversed, the tires squealing and the strong smell of burning rubber drifting into the car as she made the turn, hoping the men in the truck would miss the turnoff.

"Just like riding with Big Daddy Garlits," Lewis George said, grinning, his black eyes shining.

"Who?"

"I thought you said you didn't drag-race," he said.

"I think I said I wasn't covered for it."

Lewis nodded and pursed his mouth. "Not your first game of road tag, huh?"

"Driving reservation highways with a crazy boyfriend," she said. "I guess I picked up a few things without realizing."

The road ahead and behind was empty of traffic, and briefly she wondered about the bus, but figured it was headed to Tuba City like most of the tour buses around here. She should have stayed with the bus in the first place, she chided herself—she had missed hitting the truck only because of the roadrunner.

If she hadn't slowed to watch the large cuckoo bird...and she remembered it was Lewis George who had noticed it first.

"Good thing you saw that roadrunner," she said.

"Yep. Good thing," he said. "Nothing like being in the right place at the right time."

"These guys were playing no ordinary game of road tag. They must have waited until the tour bus passed before they pulled onto the highway to block us."

Lewis George nodded.

"They must be crazy, pulling a stunt like that," she added, though she was the one who must be crazy, crazy for making this trip at all.

Lewis George looked over as if she'd spoken out loud. "Only the brave enjoy noble and glorious deaths."

"I'm not quite ready to die yet, if it's all the same to you," she said. She should turn around—turn around *now*—and go home. It wasn't like she hadn't tried to keep her promise to Mark. "Besides, I think you mean *only the good...*" she added.

"Don't have to be good to be brave," he said. "It's the courage to continue that counts."

"You're saying I should continue? Why?"

"Those guys don't look like reservation to me," he said. "Whatever it is you're here for, they sure don't want it to happen." He shrugged. "Kinda makes you wonder why."

CHAPTER FOUR

▲▲▲

THEN:
The Ruins

Sheldon's mother and father were on a Caribbean cruise, which was why he'd been left with his aunt and uncle, something he was unhappy about and had decided to avenge by being as much trouble as he could.

As exasperating as Sheldon was there were no other kids her own age, male or female. She'd have preferred a girl for a friend but guessed she should be happy Sheldon was here at all. In a strange way the snake incident had brought them together, an alliance of sorts, in a place neither of them wanted to be.

"At least you don't have to live here," Marin told him when he complained.

They spent the summer days together, leaving the confines of the fenced compound to explore the surrounding hills or go wading in the compound's water reservoir (though it was forbidden), and most days they walked to the trading post for sodas and candy bought with Sheldon's ample supply of what he called bribe money.

It was Sheldon's aunt who told them about the ruins in the nearby cliffs east of the compound, and the two of them spent an afternoon searching them out.

It was Sheldon who spotted the broken adobe walls first, pointing up to a dark square in a crumbling rock wall that turned out to be an opening, and together they climbed up to explore.

"Wow," Sheldon breathed as they crawled through the opening and found themselves in a series of small, square rooms made of mud-brick walls and low ceilings.

Marin wiped her sweaty face and looked around, and Bailey flopped, panting, into a corner.

The square rooms, four of them, were small and deep in drifted sand, and the only room with an entryway was slightly larger than the others, its ceiling black with smoke.

"Wow...I wonder how old this place is," Marin said, crawling through the low, crumbling doorway and landing in soft sand. "Who lived here?"

"Short people," Sheldon said.

"It's cool in here," Marin said, surprised, for the rooms weren't shaded by anything other than the stucco roof. "Even the sand is cool."

"It's built into the side of the cliff... keeps it cool," Sheldon said.

He knelt beside the wall and sifted the soft sand through his hands. "Maybe there's some pottery or arrowheads in here," he said. "Something I could take home to Kansas City and show everybody."

"I don't think you're supposed to take things, Sheldon."

"This isn't exactly a major archaeological find. Besides, my aunt say no Navajo Indian would ever come in here, so nothing I find belongs to them anyway."

"That doesn't even make sense," Marin said. "Of course, it belongs to them."

"Navajos don't live all crowded together like this, in these small rooms," Sheldon said. "Didn't you read anything about the history before you moved here? These ruins were from people before the Navajos got here. And besides," he said, when Marin opened her mouth to speak, "ruins are full of ghosts. People have probably *died* in here. Navajos don't mess with places where people have died."

"How do you know that?" Marin asked, interested despite her objection to Sheldon's scavenging.

"Because, silly," Sheldon said. "Dead people turn into ghosts, evil ghosts, that can do bad things to you."

"I don't believe that," Marin said.

"It's true! My aunt says so. Dead people turn into ghosts that can harm you. And then there's the evil skinwalkers.

"The what?" Marin said.

"Skinwalkers," Sheldon said impatiently. "They're witches who wear the skins of wolves or coyotes... maybe even dogs," he added, looking at Bailey.

Bailey thumped her tail at him.

"You don't even dare to speak the name of someone who has died," Sheldon said in a lowered voice, "'cause if you do, you might call their evil ghost, their *chindii*, to you and bad things will happen to you."

"Oh, pooh," said Marin. "I think you've got things all mixed up, or you *made* it all up. And I *did* read...I read everything we were given."

"You don't believe me, ask my aunt," Sheldon said. "She told me all about the ghost *chindiis,* and about the skinwalkers."

"I still don't believe you," Marin said.

"The skinwalkers are witches that have magic powers," Sheldon said. "They can turn themselves into wolves. You gotta be careful picking up any hitchhikers at night here, 'cause it could be the *chindii* skinwalker making you *think* he's just a regular hitchhiker."

"So?" Marin asked.

"So... this..." Sheldon said, and he drew his finger across his throat, his eyes wide.

Cool air moved over Marin's bare arms, making the hair stiffen, and the silence in the room must have pressed close around Sheldon, too, for he began to whisper.

"They're real," Sheldon said. "Mr. Barber says that one winter he was out tracking a wolf... one that had been killing sheep. Anyway, he shot it, and he says he hit it, but then he couldn't find it. He tracked it down the wash in the snow for a long way, until the bloody tracks just disappeared...*poof*!"

"So what?" Marin said. She glanced at Bailey, uneasy to be talking about shooting animals.

"The *wolf* tracks disappeared," Sheldon said, "but the tracks of a *man* appeared in their place, *human* footprints...bloody ones."

"That's impossible," Marin scoffed.

"What about werewolves?" Sheldon said, his voice scornful. "You've heard about *them*, right?

Marin shrugged and leaned back against the wall.

"Maybe it sounds impossible in the daytime," Sheldon said, "but at night I bet you'd think different. *Nobody* would come to this place at night."

Marin looked at him, and then looked over his shoulder, closer, at the wall. Carved into the mud bricks about two feet up from the sandy floor was a date, *1910*, and above it she made out a crudely carved word: *September.*

"Well, *somebody's* been in here since cliff-dwelling days," Marin commented. "Navajo or not... someone like you, scratching their initials into everything."

She pointed at the wall, and Sheldon turned to look.

"Wow," he said. "This place *is* old. You think anyone's been in here since then?"

"Your aunt told you about it, so I'm guessing yes."

Marin crawled back through the small opening, stood and brushed sand from her jeans, and looked back to see Sheldon with a rock, preparing to scratch his initials into the wall—an irritating tendency he'd developed wherever they happened to go.

"Come on," she said, sorry she'd reminded him. "I'll race you down to the trading post. Let's get an orange soda."

"Okay, yeah," Sheldon agreed, and climbed out.

"You're buying!" he added, getting a head start, and Bailey rose to follow as they raced down the foothills to the wash.

CHAPTER FIVE

▲▲▲

S cattered buildings and a large gas station stood beside the highway, clustered around the intersection connecting the highway with the short stretch of road leading into Tuba City.

The tour bus was there, refueling, and Marin pulled in beside it, stopping in a flurry of dust.

Several of the bus passengers glanced at them, curious, but she didn't resent the stares; she was thankful for their company.

"Good ride," Lewis George said, opening his door. "Lot of fun."

Marin couldn't blame him for wanting to leave, but she asked him to stay anyway, reluctant to lose his company.

"You sure you don't want a ride into town? Or maybe to Shiprock?" she asked, but he smiled and shook his head, gazing into the distance.

"Looks like rain coming in the Lukachukais tonight," he said, pointing with his chin toward the mountain range to the east.

"Good to know... but I'm not going there," she said, thinking he'd forgotten her destination.

"You never know," he said. "Best to be prepared."

Not sure how to answer that, she reached for Edison's red cap and scanned the highway.

"Drive safe," he said, pulling on his old cowboy hat.

"Will I see you again?" she asked, feeling an odd affinity for her road-tag partner, and he smiled.

"I'm usually around, one way or another," he said, and he walked away.

Marin watched him go, then walked back down the road the way they'd come, looking for the Chevy truck.

The hush of the desert closed around her only a few yards from the hustle of the tourist bus, enveloping her in the remembered quiet intensity, in the potency emanating from the earth and from the vast expanse of land and sky. Sounds were magnified here, and she listened for the familiar desert noises—the trickle of sand, the clicking of small stones, and the rustle of dry brush beneath the sound of the ever-present wind, gentle now, but which could go from hushed to dust-churning with little warning. A lizard darted beneath a tumbleweed and paused, its small sides heaving, and a raven's harsh cry broke the stillness.

Like the desert creatures, she herself was a part of this immense dry ocean-bed, and she was aware of both her insignificance and her integral place in its life rhythm.

There was no sign of the Chevy truck, and she returned to the chatter of the bus passengers and the bustle of the gas station, feeling calmer now in the midst of the normal summer day.

The game of road tag had been just that, a dangerous game, and the men in the truck had obviously lost interest once she got into town.

She looked around for Lewis George but didn't see him, and she felt disappointed not to have his company, at least to Kayenta. The bus passengers usually stayed at the hotel there, about seventy miles away. She would wait and travel with them.

She drove down the main street of Tuba City following the bus, remembering the high school basketball games, the track meets and the band concerts, the school trips to nearby Red Lake or Tonalea, and the rodeos in Kaibito...usually with Edison or Vangie.

She reached up and touched the red cap.

From here on, she was on the reservation proper, back in Vangie's world—and Edison's.

She pulled in next to the bus in the parking lot of Tuba City's stone trading post and followed the tourists inside.

The interior of the trading post was cool, dark, and smelled of wood, raw wool, and saddle leather—like all the trading posts she'd ever been in. The shelves were crowded with things made of glass or feathers, and she fingered a ceramic cup with the words *Souvenir of Tuba City* on the side. She had never bought a souvenir here, not in all the years she'd lived on the reservation, and though she now qualified as a tourist, she placed the cup back on the shelf.

She didn't need souvenirs to remember her life here, it was the forgetting that was hard.

She bought a bag of chips and went back outside, listening to the bus passengers, comparing souvenirs and itineraries as they waited to reboard the bus. She let their conversations wash over her and almost wished she was part of the bus group instead of only following them to Kayenta. She turned when she heard a truck pull into the parking lot.

Not the blue Chevy, she was relieved to see, but an older truck with stock railings around the sides and a rear bumper sticker that read—*I'm not a cowboy, I just found the hat.* Three men were in the cab, each wearing a cowboy hat, and Marin smiled, remembering Edison's tired old joke about cowboy hats and trucks.

There were six children of varying ages in the back of the truck and three women seated on a tool chest next to the cab—the women in long skirts and wearing scarves which partially covered their faces and *tsiiyeels*, their traditional buns wrapped in undyed wool yarn.

The children, laughing and jostling each other, climbed over the tailgate without waiting for the older boy who tried to lower it, and they trooped en masse into the trading post behind the men. The women waited before they stood, shaking out full satin skirts and smoothing brightly colored velveteen blouses before they carefully climbed down. A cradleboard holding a blanket-wrapped baby was carefully propped beside a small girl in a red dress who stayed behind, and the girl sat on the lowered tailgate swinging her legs after the women left, her eyes bright.

Marin lifted a hand, and the girl bent her head and sent back a shy smile from beneath a curtain of dark hair, still swinging her legs and not seeming to mind being the designated babysitter.

The bus driver appeared and walked up and down the store's wooden porch rounding up his passengers, urging them back onto the bus if they wanted to reach Kayenta before dinnertime. Marin watched them lining up to board, glad she was right about the Kayenta stop.

Two women stood in the bus line, comparing the T-shirts they'd bought inside and talking as they waited to board. After overhearing their first words, Marin began listening to their conversation, noticing how close the two stood to the small girl on the tailgate, so close the girl couldn't help but overhear.

"You just don't appreciate how blessed you are until you see others in such impoverished circumstances," the first woman said, her voice lowered.

"You're right, Helen," the other agreed, not bothering to lower her voice. "All those children, and do you see that baby, strapped to a board?"

"Not so loud, Lois, she'll hear you," Helen said.

"Probably doesn't speak much English," Lois answered.

"Of course she does," Helen said, her voice still low. "It isn't the dark ages."

"Most places, anyway," Lois said, still not bothering to lower her voice, and the small girl clenched her fingers tight around the cradleboard.

"What *I* object to is how the women were sitting in the back of the truck," Lois continued. "Poverty isn't responsible for treating women like cattle! Stop shushing me, Helen," she snapped. "I don't care who hears."

"Fine," Helen said. "But a little decorum never hurts, you know?"

"Of course, Helen. Whatever you say."

"The way the people live out here, in this God-forsaken place, is just a travesty," Helen said, her voice still low, concerned. "They're

United States *citizens*, for goodness sake, they could live anywhere they wanted."

"And get what sort of job?" Lois asked.

"It's a simple matter of education," Helen said. "That's all, education."

"It takes more than education to cure idleness and a lack of ambition!" Lois said, and the two moved up in line.

Marin glanced at the girl.

She was staring at the ground, her legs no longer swinging, one small hand gripping the edge of the cradleboard and the other smoothing a crease into the skirt of the red dress.

"I just feel so sorry for the children..." Helen said. "I have some candy I bought in the store. I'll just go over there and give it to her..."

"Excuse me," Marin said, and the two women turned, as did several other passengers waiting to board.

"Yes?" Helen said, pausing in the search through her shopping bag.

"I have a question for you," Marin said, and the one called Lois bristled.

"Do we know you?" she started, but Marin interrupted.

"Why do cowboys wear their hats with the sides turned up?" Marin asked, her voice loud enough to carry.

Both women looked at Marin and at each other.

"I beg your pardon?" Helen said, looking up from her shopping bag.

"I said," Marin repeated, louder. "Why do cowboys wear their hats with the sides turned up?" She paused, looking around at the passengers. "Anybody?"

The three women were silent but a man standing in line wearing a cowboy hat grinned at her and called back.

"Your ears are up! So your horse thinks you're friendly!" he said to laughter from the group.

"Keeps the rain off your neck," another called out.

"Stops the wind from blowing it off," someone else called, and after that answers began flying faster than Marin could track.

"So your throwing rope doesn't knock it off your head!"

"Prevents sunburn!"

"Easier to pick up!"

"Makes a cowboy easier to kiss!"

The entire group of twenty or so passengers was laughing now, the small girl giggling behind her hands, and others inside the store, including the kids from the truck, had come outside to join in, laughing as the merits of each answer were judged by whistles or catcalls, until the first man yelled and waved his hands for quiet, pointing out a man wearing a faded red shirt and a beat-up cowboy hat.

"There's a man who looks like he's been around. Let's ask him to decide this issue," he called out, and the crowd clapped their approval.

Lewis George, his face and voice solemn, stepped forward, and the crowd grew quiet.

"These here are big guys," he said, indicating the three Diné men from the truck who had also stepped out on the porch. "Those hats gotta be turned up for all three of them guys to ride up front," he pronounced, and the passengers roared their approval, clapping and then cheering when the three men from the stock truck swept off their cowboy hats and bowed.

Marin glanced at the small girl, who had returned to swinging her legs, and Lewis George lifted his hand and nodded at Marin before he turned back to the store.

The bus passengers finished boarding—the two women clutching their bags and crowding up the bus steps with the rest, their faces radiating disapproval.

Forget the women, Marin ordered herself, turning to go back to her car and follow the bus back to the highway. It wasn't the first time she'd encountered ignorance—well-meaning, willful, or otherwise—in others and in herself as well.

It had been just talk.

Chaa naaghahi—those who go around—tourists with tourist talk.

She pulled off Edison's hat and put it on the seat beside her, but the red cap seemed to be a reminder of past failures...failures of her own with Edison, with Vangie.

Not fair, she argued. It wasn't fair of her psyche to accuse her. What could she say to anyone that would change a lifetime of complacent beliefs? The past was the past and she'd done the best she could.

"I did what I could, Vangie. I can't change who I am," she whispered, the same words she'd said to Vangie years ago.

The bus pulled out of the parking lot, and Marin pulled out behind it, Tuba City growing smaller beneath the words '*objects are closer than they appear*' etched in the side-view mirror.

So was the past, and the hot shame suddenly burned in her cheeks as if all the years between then and now hadn't happened.

CHAPTER SIX

▲▲

THEN:

Sweat Houses and Showers

"The gym suits are here," Vangie called from the cafeteria doors. "Hurry up so we can get ones that fit!"

Marin was filling the saltshakers, table by table, which took a while.

"You go on," she said. "I have to finish here. Hey! Save me one if you can!" she called. "Size medium!"

As usual, by the time Marin finished, Rita had the metal lunch trays washed and was rinsing them in scalding water.

"Rita," Marin complained, pulling on a heavy rubber apron and sliding the trays into a third sink of bleach and more scalding water, "Can't you wait until I get back here to help? It's not fair for you to do them all."

Rita smiled without looking up.

"I don't mind," she said. "I'm a lot faster than you are."

"Vangie says the gym suits are in," Marin said, sliding the heavy trays into the slotted draining board to dry. "Let's get over and pick one before all the good ones are taken. There's supposed to even be a few new ones this year."

"Thank you, girls," Mrs. Atcity called as she and Rita hung the heavy aprons on a hook and left the kitchen. "Good night, Nightmare," she added, chuckling to herself.

Nightmare was Marin's nickname. Everyone had a nickname, and most people had more than one—a nickname being a play on words, the actual sound of one's name, or a loose description of the person or an event, valid or not.

Marin's nickname was Mrs. Atcity's special joke, as the cook had coined the name, and it had stuck. Vangie, and most everyone else, never called her anything else.

In the gym, Marin headed for the lockers and dressed in the suit Vangie had managed to hold back for her.

The blue, one-piece cotton jumpsuit was none too flattering, definitely not one of the crisp new ones Marin noted a few older girls had nabbed, and Vangie laughed when Marin came out of the locker room with the suit's waist hanging around her hips and the shorts falling below her knees.

"Very funny," Marin said. "Thanks for your help."

"Hey, you said medium, I got medium," Vangie said. "It won't hurt your game any."

"Very funny," she said again.

Marin had played basketball in grade school gym classes before moving to the reservation, but the game here was nothing like the game she'd learned, with the niceties of rules and standard codes of conduct. For males and females alike, basketball was more than just a game; it was part rite of passage, part counting coup, and part honor duels. One's prowess in the game—the rougher the better—was imperative to proving one's worth and establishing peer status.

Basketball, in short, was serious business.

But today it seemed there wasn't going to be a game at all, for Mrs. Anderson, the Health and Hygiene teacher, stood in the center of the gym waving the girls into a loose circle.

Mrs. Anderson was one of their least favorite teachers in the school, and Marin turned to ask Vangie why she was in their gym class, but Vangie, who a moment before had been laughing at Marin's baggy gym suit, had gone quiet and still, her face closed, her expression unreadable. Mrs. Anderson flapped her hands in the air for silence and clucked her tongue to get their attention, her pale blue eyes round and slightly protruding behind her thick glasses.

Mrs. Ganderson was her nickname, or just 'Goose' but the girls were careful not to use it in her presence.

"Girls," she said briskly, "I want you to line up by the locker room where I will dispense the shower articles."

Marin groaned.

Showers.

So that was what this was all about.

"No exceptions," Mrs. Anderson said. "And no excuses."

The large shower room, separated from the toilets and sinks by a short passageway, didn't have individual stalls but was one big circular space with a cold tiled floor and ugly metal shower heads protruding from a central column of granite.

The lack of privacy was one reason—the main reason—that the showers were so hated. This year they'd gotten away with no showers, as gym class was the last period of the day and Mr. Davis, the gym teacher, was not inclined to force the issue with the older girls.

Mrs. Anderson evidently had no such inclinations.

Marin turned again to Vangie, meaning to commiserate, to join in with the others in the usual moans and complaints and add her own, but everyone, including Vangie and Rita, had lapsed into silence.

No one was speaking and, as Marin looked around the group, not a single pair of eyes looked up to meet hers; every girl was staring fixedly at the varnished gym floor.

She filed with the others to the locker room and ended up near the end of the long row of girls, their silence still puzzling, and she stepped out of line to see if she could tell what was going on up near the front.

Mrs. Anderson stood near the door leading into the shower room, handing out towels and a small bar of soap to each girl as they reached the head of the line, which seemed normal enough until Marin saw the table beside the teacher.

Towels, soap, and a number of white paper cups were lined up on the table. As each girl reached the door, Mrs. Anderson wrote a number on the cup with a black magic marker, handed it to the girl, and waved forward the next in line.

By the time Marin reached the head of the line, clouds of steam were rolling from the shower room, and the girls who had been first in line were finished and standing in front of the lockers in various stages of undress with none of the usual teasing or snatching of clothing as on ordinary gym days.

An unusual smell mingled with the smell of sweaty gym clothes and tennis shoes, and Marin couldn't identify it, though it seemed familiar.

It reminded her of coloring eggs at Easter.

When Marin's turn came, she held her hand out for the towel, the bar of soap, and the paper cup, and Mrs. Anderson looked up. "Oh Marin," she said in her distracted way, "I forgot you were in this class. You don't need to shower, dear. Go ahead and get dressed."

She waved up the next girl in line, and Rita didn't speak or look up as Mrs. Anderson handed her the towel, the soap, and a numbered paper cup.

Marin remained beside the table, watching as Mrs. Anderson crossed off Rita's cup number from the list on a clipboard.

"Twenty girls in this class, and nineteen cups gone. Good." She looked up and again saw Marin.

"Go on and get dressed, Marin," she said and lowered her voice. "I'm sure you have running water in your home."

"Well, yes," Marin said. "What does that have to do with anything?"

Mrs. Anderson began gathering up the unused towels and soap, and she leaned close.

"Lice!" she said into Marin's ear.

"Lice?" Marin repeated, not sure she'd heard correctly.

She looked toward the dressing room and saw Vangie standing in front of the locker the two of them shared. She was dressed, her long hair wrapped in a towel, and she stared back at Marin without blinking, for once her dark eyes holding Marin's own without wavering.

Marin's heart began to hammer.

"We try to get the girls to cut their hair, to wear it neat and short..." Mrs. Anderson said, shrugging. "We can't force them to do that, so we do this instead."

The teacher motioned toward the paper cups now littering the shower room floor. "Three times a year, and we keep records, but it's hardly effective, even though I stand here and make sure the entire cup goes on their hair. It's the way they live," she sighed, "dirt floors, unsanitary habits, no indoor plumbing..."

"What's in the cup?" Marin asked, her eyes still locked with Vangie's, her voice barely a whisper.

"Vinegar," Mrs. Anderson replied. "To kill the lice. But it's hardly effective," she said again, shaking her head.

Heart pounding, Marin stared at Vangie and licked her dry lips, knowing she should speak up, argue, say something in defense of Vangie, in defense of Rita, but she said nothing.

"Marin," Mrs. Anderson said when Marin hadn't moved, "unless you'd like to help clean up here, please go and get dressed."

"Yes ma'am," Marin stammered, and Vangie broke eye contact and pulled the towel from her head. With a shake of her long hair, Vangie picked up her remaining things and walked out, dropping the used towel on a bench.

Marin dressed and left the gym, going outside to get on the school bus and wait for Vangie as usual. The younger kids were already on, sitting in the desirable rear seats, laughing and leaning out the windows to shout at friends on other buses, and Marin took a seat near the front, miserable, sure Vangie would never speak to her again, would stop being her best friend.

Vangie was one of the last ones on, her long hair still damp and clinging to her shoulders as she stood by the door and took in the seating.

Marin didn't call to her as usual, she just sat there looking out the window at nothing. Even when she felt Vangie's weight settle beside her, she didn't turn from the window, aware of the sharp smell of vinegar hanging between them.

The hour it took to get home was the longest she'd ever endured. Neither she nor Vangie spoke the entire trip and Vangie got off at her stop without the usual farewell or plans to meet later.

Angry at herself and hurt at Vangie's silence, Marin got off at her own stop and took refuge with Bailey in their special place, a shady stand of cottonwood trees in the wash.

The bluff here was high, and the trees made for a secluded spot where Bailey could lie in the shade. The wash itself had only a narrow trickle of water moving down the middle, and Marin closed her eyes and hugged her knees, listening to the water's quiet ripples.

Why did she feel condemned for who and what she was? Why did Vangie expect her to be otherwise? She didn't ask for special treatment from the teachers, though she knew she often received it as one of the few Anglo students.

"I can't change who I am," Marin said, and Bailey looked up and whined. "Prejudice works both ways...you think it's easy for me to live here?" she added, but the words sounded thin to her ears, and instead of anger she felt only loss.

The late afternoon sunlight warmed her face, slanting through her blond hair, and she thought of Vangie's blue-black curtain of shining hair.

She'd never been in Vangie's house, wasn't even sure which one was hers in the family cluster of houses and hogans where Vangie got off the bus, and she thought about that now, wondered if the floors were dirt, wondered if Vangie had indoor plumbing, wondered if Mrs. Anderson had ever bothered to ask.

A wagon was coming along the bluff above, rattling along the dirt road leading into and across the wash. Marin heard the creak of harness as it drew near, and beside her, Bailey sat up and pricked her ears as a team of horses came into sight pulling a buckboard with two large metal drums in the wagon-bed, water sloshing gently from their open tops.

A woman was driving—an older woman with gray hair yarn-wrapped into a *tsiiyeel* and long skirts worn under a velveteen blouse. She held the reins loosely between gnarled hands as if the horses didn't need any help from her, and she rocked side-to-side with the movement of the wagon. A younger woman, dressed in jeans, sat on the seat beside her and seemed to be asleep, leaning against the backrest with her booted feet propped on several boxes of canned food.

Marin often saw wagons or trucks hauling water barrels, both at the trading post and the school compound, and sometimes the drivers stopped at her house, asking to use their outside water spigot. She hadn't thought much about it until her father told her not everyone had running water in their home—something she'd always taken for granted.

"Water is a scarce commodity in the desert," her father had explained, telling her water wells were expensive and relatively rare.

Marin thought of that now, watching the wagon draw closer, and she wondered how far these two women had to go for water.

Bailey gave a short bark, and the old woman looked up as the wagon cleared the sandy bank leading down to the cottonwoods. She chuckled and nudged the sleeping woman beside her, saying something that made the younger woman smile before she opened her eyes and sat up.

As the wagon drew abreast of Marin, the old woman began to laugh out loud, her laugh a rusty cackle. She called out to Marin, pointed down the wash, and laughed some more, even going so far as to slap one leg hidden beneath the full skirts.

Marin felt foolish, as if a joke was being played on her that she did not understand and, as the old woman continued to laugh, the younger woman smiled broadly at Marin before she called over.

"It's where you are sitting," she said and pointed with her mouth and chin down the wash.

Marin shook her head, still not understanding.

"It's where you are," the younger woman said again. "The sweat house, it's just beyond you. My grandmother says you are sitting here hoping to catch a glimpse of the naked men as they come out!"

Marin felt the heat come up in her face.

She didn't say anything, couldn't think of anything *to* say as the wagon rattled past with its load of water sloshing from the open barrels, and the younger woman turned in the seat and called again.

"My grandmother says the men come here to bathe about this time of day, so maybe we'll catch a glimpse of them, too!"

She laughed and waved, and Marin waved back, the softly rippling water in the wash the only sound after the wagon crossed and climbed back up to the main road.

She knew the place the women meant, had noticed the small mud and stick hut built near the water, but she hadn't known it was some kind of bath house. She'd never seen anyone naked here, but the woman spoke as if the sweathouse was in daily use.

Her face hot with a pressing need to get out of the vicinity, she stood and brushed the sand off her jeans and called Bailey to her.

So much for her special place by the cottonwoods.

She walked home, thinking about sweathouses, about ways of bathing she'd never heard of, about showers and running water and definitions of cleanliness.

What could she say to Vangie—if she *could* say anything to make things right again.

In her mind's eye she saw herself standing beside Mrs. Anderson in the locker room, saw herself insist on taking the towel and the soap and the paper cup of vinegar and follow Rita into the shower room, saw herself getting dressed at the lockers. She'd held Vangie's gaze with her own, and they'd ridden home as usual on the bus, joking about the showers and laughing at the strange ways of teachers.

▲▲

CHAPTER SEVEN

M arin checked to make sure the blue Chevy truck wasn't behind her, and she relaxed, feeling she had found a good traveling companion in the tour bus for the stretch to Kayenta.

She turned on the radio for company, but even with its cheerful patter a kind of guilty despair settled over her, almost certainly a result of the conversation she'd heard at the trading post.

She concentrated on the open vistas to clear her mind, admiring the wide plateau of sweeping desert punctuated by broad fingers of red rock pointing into the sky.

And what a sky...

Nowhere else had she seen skies of such brilliant, deep blue, accented by red rocks and the white billowing clouds.

She passed the little round house where Zane Grey had written one of his books—she didn't know which one, didn't know if the story was true. She had never asked or checked.

The tour bus ahead of her began to slow, turning into the combination gas station and store at Tonalea, and Marin followed, parking in the graveled lot in back in the narrow band of shade provided by the roof overhang.

She walked around to the front and watched the bus passengers file out, stretching and yawning, though they'd traveled less than twenty-five miles from Tuba City, and she wondered how many times the bus was scheduled to stop before they reached Kayenta.

This was a place they'd always stopped for snacks and sodas on the high school trips—Baby Rocks—though the actual Baby Rocks mesa was further along the highway and would likely be yet another stop, as would Elephant's Feet: two giant rock formations that looked like the legs and toes of a huge elephant.

The passengers wandered around the area taking photos of the stacks of small rocks, and Marin went into the store to get a cold drink while she waited.

A raven, large and inky-black, sat perched on the railing preening its feathers and seemingly admiring his reflection in the glass window. The bird hopped away at her approach, and she glanced at her own reflection—a white cotton shirt worn over jeans, her long hair tied back—but the face beneath the red cap was one she barely recognized, drawn and thin and pale.

A buzzer went off when she pushed open the door, and the sound of wind flutes floated from the ceiling speakers, accompanied by an overhead fan making soft chirring noises.

She heard the tour group folks chatting in the aisles, discussing the merits of rocks and post cards as she selected two cans of cold soda, one for now and one for the road, and she picked out a plastic-wrapped sweet roll before going the counter to pay, determined to listen to no more passengers' conversations.

A girl in her teens was at the register, thumbing through a fashion magazine lying on the counter, and a radio on a high shelf was playing oldies and goldies from the "Station of the Navajo Nation." Dark eyes looked up to meet hers, and Marin politely glanced away but the girl regarded her steadily.

"This do it for you?" she asked, turning down a corner of the magazine, and Marin nodded as she handed across her money.

"I'm listening to this station in my car," Marin said, nodding toward the radio. "The songs weren't oldies and goldies, though, in my day."

"Mmm-hmm," the girl said.

"Gas?" she asked, glancing at the pump register, and Marin shook her head.

"I must not have seen you drive in," the girl said, brushing Marin's hand with cool fingers as she handed back her change. "You're not with the bus?"

"I'm not a tourist," Marin said, and immediately felt foolish for saying such a thing.

The girl nodded, pushed across the sodas and the bagged sweet roll, and went back to her magazine.

The sun was blazing down with summer heat, and the interior of the car was hot despite the strip of shade.

She hoped the bus wouldn't linger.

For lack of anything else to do while she waited, she popped opened a soda and pulled out the automobile manual from the glove compartment to read about the car's virtues.

"Road tag indeed," she murmured out loud, finding herself impressed with the car's stats, and she wondered if the man at the rental agency had been trying to make amends by giving her a car with a V-8 engine and a six-speed manual transmission.

The section concerning the keyless start caught her attention, and she punched in a series of commands as instructed and gave it a try, satisfied when the car immediately started without the keys in the ignition. She got out and experimented with the distance by leaving the keys here and there, finding the keys had to be within about three feet before the car would start.

That done, she played around with the alarm system, activated it, and put the manual back in the glove compartment.

She finished the soda and was once more at a loss.

The tour bus showed no signs of leaving anytime soon—most of the bus tourists were still taking pictures—and the driver had shown up with a long squeegee and a bucket of water, preparing to wash the windows.

She sighed, debating whether she should drive to Kayenta on her own, and she pulled out the reunion invitation. She'd meant to call Vangie, or someone listed on the card, to say she was coming, but there was no RSVP information on the card, no names, and no phone numbers. She looked again at the courthouse address, turning the card over in her hands and still not completely sure she wanted to commit to—whatever this was—despite Vangie's written appeal.

So far, this journey hadn't done anything to convince her not to turn around and go home. It's not like Mark would know, and maybe it would be the smart thing to do.

But could she ignore her promise, ignore Vangie's call for help?

She thought of the two men in the Chevy—not just bored kids looking for kicks—but how could they be connected to the reunion? Road tag wasn't that unusual, but what had happened today wasn't anywhere close to usual.

She studied the card, seeing nothing she hadn't seen before, but what if someone had forged Vangie's handwriting, and if so, why?

Please come, Marin. I need to see you...

Why would Vangie need, or want, to see her after all these years? The things that had kept them apart hadn't changed. To see Vangie now would be embarrassing to them both. Still, Vangie had written 'Marin' and not 'Nightmare' and that had to mean something, even if it was only intended to get her attention, and someone did break into the apartment...

It was futile to continue an argument with herself, and she was so tired. The heat and the aftermath of the earlier adrenalin surge made her thinking slow, sluggish, and that, added to her recent lack of sleep, began making the heavy lassitude irresistible.

The remaining can of soda was on the dashboard, sitting in the full sun, but she didn't have the energy either to drink it or move it, and she pulled the red cap down over her eyes and slumped in the seat, letting her mind drift. The car door and the windows were open, and the noise of the bus engine and the chatter of the tourists were sure to alert her when they departed.

The bus driver was now washing the wide windows with the long-handled squeegee—up and down, up and down—and she closed her eyes.

CHAPTER EIGHT

THEN:
The Mesa

M arin planned to attempt climbing the mesa again today, in the
company of Sheldon. Not that Marin particularly wanted Sheldon's company, but her father had forbidden her to go alone anymore,
and that left Sheldon, exasperating as he was.

"Hey," Sheldon called, walking over from next door. "Ready to go?"

"Waiting for you, slowpoke," she said from the porch steps, standing and dusting off her jeans.

"Let's go, Bailey."

It took them a few tries to get over the fence stile, and they tried
first coaxing and then shoving Bailey up and over the steep steps, and
then Sheldon had to prove he could jump the fence without using the
stile at all.

It was hot and dry and almost noon when they at last got started,
the dust rising in small puffs beneath their feet as they walked
cross-country toward the mesa. The air smelled of dust and sagebrush and, faintly, of juniper as they made their way around clumps of
tumbleweed and the sharp limbs of greasewood bushes, hiking over
ground that was uneven and rocky.

Bailey scouted ahead, flushing imaginary rabbits, but as the
ground grew steeper, the dog slowed to a walk, panting as she trotted beside Marin. The heat was dry, but sweat soaked their hair and

skin and their steps grew slower, the mesa ahead dancing in the heat waves, looming before them but seemingly impossible to reach. They stopped for a rest in the lower foothills, the mesa walls still ahead of them, jutting straight into the blue sky over their heads.

"Whew," panted Sheldon, mopping his forehead. "This is some climb. When do we get to the actual mesa? How about a break?"

"We haven't even started to climb, Sheldon," Marin said. "See that narrow path going up the foothills? That's the one I followed before, but it didn't take me to the top. We'll have to find another."

Bailey plopped down in the shade of an overhanging ledge and rested her head on her front paws, panting, and Marin handed out cheese sandwiches and water.

They ate and rested, listening to the intense, pressing quiet. There was a feeling of complete stillness here in the shadow of the mesa walls, and the air was cooler in the deep shade. Even the wind seemed to be muffled, and the only sound other than Bailey's panting was the strident scream of an eagle high overhead.

"It's sort of eerie here, isn't it?" Sheldon said. "So quiet and all. It's like the mesa is listening to us."

"I like it," Marin answered.

She studied the base of the mesa and considered, then pointed. "I haven't tried the trail from that side yet. It looks like it leads into the fallen rocks, but maybe we can climb them, get to the top that way."

"It looks too hard," was Sheldon's doubtful response, but he stood, waiting while Marin knelt and poured more water for Bailey into the lid of the water bottle.

"Sheldon, what are you wearing on your feet?" she said.

Sheldon held up one foot.

"My new cowboy boots," he said proudly. "Real snakeskin. They were a present for my thirteenth birthday...since I was coming out here and all."

"You and your snakes!" she muttered. "You can climb in cowboy boots?"

"Hey," Sheldon said. "I can go anywhere you can in your dumb tennis shoes!"

"I doubt it. And don't expect me to wait for you if you can't."

She led off up the steep hillside and they climbed steadily for a while, scrambling up and over boulders they couldn't get around or squeezing themselves between the cracks and crevices.

Marin stopped on the top of a boulder to rest, and she looked around.

It was like she was in the middle of a rocky ocean. Massive blocks of red and black sandstone lay scattered for as far as she could see, rocks from the mesa wall that had split and fallen away, who knew when, and had landed in a heap at the mesa's base.

"Just think," Marin said, "if we could put these rocks back together again like a puzzle, we'd know what the mesa looked like hundreds, maybe thousands of years ago."

Sheldon didn't answer and Marin looked around.

He was crouched a few feet below her, a rock in his hand, busy scouring his initials into the mesa wall.

"Sheldon!" Marin said.

"What?" Sheldon answered, looking up, rock in hand.

"Do you *have* to do that? You're defacing the wall!"

"We can't climb any higher," he pointed out. "The boulders end here and the walls go straight up, and we don't have ropes. I want to show how high we made it."

He went back to sanding out his initials, and Marin looked up at the steep walls where streaks of black water marks stained the red sandstone in long, unbroken lines from the top all the way down to where she stood.

She sighed, defeated.

This was as high as they were going to get, and there was nothing to do but make the climb back down again.

She looked up at the rocks a final time and straight into a pair of dark eyes.

"Hey!" she cried, startled, and below her, Bailey stiffened.

"Hey, yourself," a voice answered.

An entire face appeared—and long dark hair to match the dark eyes—then arms and shoulders, until a girl about Marin's age stood smiling down.

"Who're you?" Marin said. "How did you get in there?"

"Who are *you*?" the girl returned, her smile remaining.

"I'm Marin. That's Sheldon. We're rock climbing."

The girl cocked her head. "Funny way to rock climb," she said, "Are you marking out a path, so you don't get lost?"

"We're *trying* to find a way to the top," Sheldon said from below her.

"Why not take the trail?" the girl said.

"Oh, the *trail*," Sheldon said. "Why didn't we think of that? And just where would that be?"

"I'm standing in it," the girl said.

Marin studied the position of the girl, puzzled. "Where *are* you standing, anyway?" she asked. "You look like you're inside the rock."

"So I am," the girl replied, and she vanished again into what appeared to be a solid rock wall.

Marin and Sheldon looked at one another, Sheldon shrugging, but Marin began to climb toward the exact place the girl had disappeared. She called down to Sheldon to hold Bailey, for the dog would try to follow and Marin was scrambling for every hold, forcing herself up with fingers and toes jammed against the rock. She wouldn't be able to go far like this, but she kept her eyes fixed on the spot the girl had been, and suddenly there was only open space beneath her reaching hand.

She cried out as she fell.

Sheldon was calling to her from below, but Marin didn't answer; she was too busy looking around in wonder, on her knees in deep, soft sand.

She had fallen into a crevice in the face of the wall, a vertical split going to the top of the mesa, for she could see a strip of blue sky far above her head. The split was narrow—she could touch each side with her outstretched arms—and undetectable from below looking up, as a slight overlap disguised the break, making the wall from the outside appear unbroken. The sandy floor inside sloped gently upward and the passageway was much like a narrow cave except for the slice of sky overhead. Marin shivered as her sweat cooled, and she looked around for the girl, but she was alone. The only sound was Sheldon's voice calling from outside.

She looked out and laughed to see Sheldon standing directly beneath her, pushing Bailey upward with both hands on the dog's rump, trying to avoid the scrabbling claws as the dog climbed, for Bailey knew exactly where she was.

"Hey!" she called down as Bailey scrambled into the crevice along-side Marin, her tail wagging as if to say "aren't I clever?" and Sheldon's head appeared a moment later.

"Where are we?" he began as his eyes adjusted to the deep shade within the split. "Wow," he said as he dropped inside. "A split right up the cliff wall! It's like a 3-D puzzle. You have to know it's here to see it."

He sat down and began sifting the cool sand through his fingers. "Where's the girl?" he asked.

"Don't know," said Marin. "But this must be the way to the top, and I'm going up."

The split narrowed the higher they climbed, until their out-stretched hands easily brushed both sides of the wall, and still the path wound steadily upward, the patch of blue sky bright above them as they climbed.

Inside, all sound was hushed, the deep sand deadening their foot-steps and their voices. Even the wind didn't penetrate and break the stillness. The absolute quiet was eerie even with the strip of daylight overhead, and the stillness had a watchful quality about it that made Marin glance behind her more than once, but there was only Sheldon and Bailey.

"I'm beat," Sheldon said as he stopped and dropped to the sand. "Does this ever come out on top?"

"The top must be getting close. I'm going to keep going."

She continued climbing as she spoke, Bailey close behind her, and in another few yards she stepped between the two edges of overlapping rock, and found herself standing in glaring sunshine with the sound of the wind around her, the bright day dazzling after the shadowed split.

She was near the edge of one end of the mesa, the land below spread in sheets of green and brown from horizon to horizon, the mountains to the west great curves of blue. The school complex made up small, interconnecting circles, spirals of identical toy houses with the school buildings in their center, the whole intertwined and surrounded by its narrow black ribbon of pavement.

At last, she was standing on the top of the mesa.

Marin raised both arms and shouted for the pure joy of it, Bailey dancing around her legs and barking.

"Sheldon, come look! We made it! It's great!"

Sheldon emerged from the rock split, squinting in the bright sunlight and shading his eyes with one hand.

"Wow," he said.

"Yeah, wow!" Marin cried, spreading her arms wide and letting the wind tear through her long hair. The updraft at the rock's edge pushed against her, holding her in place like a strong hand, and she felt the urge to jump into the wind and let it blow her back again.

"Hey," Sheldon said. "Look at this rock we're on. It looks like a giant turtle!"

The rock formation hanging out over the cliff's edge did look like a turtle, with she and Sheldon standing on its back and its head a smaller rock beyond the mesa rim.

"We name you Turtle Rock," shouted Marin, abandoning the idea of windsurfing and deciding instead to explore the mesa's edge.

"Turtle Rock," Sheldon echoed, jumping up and down.

"Sheldon," Marin said, suddenly aware of just how far the 'turtle' hung over the mesa's edge. "Maybe we shouldn't stand quite so near the edge."

She pointed to the jumbled boulders of the canyon far below.

"All those rocks down there came from up here, remember."

"Oh, this turtle's as steady as a rock, Marin," Sheldon said, but he moved back.

The mesa top was broader than they had imagined, the flat rocks nearer the edge giving way to a new, higher landscape of gnarled cedar and pinions, and they ventured a ways toward the center, but Marin worried they'd get turned around and be unable to find their way back. They both were more interested in exploring along the edge anyway, and the flat rocks, layered like giant playing cards, were easier to navigate than sagebrush and rough dirt.

The rocks were scarred and pitted with erosion holes or shallow basins filled with several inches of rainwater, and the wind blew across the deeper holes, making a hollow moaning sound that caused Bailey to cock her head and whine.

Together they walked the entire length of the mesa wall, a mile or more, skirting the occasional ravines until the afternoon sun was low and shining almost directly into their faces. Bailey had been running far ahead, doing her own exploring, and now the dog was trotting back and forth, her way blocked by the edge of a deep ravine.

Like a miniature canyon, the ravine walls rose thirty feet or so above a sand-covered rock floor stretching all the way to the mesa's rim, and there was a pool of water at the end nearest them, beneath a rock shelf about five feet above the water. A twisted cedar tree had grown out of the wall alongside the shelf, its gnarled branches leaning over the pool.

"We should go back," she said but Sheldon was already climbing down, jumping from rock to rock to reach the overhanging ledge.

"Sheldon!"

"I'm going to swim!" he shouted. "I can jump from the tree!"

"You don't know how deep that water is," she said. "Besides, it's time to go back."

"Scared?" Sheldon called up. "It looks deep enough. The bottom will be sandy anyway."

"You don't know that. I'll climb down," she said. "Wait, and I'll wade out and check."

"Okay, I'll wait, but I think it's just 'cause you're a scaredy-cat."

"Really? Well, *you* better watch out for snakes, Sheldon," she said, returning the taunt. "They like the shade under the rocks."

The climb down into the ravine was steep and uneven, but there was a sandy chute part of the way down, and below that were the stacked rocks again, so there were good handholds. Marin eased from rock to rock, bracing her feet to keep from sliding, while Bailey was forced to remain on top, the dog's anxious eyes watching Marin.

"It's okay, girl," Marin soothed when Bailey scooted to the edge, whining. "I'm okay. Just stay there."

She reached the bottom, jumping the last few feet, and looked up. Sheldon was on the rock ledge, crouched near the cedar tree, etching his initials into the rock wall.

"Sheldon, really! Do you *have* to deface every rock on the reservation?"

He waved her away without turning, and Marin left to explore on her own, following the gentle slope to the shallow hollow at the mesa's rim where the wind had scoured the rock smooth. The mesa walls loomed high overhead, blocking the afternoon sun, and the wind was cold as it tore at her hair and clothes and whistled up the ravine behind.

She stood on the rim, buffeted as she leaned into the wind's strength and stared down at the boulders jumbled against the cleanly-sliced cliff walls. Above her an eagle screamed, the sound echoing as the bird rode the air currents and floated close to her, so very close, and she knew this was the closest she would ever come to flying.

She swayed, the space and the wind dizzying, again tempted to trust herself completely to the push of the wind, but she slowly backed against the sandstone wall and slid into a sitting position. She sat there, her knees to her chest, absorbing the unbroken view all the way to the mountains on the western horizon as sand devils raced up the ravine beside her, etching tiny whorls into the sand and reminding her of Sheldon.

She had forgotten all about him.

Sheldon was still perched on the ledge beside the twisted cedar tree, surveying the pool of water beneath him when she returned, and she waded out, stopping when the water reached about mid-thigh.

"I'm not going in any further. I guess it's deep enough in the center," she said. "You're not that high, anyway."

"I'm going to climb down a little more first," Sheldon said, scooting along the ledge, and Marin could see his large, uneven initials etched into the rock wall behind him.

She was suddenly angry, annoyed by Sheldon's lack of respect, his lack of awe for this place of sky and wind, and she wished he *would* go back home, back to his precious Kansas City.

"I thought you were going to jump from the ledge," she said. "Don't tell me you're scared after all."

Sheldon leaned out and studied the pool. "I am going to jump. I just don't want to get my new boots wet," he said, and he bent down to remove a boot, but it resisted his pull.

"Sheldon," Marin said, aware he was serious. "Don't jump. I was only teasing. It's too high. I'm scared there might be rocks down there...the sand is shallow here—"

Sheldon didn't let her finish.

"Marin," he said, still struggling with a boot, "is there *anything* in the whole world you are *not* afraid of?" He laughed, and Marin's annoyance returned to anger.

Freezing, exaggerating her fear, she pointed at the cedar branches beside him, staring at a spot just behind his head.

"Sheldon," she whispered. "Don't move! Behind you... on the tree branch. There's a snake!"

Still in the boots, Sheldon gave a cry and came flying off the ledge, windmilling his arms for balance and missing the pool completely, landing face-down in the ravine. He hit the ground hard enough that dust billowed around him like a TV cartoon, and Marin laughed, satisfied with her revenge.

Sheldon struggled for a moment, pushing himself partway up before he crumpled back to the ground with a moan, one leg with its booted foot twisted beneath him.

"Come on, Sheldon," Marin said. "You might as well get up. I know you're faking." Sheldon didn't move, and above her, Bailey began a frantic barking, running back and forth along the top of the ravine wall.

Marin crossed to Sheldon and knelt beside him. "You're not really hurt, are you?" she asked, getting a little worried. Sheldon didn't look good, and he wasn't moving. His eyes were closed, and his face was so pale every freckle stood out against his white skin.

"Come on, Sheldon," she said. "I'll help you. You're okay."

She touched his shoulder and shook him lightly. "This is *not* funny! Come on! Get up!"

There was no response and she looked at the ground around him.

There was no blood, and he was breathing, so that was good, but she could feel the hard rock underneath the thin layer of sand.

She shook his shoulder harder, and this time he moaned, his eyelids fluttering.

"My leg," he said hoarsely, and she looked down.

One leg was turned in an odd position for a leg, twisted, and she took the heel and toe of his boot to try and straighten it, but Sheldon screamed and grabbed her hand.

"Don't touch it!" he cried in almost his old voice, his face going even whiter than before as he fell back.

"Sheldon, I think your leg may be broken," Marin said. "What should I do?"

Sheldon didn't answer. His eyes were closed, and he was breathing with hard, short puffs.

"Oh, dear God, please let it be okay," she prayed. "Let him be okay."

Sheldon groaned, and his eyelids fluttered, then he seemed to fall asleep, his body going limp and his breathing changing to deep, gasping breaths.

He didn't speak again after that, even with Marin's coaxing.

Marin sat back on her heels and looked at the steep walls of rock around them, and she punched the sand beside Sheldon's shoulder.

"Stupid, stupid, stupid!" she said, talking both to herself and to him, but immediately she felt ashamed and hoped he hadn't heard.

What should she do?

She couldn't carry him out of the ravine. She'd have to go for help, go home and find her father.

"Sheldon," she said, trying to shake him gently when she really wanted to shake him into awareness of their situation.

"Sheldon, can you hear me?" she said. "I'll have to go for help. I'll have to leave you behind if you don't wake up."

He didn't answer and Marin thought of the walk down the mesa and the longer walk cross country to get home.

How quickly could she do it? Would Sheldon be okay alone?

"Well, he'll just have to be," she said out loud just as something cold and wet touched the back of her neck.

She yelped, but it was only Bailey, tail wagging and tongue hanging.

"Oh, Bailey!" she cried, throwing her arms around the dog's neck. "What are we going to do?"

Bailey licked her face and then licked Sheldon's, too, looking at Marin as if waiting for her to explain this new game.

"You'll have to stay here with Sheldon while I go for help," Marin said, and added, puzzled, "How did you get down here, anyway?"

"She came down with me," someone said, and Marin turned to see the girl in the rock sliding down the sandy chute.

"I guess you found the way up after all," the girl said. "But this ravine is not a good place to be," she added, and her eyes went to Sheldon.

"Is he alright?" she asked.

"No," Marin said in a rush, "He's not. He jumped, from up there," she said, pointing to the ledge above the pool and leaving out the part about the snake.

"His leg is maybe broken, and I've got to go for help, but I can't just leave him here alone, so if you could stay...?" She trailed off, aware of the girl's silence.

For a few seconds there was no sound save the wind whistling up from the mesa's edge, covering the sound of Sheldon's labored breathing, and Marin felt the timelessness of this place—the wind, the sun, the rocks—and her own insignificance.

"Okay," the girl said, just the one word before she stood and started back up the way she'd come.

"Hey," Marin said, startled into finding her voice. "Hey!" she said again. "Wait!"

I'll be back," the girl said from the top of the ravine, and she disappeared over the edge and out of sight.

Marin stood, meaning to follow, and looked down at Sheldon. She couldn't leave him here, as much as she wanted to do so.

She had to stay here with him, and she sank down in the sand.

The girl said she'd be back, so she must be going for help.

"I sure hope so," she murmured, wishing her dad was here.

Bailey sat beside her, and Marin wrapped her hand in the dog's warm ruff.

The stillness of the mesa, the wind and the blowing sand, encircled her, and she sat close to Sheldon to keep him warm, pulling Bailey close to them both.

The sun dropped lower, touching the tips of the western mountains, and Sheldon didn't move or make a sound other than his hoarse breathing.

"Sheldon," Marin whispered. "I'm so sorry. Please be okay. Please God, let Sheldon be okay."

She'd caused a terrible thing to happen because of a moment of anger, a moment she could never take back, could never do over.

"No do-overs," she whispered, and she wished she had been the one to go for help and not the one who had to stay and wait.

CHAPTER NINE

▲▲▲

The strident cries of the raven woke Marin—the black bird was strutting around the car, flapping its wings and crowing as raucously as a rooster at dawn. It hopped closer and croaked into her open window, and she came fully awake to a late afternoon sun slanting long shadows across the gravel.

She was alone in an empty lot, and the tour bus was gone.

She glanced at her watch.

She'd slept for over an hour, and at some point during that time the bus had left.

Maybe she could catch them. She was fairly sure the tour bus would stop either at Baby Rocks Mesa or Elephant's Feet, probably both, before continuing to Kayenta, and those sites were nearby.

"The girl inside will know when they left," she said, and the raven flapped its wings and flew the few feet to the curb, cocking its head and looking at her with bright black eyes.

"You could have made all that noise a little earlier," she added, and the raven flapped its wings harder and croaked again.

"Are you trying to talk?" Marin began, and she heard the crunch of gravel.

The raven took wing with a final croak, and a dark haired and darkly tanned man leaned into Marin's open passenger window, the smile beneath his dark sunglasses revealing perfect teeth.

She was alone in an empty lot...with the driver of the blue Chevy.

She swallowed. "You must have worn braces for years to get teeth like that," she said, the fear lurching from her stomach to her throat. "Or maybe it's the tan that make your teeth look so white..." she stammered, her attempts at casual failing even to her own ears.

The driver of the Chevy truck folded his arms across the window frame, his smile turning to a smirk. "Sorry to bother you," he said, his voice smooth, "but I was wondering if I might catch a ride into Kayenta."

His mocking tone gave lie to the oh-so-polite words, that and the lazy way he examined her, and she knew this man wasn't here to play games. A quick glance behind him revealed no sign of the blue Chevy, but she was sure it was close by—and so was the blond man.

No one in the store could see her, and even if she shouted, she doubted anyone inside would hear, but the keys were clutched in her hand, and the car should start.

Instinctively she again spoke with a calmness she was far from feeling, hoping that if she made no sign she recognized him, she could make an escape.

"I make it a practice never to pick up strangers," she said in the most normal voice she could manage. "Sorry," she added, and pressed the ignition button.

Nothing happened.

She pressed again...and again nothing.

"Well," he said, reaching through the open window and catching her hand before she could try again, "If I introduce myself, we won't *be* strangers, now will we?"

Perfect teeth, she thought, and before she could move he had opened the door and was in the seat beside her.

"Get out!" she said, but her voice was shaky, unconvincing.

Her move to get out her door was more decisive but too late and—smiling—he reached across and seized her hair, pulling her back inside the car as he wrenched the key fob from her hand and dropped it to the floor.

She managed to hit the steering wheel with her left hand, and the car horn sounded with one short burst before he grabbed her wrists and pulled, and she cried out as the small bones of her wrists grated painfully in his grip. He ignored her cry and continued to squeeze.

Desperately she tried to pull her wrists free of his crushing hold.

"We could do this the easy way," he said, his words casual and his voice cruel, "but I find the hard way is always so much more entertaining."

Marin's mind went blank, stopping the pain her only coherent thought, and she didn't notice the raven until it gave a hoarse croak directly beside the open passenger window.

The man jerked around, swearing, and Marin raised his hands to her mouth and bit down, hard, on the fleshy heel of his hand.

He turned when her teeth sank in, but instead of pulling away, he pushed the heel of his hand against her mouth, against her lips and teeth, until she tasted blood, laughing when she opened her mouth to scream and pushing his hand into the back of her throat.

Marin's fear gave way to panic, and she gagged, fighting to get free, fighting to breathe, her arms trapped between her body and his. His fist blocked her air, and she pushed against him, throwing herself to one side, a blackness spreading behind her eyes. His sunglasses were gone, and she could see blue, blue eyes scant inches from her own as her struggles grew weaker and his face began to blur.

"Such a pretty girl," she heard him say as a black wave crested and another began.

"Don't pass out on me," he said, and he pulled his hand from her mouth and dropped it to her breast.

"Your heart's beating fast," he said in a detached voice, and Marin felt the blessed rush of air into her lungs and a fresh burst of terror at his touch.

She coughed, trying to speak, trying to push him away, but he held her too tightly.

"Guess you should have stayed home," he said, and he squeezed her breast, painfully kneading the soft flesh.

A sound reached her ears, and from the corner of her eye she saw a car pull into the parking lot, a car with the insignia of the Navajo Nation Police on the door, and she heard the raven cawing loudly in his raucous voice.

The blue eyes flicked away from hers as the man turned his head, giving her the vital few inches she needed.

Instantly she pushed herself back against the door, getting one foot on the seat underneath her and levering herself up and halfway out the driver's window before he again caught her hair and pulled.

"You're not going anywhere," he hissed, one hand in her hair and the other beneath her jaw, and she cried out as hard fingers dug into the sensitive joint just below her ear. Tears blurred her vision as pain shot through her face, her scream only a strangled, feeble cry.

A bright red light on the dashboard was blinking steadily, and she focused on it, focused on fighting the pain as the light flashed faster, and suddenly a shrill blast of sound erupted inside the car.

The car alarm.

It must have been triggered when the man opened the door.

He cursed and yanked her down with a jerk on her shirt, and she heard the *spang* of a button as it came loose and hit the steering wheel.

One hand still twisted in her hair, he slapped the red cap on her head and began pressing console buttons with the other until the alarm stopped as abruptly as it had begun.

For a few seconds Marin heard nothing but the ringing in her ears until she heard the crunch of gravel and got a sideways view of boots approaching the car.

"If you know what's good for you..." the man growled in her ear an instant before another voice spoke from behind her head.

"What seems to be the problem?" a man asked, and she strained to turn until she could see the badge and the police uniform—and a face she knew.

Justin Blue Eyes.

CHAPTER TEN

▲▲

THEN:
The Mesa

Marin wasn't aware of the passing of time until she began shivering, and she saw that the sun had completely left the ravine, leaving it in deep shade with the sand quickly growing cold. She stood and walked down to the mesa's edge, leaving Bailey beside Sheldon. The sun hung low in the west now, resting on the mountaintops, and the entire horizon was deep blue sky and golden sun. She shivered in the wind and walked back to Sheldon.

"Are you awake?" she whispered.

No answer.

"Are you cold?"

Nothing.

She leaned close to see if Sheldon was still breathing. His breath was raspy and very shallow, but it was there.

Maybe he didn't feel the cold, but it worried her. Someone sick or hurt was supposed to be kept warm, and neither she nor Sheldon had jackets with them. She started scooping the still-warm sand around him, patting it against his sides and arms and even around his neck and head, trying to avoid touching the hurt leg. She pulled out the folded paper sack from her jeans pocket, the sack that earlier had held their sandwiches, and filled it partway with sand. Gently she pushed it under Sheldon's head for a pillow and coaxed Bailey over to lie partially across Sheldon's chest to provide some heat.

Sheldon groaned and moved a little under Bailey's weight but didn't open his eyes. Maybe Bailey was too heavy and he couldn't breathe now, Marin worried, and she called Bailey off again, and scooted herself as close as she could to Sheldon's side. Hopefully she, with Bailey on the other side, would give him a little warmth. Maybe she should be doing something else for him, but she couldn't think what, and she was so tired of worrying.

Was the girl down the mesa yet? Was she on her way back?

"Please, please, God, let her hurry," she prayed.

She was scared and cold and wanted to be home.

"Please help us, God, please let it be okay."

She reached across Sheldon to stroke Bailey's fur. It was so quiet here, so very still as the shadows grew long.

Too still.

"Sheldon," she whispered, "wake up and talk to me."

She thought of the snake on the playground, how Sheldon had treated the whole thing as a joke.

"You should have seen your face when it hit the ground," he'd said to Marin when they examined the dead snake in the jar. "You take everything way too serious."

But if he had seen her face, she had seen his as well, and she told him so.

She looked at Sheldon, his face as white now as it had been that day on the playground, and she squeezed her eyes hard shut and prayed over and over for Sheldon to be okay. Surely God would hear her prayers, would know how sorry she was and make things right again.

The sun sank lower and the shadows deepened, and still she waited, her head sinking onto her knees. "Life *is* serious here, Sheldon," she whispered, thinking of dead dogs and ravaged sheep, snakes and witches and skinwalkers. In her head she could hear her father's voice repeating something he often said: "the world is not a perfect place, Marin...not a perfect place."

Her eyes grew heavy as she waited, thinking that this particular world was not only imperfect, it was dangerous...a very dangerous place.

Marin opened her eyes with a snap. Bailey was growling a low-pitched growl, her ears pointed, nose lifted, and Marin put a hand on the dog's shoulder.

"What is it, girl?" she whispered. Then she, too, heard the faint noise and a soft rustle.

Bailey leaped up and gave a short, sharp bark, her ruff erect.

It was the girl. She carried something in her arms but hesitated to come close to the bristling dog.

"Hush, Bailey, it's okay," Marin said, relieved at the girl's reappearance. "Am I glad to see you! Did you bring help?" she asked eagerly, standing to peer into the half-darkness beyond the girl, looking for the others.

"Yes and no," the girl said, stepping closer. She held a blanket, and she stooped to unfold it next to Sheldon while Bailey walked stiffly around her, sniffing the legs of this new arrival.

There was no one with the girl.

"You're alone?" Marin asked, not believing the girl would come back without help.

The girl nodded and finished spreading the blanket flat on the ground. Marin watched, thinking she intended to cover Sheldon with it, but the girl did not pull the blanket across Sheldon, leaving it stretched on the ground beside him.

"You'll have to help," the girl said, pursing her mouth and pointing with her chin toward the blanket. She stooped and pulled Sheldon's arm onto the blanket, then paused and looked at Marin.

Marin fell to her knees beside the girl.

"I don't think he should be moved," she protested. "What are you doing?"

"We have to carry him to the horse," the girl said.

"You brought a horse?"

"No."

Marin waited for her to explain, but the girl didn't, she just reached for Sheldon's other arm and began to shift his shoulders onto the blanket.

"Wait a minute," Marin said, alarmed. "Wait."

She reached out and caught the girl by the wrist. "What horse?"

"The one my uncle is bringing," the girl replied.

She spoke as if Marin was a little slow, and Marin did feel she was somehow missing something.

"And where is your uncle?" Marin asked.

"He will meet us at the rock split," the girl said.

She looked at Marin's puzzled expression and frowned. "The horse cannot come here," she said. "It's too rocky, and it's dark."

"At the rock split," Marin repeated. "You mean *carry* him, to the rock split."

She thought of the mesa top, the layers of uneven, pitted rock, the gullies she and Sheldon had crossed or climbed, the shallow ravines they had navigated through or around that afternoon.

Too hard for a horse to manage in the dark, but not for two girls?

"I don't think it's a good idea to move him," she repeated. "Maybe we should just wait. Someone will come."

The girl sat very still, looking directly into her face for what Marin realized was the first time.

Neither spoke.

Even in the near-dark, Marin could see the tiny twin points of light in the girl's dark eyes, and they sat in the sand, knee to knee, staring at one another over the still form of Sheldon.

She wanted to be home. She didn't want to do this, didn't think she *could* do this, and she suddenly knew the girl was thinking the same thing.

"There is no one else," the girl said, answering Marin's unspoken thought. "My uncle will tell the people at the school, but it will take too long for anyone to get to us."

Marin looked at Sheldon.

The injured leg was beginning to swell; she could see a growing bulge above one boot top and his jeans were stretched tight to just below his knee.

Hours for anyone else to get here, then more time to get Sheldon to the rock split and down the mesa...and how long to get to a hospital? Sheldon needed to get started now, and they were the only ones here.

"You're right," Marin said at last, finding she held the girl's wrist in one hand. She released it, holding the girl's eyes with her own.

"There's just no other way, is there?" Marin said, and the girl shook her head.

"This is going to hurt him," Marin said, helping to stuff the corners of the wool blanket under Sheldon. As would dragging him across the rocks, she thought but didn't say. "I hope this blanket is strong."

"The best the trading post has to offer," the girl replied, and Marin glanced at her, not sure if she was joking.

"I don't want to make it worse by dropping him once we get started," Marin said.

Together they grasped the waistband of Sheldon's jeans and pulled him as gently as they could onto his side. Marin tried not to jar his leg—twisted beneath him, the foot still in the snake-skin boot—but Sheldon woke and cried out, pushing at Marin weakly with his free arm.

"Sheldon, we've got to move you," Marin gasped, struggling to hold him while the girl pushed the blanket beneath Sheldon's shoulders and head.

"We're trying to help you. Try to help us, okay?" she said, but Sheldon continued to flail, striking out blindly, hitting her on the arms and once in the face.

Marin barely felt it.

Bailey whined, standing close to Marin's shoulder, each cry from Sheldon causing the dog to pace nervously a few steps away and then back again to crowd against Marin.

She ordered the dog away, holding Sheldon on his side. He was no longer fighting and his moans sounded deep in his throat.

"Hang on, Sheldon," she whispered. "Hang on."

The girl spoke. "He's on."

As gently as they could, they levered Sheldon back again onto his back, now on the blanket, where he lay quietly, no longer resisting.

"Okay," Marin said. "Now what? You think we can drag him out of here?"

"We'll have to," the girl panted. "Hurry."

Marin glanced over. "Won't your uncle wait for us?"

"It will be full dark soon and it is not a good thing to be here in the dark," the girl answered.

Marin opened her mouth to ask, "How come?" then thought better of it and remained silent. She wasn't crazy about the idea of being here in the dark herself.

The girl took one corner of the blanket, Marin took the other, and together they pulled Sheldon to the sandy chute and started up.

They pulled hard, side by side, using one hand to hold the blanket and the other to pull themselves up the ravine as they worked their way to the top. The sand hampered Marin's every step, and for every inch she gained, she slid back several more.

"Like this," the girl said from beside her, and turned, stepping sideways into the sand, lifting her other foot into her footprint as soon as she moved upward.

As the slope became steeper, Sheldon began to slide, and the downward motion caused his injured leg to twist.

Sheldon cried out in a hoarse voice and tried to sit up.

"Sheldon," Marin said. "Sheldon, lie down. You've got to be still!"

His eyes rolled back into his head, and he slumped backward but he remained on the lower part of the blanket.

"I think he's passed out," she said to the girl. "We're only making things worse."

"We must take him out of this place."

"It's too steep. We'll have to wait for help."

"We cannot," she said. "It will be dark soon. This is a place of *chindiis*."

"What?" Marin asked, remembering Sheldon's talk of witches and ghosts.

"Evil spirits," the girl said. "We must go. You stay there, push while I pull. Can you do that?"

Marin nodded and pulled the lower edges of the blanket across Sheldon's legs, and the girl dug both heels into the sand and braced, pulling as Marin pushed. Gradually the blanket began to inch upward with their combined efforts.

Sheldon was a heavy weight, and even though Marin heaved upward with all her might, the sand melted away under her feet at each step until bright lights began to pulse behind her eyes. She tried to coordinate her efforts with those of the girl above, but gave up and just concentrated on not sliding too far back, certain they weren't moving upward at all, until suddenly the girl above her stopped.

"We're up," she said.

Marin's heart was thudding inside her chest, and she could hear the girl's heavy breathing as they managed to move Sheldon the last few steps, the two of them putting him down gently before sinking to sit on the rocks beside him.

Sheldon lay very still, his face white and sweaty, and Marin touched his cheek. It felt clammy and she shivered, looked at the girl.

"I don't even know your name," Marin said, noticing that Bailey was walking around and around Sheldon, shoving her nose into the wrapped blanket, snuffling at Sheldon's face and whining, and Marin wrapped the ends of the blanket as securely as she could about Sheldon's legs and body.

"Well," Marin asked again. "What do I call you?"

The breeze stirred the branches of a nearby juniper tree, the dry rasping noise loud in the silence, and the girl started nervously.

"Here in the dark," she whispered, "it is not a smart thing to talk about names."

"What?" Marin asked.

"This place is haunted...evil spirits," she said. "Do not call them to us."

It seemed to Marin this girl spoke in riddles. "Then what do I call you?" Marin asked.

The girl looked at the still form of Sheldon wrapped head to foot in the heavy wool blanket before she stood, bent, and again picked up the blanket at Sheldon's head, wrapping the edges securely around both hands.

"Call me 'blanket carrier,' tonight," she said, straightening, holding the blanket tightly in both hands. "For that's who I am right now."

CHAPTER ELEVEN

‘Sgt. J. Blue Eyes,’ was printed on the name tag above the words ‘Navajo Nation Police and Law Enforcement Agency,’ and the Sergeant stopped, standing close to the car but not too close. He didn't comment, and Marin didn't speak, watching his eyes move from her face to her gaping shirt and up again before they shifted to the man's hand twisted in her hair.

"Let her go, sir," Sergeant Blue Eyes said, his words polite enough but spoken with authority, and the man smiled and opened both hands.

The instant she was free, Marin pushed herself from the car window, but she kicked out before dropping to the ground, catching the man on the chin hard enough that his perfect teeth snapped together.

She hoped she'd broken a tooth, and she dropped to the gravel.

Sergeant Blue Eyes took a step back as the man flung himself from the passenger door, but Marin barely spared either of them a glance, making two stumbling steps before the hot saliva filled her mouth. She grasped the front bumper and retched into the gravel.

When the worst of the nausea had passed, she raised her head and wiped her mouth on her shirt sleeve but didn't move.

Justin Blue Eyes had moved, she noticed. He was now standing exactly halfway between herself and the man, a hand resting lightly on his uniform belt near his sidearm, his eyes on them both.

"What seems to be the problem?" Justin asked, the soft tones belying the sharp eyes. "Keep your hands on the roof, sir," he ordered. "I can hear you from there."

"No problem, officer," the man said, his arms now folded on the roof. "Just a domestic misunderstanding, you know? It's a private matter."

Justin looked at Marin, and she looked back, unable to speak up for herself just yet but relieved to see him—and saw nothing in his face.

He didn't recognize her.

His eyes left hers, and she followed his gaze to the man's hands resting on the car roof, to the red half-circle of teeth marks.

Marin pressed her hands against the hot metal of the hood to ground herself and took deep breaths to keep the nausea at bay. She knew she had to speak up, had to at least stand up, but her knees had started to quiver with a life of their own.

"May I see some identification, sir?" Justin said. "You, too, ma'am," he added.

Marin straightened, supporting herself against the bumper, and hesitated to get too close to the car.

"Move away a few steps, sir," Justin directed, and the man did so, taking a wallet from his pocket.

Marin levered herself to the driver's door with one hand on the car, not trusting her shaky legs, and reached for her bag in the back seat.

"Leave your IDs on the hood, please, and step away," Justin said, and the man did so, pulling a cigarette pack from his shirt pocket and lighting up as he stepped back.

"I... I... have to sit," Marin said, placing her license on the hood and sagging down into the driver's seat.

Justin looked briefly at each license, then from the photos to each face.

Marin stared back, thinking he moved with the same grace as the rodeo star he'd been when Vangie and herself, and Justin's sister, Frannie, were in high school together.

His uniform looked fresh, the leg creases crisp and the buttoned-down collar stiff, and she wondered how long he'd been with the police and when he'd stopped following the rodeo circuit.

Of course, they were all a lot older now.

His face was harder to read, but there was experience in the lines at the corners of his eyes and mouth.

"Want to tell me the problem?" he said. "Mr. Tolliver, Ms. Sinclair?"

The problem?

She had no idea of the problem. How could she explain what was going on when she didn't understand it herself?

"Tolliver," she repeated. She didn't recognize the name.

She looked at Justin.

"I don't know this man," she said. "He...assaulted me," she managed before the bile again rose in her throat.

He was the man driving the Chevy truck, she was sure of that, but where was the truck, where was his blond passenger? She bent her head to the steering wheel, her lip and jaw throbbing, and wanted to be anywhere but here.

Guess you should have stayed home, he'd said...

Did that mean anything?

"Ms. Sinclair?" Justin said.

"He... they..." she stopped, swallowed. "He said I should have stayed home..."

Tolliver exhaled a stream of smoke and flicked the butt away.

"This is too much," Tolliver said. "I'm not sure what it is you're trying to prove, but I guess I'll play."

He turned to Justin Blue Eyes.

"We had a disagreement. She ordered me out of the car." He shrugged. "I didn't want to go."

Justin looked at Marin.

"I don't know this man!" she said, leaning on the door. She heard the note of hysteria in her voice and tried to rein it back. "He got into my car, demanded a ride. I said no but he wouldn't get out, and then he..."

"Be nice, Marin," Tolliver said, and her surprise cut through her confusion.

"How do you know my name?"

He shrugged and sighed, and he exchanged a glance with Justin as he lit another cigarette.

"I don't know this man," she said again. "They've been following me since Cameron. A big Chevy truck, a blue Chevy truck. They—there are two of them—we thought they were playing road tag until they stopped in the middle of the road, and I almost hit them."

"We?" Justin asked, narrowing his eyes at the words 'road tag.'

"I have a witness, a passenger...he's not here now," she said, looking around, hoping Lewis George might suddenly appear.

Taking out a black notebook and motioning toward the store, Justin said, "Maybe we'd better go inside and get this sorted out."

"That won't be necessary, Officer," Tolliver said. "I will willingly take myself out of the picture and sit here if that's what she wants. If I could just have my license back..."

He held out his hand.

"You can't assault me and just waltz off!" Marin cried.

"Just a moment, sir," Justin said, glancing at the license.

He made a note in a black notebook and handed back Tolliver's license, then turned to Marin and handed across her license as well.

"Do you wish to press charges?" he asked her. "We can all take a ride back to Tuba City and file a complaint. It's up to you."

He stood waiting for her answer, and she saw his gaze following the raven, now jumping from rock to rock, scratching in the gravel.

Justin's eyes were as dark and inscrutable as the bird's, and she watched him, feeling.... what, exactly?

Sad. She was sad that he didn't remember her when he'd been such a prominent person in her life. She and Vangie had gone with Frannie to almost every rodeo Justin Blue Eyes had performed in. Now she represented little more than a distasteful domestic scene he'd had the bad luck to happen upon.

She frowned and looked at him again.

Happened upon? "How did you know where..." she started.

"Before you decide," Justin said at the same time, "I didn't see much that I could testify to, and the contradiction between your two statements makes it your word against his."

He paused and pushed his hat brim back a few inches. "Unless you've got a witness?"

Only the raven.

She reached up to touch her jaw. She would bruise, but what would that prove? Her bruises against Tolliver's bite mark...his word against hers.

The reunion invitation lay on the dash, her name on the envelope, and she picked it up and handed it to Justin.

"This could be how he knows my name."

"Oh, Marin, Marin," Tolliver said, shaking his head. "Maybe we should just meet you in Shiprock as planned. We can talk this out there."

As planned?

"I don't know this man," she repeated.

She watched Justin read the invitation and she focused on his name tag above the shirt pocket—*Sgt. J. Blue Eyes*—and she heard Vangie's laugh as clearly as if she were standing beside her.

"J for *jeeshoo*..." Marin said under her breath, and he looked up.

The word meant turkey buzzard—it was Justin's nickname—she'd heard it shouted often enough at his rodeo performances.

He frowned as he slid the invitation back into the envelope, then stood smoothing the paper between his thumb and finger.

"You're on your way to Shiprock?" he asked her.

"For that," she nodded, pushing her chin to indicate the envelope.

Tolliver interrupted. "If you insist on pursuing this, Marin, I will be forced to file a complaint as well. You *did* bite me," he said, and he held up his hand, her teeth marks plainly visible. "In fact, *Officer*, if I am under arrest, I would like to know now in order to contact my lawyer." He paused a moment as if considering. "I wonder, though, if your superiors will think it a worthwhile activity on your part. I mean, putting in a call to the county sheriff or the state police, and waiting until they respond to a minor domestic incident..."

Marin saw the truth on Justin's face, and she glared at Tolliver and wished she'd kicked him harder. "What does he mean," she asked Justin.

"It's illegal to arrest a non-native on federal reservation lands," Tolliver answered before Justin spoke.

"You mean you can't hold him if I file a complaint?" she said to Justin, incredulous.

"I can hold him for a while, but it's still his word against yours. And, saying you don't know him doesn't look good."

The raven hopped nearer, a piece of debris in one claw, and picked at the gravel with jerky motions of his beak as heat waves shimmered from the top of the red car and disappeared into the bright air, the entire scene like a dream from which Marin couldn't wake.

Justin held out both licenses. "Same address is on both of these," he said, and she looked down.

"How is that possible?" she said at last, and she put her hand to her cut lip and pressed. The pain was real enough, even if the rest of the scenario wasn't.

"But... I don't know this man," she said, the words beginning to sound like a mantra.

Robert Tolliver's photo stared out at her from his license—the blue eyes, the dark face clean-shaven but definitely the same man—and the address beneath his photo was her own. The apartment address, she saw, and not the house, which was something anyway.

She opened her mouth, and another man, shorter and blond, rounded the corner of the store.

"The passenger," she murmured, and Justin glanced up.

"Here we go!" the blond man said, lifting three soft drinks and raising an eyebrow. "What's up?"

"Anything wrong?" he asked when no one spoke. "Bud?"

"Ask Marin," Tolliver said, leaning against the trunk with his back to them, still smoking.

"Do you have some ID, sir?" Justin asked the blond man.

"Sure," he said agreeably. "Did we break some kind of reservation law or something?"

The blond pulled his license from a wallet and handed it over, and Marin looked around for the blue Chevy truck.

"Hey guys," the blond said when Justin handed back his license without comment. "We gotta go if we're going to make Kayenta before dark."

Bud Tolliver turned to Justin. "That's if it's okay with you, Sergeant, of course," Tolliver added, taking one of the soft drinks.

"We aren't traveling together," she said to Justin, unable to read his face.

"Not all three of us in this little car anyway," the blond man said, and winked. "We're following you in the truck... right, Bud?"

"I don't *know these men*," Marin said, her voice picking up heat. "These two almost killed us by stopping in the road," she said to Justin. "I don't know what this is about, but we are *not* traveling together."

The blond frowned and turned to Tolliver. "What's up with her?" he said, and Marin took a step and knocked the remaining two soft drinks from his hands. He swore and jumped back as soda splashed across his shirt and pants. "What the hell, Marin..." he started, and she turned on him.

"*Enough!*" she said. "I am *finished* with this charade. Don't you dare call me Marin! I don't *know* you!"

She whirled around to Tolliver. "And *you*," she said. "You wretched excuse for a man...get away from my car before I decide to run you over with it."

Tolliver threw the cigarette down and took a step toward her, his expression ugly, and Justin's hand went to his sidearm.

"Sir," Justin said.

"Whatever you want," Tolliver said, backing off, his hands up and his voice thick with anger. He glanced at the blond still brushing at his pants leg. "Come on Cecil. Let her cool off awhile. We'll see you later," he said to Marin. "Count on it."

Cecil snatched the remaining drink from the trunk and followed Tolliver toward the store, and Marin turned to Justin, angry.

"This man *assaulted* me, and you—the police—can do nothing?"

Justin's mouth tightened. "Like I said, I can hold him, but anything further has to come from local or state law enforcement...and like *he* says, they don't always take our problems seriously."

He narrowed his eyes, looking toward Tolliver and Cecil rounding the store's corner. "I'll do it if you want," he added.

Marin considered the necessary neutrality of the police, considered eye witnesses and counter charges. It was Tolliver's word against hers, and Cecil's, too, no doubt.

She shook her head, fingering the loose thread from her missing shirt button, and felt the tears beginning to burn. She would *not* cry, and she blinked rapidly.

"Wait here," Justin said.

He turned and walked across the graveled lot, boots crunching, and the raven skipped off the curb and made a hoarse sound. She looked up at the sound, and a bright color caught the corner of her eye—the blue Chevy pulling around from the other side of the store, stopping near the entrance. Cecil emerged from behind the wheel, leaving the motor running, and entered the store.

*Guess you should have stayed home...*Tolliver had said. Robert Tolliver. The blond, Cecil, had called him Bud.

Neither name was familiar, but they knew who *she* was, and for some reason wanted to keep her from reaching Shiprock.

Shiprock, and Vangie Tso.

"Vangie, Vangie...what is going on here?" she murmured.

It was hot and still and more than quiet, the silence weighted, as if the words and actions here had been absorbed whole into the timeless desert just as they had been for countless ages. She felt hollow, the anger draining away with the adrenaline, the events here no more in her control than those silent revolutions of the earth circling the hub of the sun.

She wondered what would happen next.

The car keys were on the floormat, and she picked them up and put the forgotten can of soda, now too warm to drink, in the back, then sat down to wait.

Before too long Justin came back around the corner, two cans of soda in one hand, a sandwich in the other, and he squatted beside her open door.

"Drink this," he said, handing her a soda. "The sugar will help. The sandwich you can save for later if you don't feel like you can eat it now."

She felt his gaze on her face and glanced in the side-view mirror, at her bloody lip and swelling jaw, and suddenly hot tears were running down her face.

"Let me take you to the clinic," Justin said, and she shook her head, swiping at her face with her hand.

"It's anger as much as reaction," Marin said.

"I got that," he said. "Vangie said your temper is the reason you were called 'Nightmare'..."

She looked at him. "I thought you didn't remember me...and it's a play on the sound of my name, nothing more."

"Marin Sinclair, Vangie's *Bilagáana* friend," he said.

"Justin Blue Eyes, Vangie's rodeo-star cousin," she returned. "Anyway, you should talk, *Jeshoo*."

He shrugged and nodded. "Nicknames always have a story, I guess."

"This is the second time you've come to my rescue," Marin said.

Justin frowned and shook his head.

"The Fair in Shiprock—my Junior year in high school—the runaway horse in the rodeo arena," she said. "You don't remember?"

"I don't remember some things—a lot of 'somethings'—from those years," he said.

"You seem good now. I mean—a policeman and all."

"It took a while."

"Seems odd, you just passing by like this... of all the trading posts, in all the towns, in all the reservations..." she said. "Care to explain?"

He smiled. "Susan, inside, called. She heard your horn and took a look. I happened to be in Tuba."

"She heard the horn from inside the store?" Marin asked, thinking of the flutes and the overhead fans, and Justin shook his head.

"She happened to be outside...shooing that big raven off the porch," he said, thrusting his chin at the raven still pecking at the gravel. "It was making a racket."

"I'll go in and thank her." Marin said and opened the soda can. "Orange...now I know I'm back on the rez."

"If you don't want it..."

"No," she said, "*shilikan*."

He smiled. "Glad you like it... and not bad pronunciation for a *bilagáana*. You feel up to a few questions?" he asked as he stood.

She held the cold soda can to her jaw and nodded. "Yeah, I'm just a little shaky."

"Susan says you came in with a tour bus group," Justin said, pushing his chin to indicate the store. "She's never seen the other two—they left just now, headed toward Kayenta."

"Great," she said. "I'm thinking I should go the other way...head home."

"Tell me about the road tag."

"Started when we left Cameron... oh, and I did have a passenger," she said, reminded. "His name is Lewis George. He's a witness—to the road tag anyway. He needed a ride to Tuba. He got out there."

"Don't know him," Justin said. "I'll ask around."

"We ate at the Cameron Post... they may know him. Older man, cowboy hat and gray hair in a *tsiiyeel*. We were staying close to the tour bus after almost hitting the truck when they stopped in the road."

"What do you think is going on?" he asked.

"I don't know, but I think it might have something to do with the invitation."

She handed him the card again.

"Is this reunion legit?" he asked.

"Not unless Vangie has forgotten which year we graduated... and the reception address is the courthouse in Aztec."

"So, not legit, then," Justin considered, handing the card back. "But Vangie wants to see you."

"It's her handwriting," she said. "I'm sure of that, and Tolliver told me I should have stayed home. Flagstaff," she added to his raised eyebrow. "Someone broke into my apartment recently. I don't know why. Nothing seemed to be missing."

"Recently? You don't know when?"

"I'm not often there," she said. "I work... away from home."

"You're thinking the two are connected?" he asked.

"Well, I'm heading to Shiprock to see Vangie for a fake reunion, and those two seem to be trying to stop me getting there."

He nodded and seemed about to speak but she spoke first. "I realize I'm linking incidents with little reason to do so. Go ahead and say it."

He held up his hand. "I was under the impression you and Vangie hadn't seen each other for a while," he said after a pause.

"All the more reason to check it out," she said.

They were quiet then, Marin drinking her orange soda and Justin staring off into the distance.

"I never did know how you and Vangie were related," Marin said, wondering what he was thinking and how much he knew about herself and Vangie.

"My maternal aunt was married to Vangie's paternal uncle."

"Was?"

"Vangie's uncle died awhile back."

"I didn't know," she said.

"No reason you should," he said, and they were back where they'd started.

"Road tag, huh?" Justin said after a minute. "Tolliver didn't strike me as reservation."

She shivered. "How hard is it to fake an address on a driver's license?"

"Guess you can give any information you want. But..." Justin pulled out the black notebook and tapped the cover, "I'll be getting a call back about the license numbers. If they have any kind of police record, I'll know it—if the IDs are valid."

His eyes met hers, his statement including her as well.

"Mine is valid," she said her tone grim.

Justin picked up a small piece of rock and turned it between his fingers, his eyes on the raven.

"I'm headed toward Kayenta myself," he said. "Why don't you go inside, let Susan help you clean up...do whatever you need to do, and you can follow me over, check in to the hotel there, rest. You might decide you do want a clinic visit...and we need to talk."

"About Vangie?"

He nodded.

"I'm not sure how, or if, these two are connected but there's some things you should know," he said, and the raven hopped up beside Marin and dropped several cigarette butts into her lap.

"Friend of yours?" Justin asked, placing a hand on hers as she moved to brush the butts away.

"The raven?" she asked, thinking of its raucous croaks when Tolliver...she stopped the thought—it was too soon to go there. "I think it must be a friend...he's sounded the alarm several times today."

"The one Susan shooed off the porch, probably," Justin said.

"Thanks," Marin said to the raven, and the bird flapped its wings.

Justin knelt and ripped a page from his notebook and folded it in quarters.

"What are you doing?" she asked as he unfolded the paper, took a pen from his shirt pocket, and used it to push the cigarette butts onto the paper before he folded it again and placed it in a pocket.

"Tolliver's?" she asked, looking at the raven now preening its feathers.

"Tolliver's," he agreed, rising. "Those brown cigarettes he was smoking."

"You're going to test for DNA? That will take a while."

"I have a few contacts at the state lab," he said, turning toward the store. "Be nice to know for certain who he is. I'll be out front when you're ready," he added.

"I haven't decided yet if I'm going on..." she started and stopped. She had to keep going—for Vangie, for Mark, for herself. "Okay, but wait. What do we do about Cecil and Tolliver?" she called to Justin's back.

"*Aťaa aťeego*," he said over his shoulder. "It is what it is."

CHAPTER TWELVE

▲▲▲

THEN:
The Rodeo

T he Northern Navajo Nation Fair in Shiprock was going strong, the sun summertime-hot and the air redolent with the smell of fry bread and hot oil, horses, hay, popcorn, and the smell of dust.

The smell of sweat was Marin's own; she was sweltering in the wool jacket of the marching-band uniform, relieved the long parade through town was finished.

The parade had started at one end of Shiprock, continued across the San Juan River bridge, and ended near the fairgrounds on the other side, and now at last 'break formation' had been called and she was free to remove the heavy coat and the braided hat.

She looked around for her father—he'd been on the bridge with a crowd of bystanders—but she didn't see him anywhere.

Vangie, falling out of marching formation behind her, poked her in the back with her clarinet.

"I'm hot," Vangie said, shrugging off the uniform coat and gathering her long hair away from her neck.

Marin nodded, still scanning the crowd.

"I didn't see Edison on the bridge. He told me he'd be watching from there," Marin said. "I don't see my dad either, and I need him to put my stuff in the car."

"Let's find them later," Vangie said, fanning herself with the braided hat. "We can leave our stuff on the band bus for now. I want a cold soda. I'm so hot I almost jumped in the river when we got to the bridge."

Marin agreed, and they threaded their way through fairgoers toward a concession stand.

The fair was already crowded and it wasn't yet noon.

"What'll it be," the teenage boy at the counter asked, busy filling orders for food and drink and not looking up.

"Got anything cold to drink?" Vangie asked, and the boy glanced up, then quickly down again.

"Hey, Vangie," he said.

"Hey, Mel," Vangie answered, her voice cool, and Marin looked at her and frowned.

"Seen Edison around?" Vangie asked.

His eyes flicked up, first to Vangie, then across to Marin.

"He was here earlier," he said.

"And you think he might be…where now?"

"Aahh—at the rodeo grounds?"

"Too early," Vangie said, shaking her head. "AIR isn't 'til three."

The rodeo, known locally as AIR, was shorthand for the All Indian Rodeo Cowboys Association. Vangie had tickets for today's performance—free of charge—from her rodeo-star cousin, Justin Blue Eyes.

Melvin slid two sodas across the counter. "On the house," he said.

"We don't want to get you fired," Vangie said, handing across the money.

"Nah, they want us local kids working," Melvin said.

"Melvin," Vangie said, not moving away from the counter window. "Edison?"

Melvin looked at the line of people behind Vangie and sighed. "I think he said he might catch a ride to the line with a few of the guys."

"The line," Vangie said, and Marin knew they meant the bar just across the reservation boundary line, as it was illegal to sell alcohol on the reservation. If so, Edison wouldn't be back for the rest of the day, and probably not for the rodeo tonight.

Melvin gestured to the growing line behind them. "If you wouldn't mind..." he said.

"Later, then," Vangie said, and Marin turned directly into a tall man standing behind her.

"Sorry!" she said, grabbing at her drink, most of which had splashed onto the man's boots.

"Geez, Nightmare, that's the oldest ploy in the book," Vangie said, laughing, and Marin felt her face flush.

"I wasn't trying to..."

"No problem," the man said, taking Marin's arm to steady her before he stepped away to rub one boot and then the other against his pants leg. "These boots have had a lot worse than pop on them today," he said.

He frowned down. "And looks like they still do," he added.

"Where's your horse?" Vangie said, and Marin looked up.

"You're Vangie's rodeo-star cousin," she said without thinking.

"Hardly a star," Justin Blue Eyes said, offering his hand to Marin with a smile that was pure Hollywood, even to the hint of a dimple in one cheek.

"This is Nightmare," Vangie said. "I've told you about her."

"Star Justin... I mean, Justin. I'm nice to meet you," Marin stammered, raising her hand to brush her palm against the hand he offered.

"He has this effect on women," Vangie said, and Marin felt her face flush. "It comes from being so good-looking."

"You didn't tell me she was so pretty," Justin said to Vangie.

Vangie poked her when she didn't speak, and Marin blinked, wondering what Vangie had said to him about her.

"Aahh...Vangie talks about you, too," she stammered. "Nice to meet you."

"You said that already," Vangie pointed out, but Justin Blue Eyes smiled.

"You get the tickets I had held for you?" Justin asked, and Vangie took them from a pocket.

"Yep," she said. "We'll be there in the grandstand, so try not to let some crazy horse stomp you to death."

"It's a living," Justin Blue Eyes said, smiling at Marin before he walked away toward the rodeo grounds.

"Don't come running to me if you break a leg!" Vangie called, and he lifted a hand without turning.

"That's so lame," Marin said, but Vangie only shrugged, and they headed toward the staging area where they'd left bags and clothes.

"He's gorgeous, I know," Vangie said. "But don't get involved, okay?"

"Wasn't planning on it," Marin said. "And hardly likely to happen even if I was. But why not?"

"He's too old for you," she said. "And besides…"

"What?" Marin said when Vangie hesitated.

"Let's just say Edison looks like a teetotaler next to Justin's issues with alcohol."

"He competes in rodeos," Marin said. "How's he manage that?"

Vangie shrugged. "I think his horse does all the work for him," she said. "Blue's Boy. He's the best roping horse on the rez."

"Justin still has to throw the rope," Marin pointed out.

"Let's head toward the rodeo grounds," Vangie said after they'd changed clothes and deposited their uniforms and instruments on the school bus.

"It's still pretty early," Marin said.

"I've got my reasons."

"Yeah, I bet…a reason named Nelson, right? Or is it Harrison this week?" Marin asked.

"You'll have time to pick out good spots for taking yearbook photos," Vangie said. "Get us a seat next to the corridor where the wall is low enough to jump so we can leave whenever we want," she added.

"Sure," Marin said. "I'll just sit there and save you a seat—*if* no one more interesting comes along," she said.

It was possible Edison could still show.

"It's a bench," Vangie said as she walked away, and Marin made a face at her back and turned toward the rodeo grounds.

There weren't assigned seats for the rodeo stands, just wooden benches on graduated risers and a ticket that specified general admission or the covered grandstand, and Marin took her time walking around the still empty seating area—debating between photographing the action at mid-ring or from near the arena gates where she could see the riders up close.

The gates, she decided—and wondered if Justin Blue Eyes was a grim-faced rider or one of those devil-may-care types who grinned and joked with the handlers before the gates shot open. Devil-may-care, judging from his smile and easy demeanor.

How was it they'd never met?

His sister, Frannie, was a good friend, a year ahead of herself and Vangie in school, and she guessed Justin was several years older than Frannie. She didn't remember him graduating...maybe because of the drinking issue, which brought her full circle back to Edison.

Edison had been drinking more than usual—blaming it on the stress of his Senior year and the difficulties involving preparations to leave home, as he'd been accepted to the prestigious University of Chicago. He was conflicted about leaving, worried about his performance once there, and he excused the drinking by telling Marin he needed to have some fun before he left his friends and family—though he wasn't leaving until August.

Unlike Edison, Marin wasn't a life-of-the-party kind of person. She didn't enjoy the kind of fun he had in mind—being neither a drinker nor an extrovert—so she'd been spending most of her free time with Vangie and Frannie Blue Eyes since the school year had started.

Today, though, she had planned on Edison being with her, and he'd promised to bring his new, expensive camera to take yearbook photos. She'd hoped for some good photos for the yearbook, especially of the rodeo clowns doing their job of distraction, giving a fallen rider time to recover. It wasn't the first time Edison hadn't followed through, and she had the school's camera with her, just in case.

Today's performance was the second qualifying round for the championship rides on Sunday, and she wondered where Justin Blue Eyes ranked in the saddle bronc contest he'd entered. She figured it was close to the top, although Vangie said he preferred roping events. He'd won last year's contest: a money purse and a silver belt buckle.

Vangie had brought the buckle to school one day and showed it around... a big, silver buckle stamped with a bucking horse with all four feet off the ground and a cowboy up top with one arm in the air. The word *Champion* was engraved under Justin's name, and she should have thought to notice if he was wearing the buckle today—though probably he didn't wear such finery for competing. It would have been a great photo for the yearbook though.

Darn that Edison! She'd been looking forward to seeing him, and he knew she was counting on him to be here today.

She walked down the corridor toward the big, circular arena, stopping beside its open gate to check more photo angles, then walked partway back down the corridor. She wouldn't be allowed to stand here once the fancy-dress riders—the flag-bearers for the opening ceremony—were mounted for the entry parade. Maybe she should go higher and shoot from above...

She raised the camera to check one more angle and smiled when she saw she wasn't the only early patron. A small boy, maybe six or seven years old, stood in the packed-dirt corridor, eating cotton candy from a paper cone and sharing small pieces with a large crow hopping about near the boy's feet.

She flipped the flash up and snapped a quick picture, mentally captioning the shot *Everyone Enjoys Fair Treats* when the boy suddenly squeezed his eyes shut and thrust the paper cone in front of him, holding it out with both hands like a small, conical sword.

Shouts and whistles erupted behind her, and she turned and caught the blurred streak of a sorrel horse, a very big sorrel horse, charging straight toward the open gate, already halfway across the arena, nostrils flared and all four hooves churning dirt.

Too late to close the gate.

Too late to jump for the risers, and there was the boy...

The horse shot through the open gate and into the corridor, and Marin lifted the camera and pressed the flash button at the same moment the large crow flew straight up, wings flapping.

The panicked horse reared and crashed sideways into the lowest row of benches, scrambled to his feet and tried to jump the risers, his full bulk coming down solidly on a narrow wooden bench. The bench cracked beneath his weight, trapping a foreleg between the broken pieces of wood, and the sorrel squealed, the sound high and shrill. Kicking, rearing, the big horse succeeded in freeing his foreleg but immediately came down between another row of benches. He floundered, thrashing between the rows, unable to turn around.

"Oh God, oh God," Marin chanted, trying to push the boy down the corridor, his eyes closed and his mouth open in a perfect 'O' one second before his high-pitched screams began. The sorrel horse reared and whistled back, both ears plastered flat against his head, his shrill scream matching the boy's as the frantic horse lunged again—and landed in the corridor.

"Run!" Marin shouted, her eyes on the horse as it struggled to get all four legs steady on the ground, but the boy didn't move. He stood still, screaming, his eyes closed.

"Go, go!" she shouted, grabbing the boy by an arm and one leg and half-lifting, half-shoving him up the head-high corridor wall into a row of benches. "Climb!" she ordered and pointed toward the upper rows, and the boy did so, scrambling on hands and knees from row to row toward the top riser.

It was too late for Marin to do the same—she was backed against the corridor wall—the wall too high for her to jump. She was afraid to breathe as the big sorrel snorted and blew froth almost into her face, his ears flat against his head and his front legs splayed and trembling.

The whites of the horse's eyes rolled, and he snorted a warning when she tried to sidle along the wall, his long upper lip curled and showing teeth.

She stood still, and though the wall behind her stood at least five feet high, she was going to have to jump for it if the sorrel decided to charge.

The horse shook itself like a big dog, pawing at the dirt with a shod hoof, and she bent her knees, ready.

"Don't move," a quiet voice said from over her head, and at the outer edge of her vision she saw Justin Blue Eyes standing above her, hatless, one boot on the top edge of the corridor wall and the other braced against a bench.

"Steady, Crackerjack...steady big fellow," Justin crooned, and the sorrel flicked one ear. "Easy now, boy. I've got you. Everything's okay. We know you don't want to hurt anybody," Justin said in the same soothing tones.

"Hey, Marin Sinclair, you okay?" Justin said without changing his voice inflection, and she barely moved her head in acknowledgment, her eyes on the horse.

"You're doing fine," Justin said in the same crooning voice, and she wasn't sure if he meant her or the horse.

"Stand still," Justin said, and before she could nod her agreement, a loop of rope floated over her head and landed around the horse's neck. At the same moment, Justin Blue Eyes jumped lightly down and tossed a woven saddle blanket over the horse's head, cinching the rope around the horse's neck with one hand and gathering the blanket ends with the other before the horse had a chance to move, all the while talking steadily in the same low croon.

"Easy now, easy. I've got you, big fella. Everything's gonna be okay... nothing to be scared about."

The big horse suddenly sagged against Justin, who took a quick step back and braced against the weight, but his voice never wavered, talking quietly as he stroked the horse's neck. Slowly the horse calmed, and when Justin gently pushed the big head toward the center ring, the sorrel turned willingly and followed him meekly down the corridor.

Only then did Justin look back and meet her eyes.

"You okay?" he asked, his voice still soft.

She nodded, her mouth dry.

"Couple of kids with noisemakers spooked him," he said, and Marin barely had time to nod again before Justin, the horse now docile beneath the eye-shielding blanket, reached the gate and the two were swallowed up amid a flurry of rodeo wranglers.

An older man in a faded red shirt and a battered cowboy hat spoke to her from beside the arena gate. "Good job with the boy," he said, "That was a brave thing to do, Marin Sinclair."

"I was so scared," she said. "I wanted to run."

"That's what makes it brave," he said.

Slowly Marin pushed away from the corridor wall and looked at the boy still standing behind the top row of benches.

"You okay?" she asked, and he nodded.

"Maybe you should go find your mom," she said.

He stared at her a moment before he scrambled over the benches and ran down the corridor.

Marin watched him go, and it occurred to her to ask the older man how he knew her name, but when she turned back the man was gone.

It also occurred to her that Justin Blue Eyes had thrown that rope with no help from his horse.

CHAPTER THIRTEEN

▲▲

T he sun was low in the sky when Marin, following Justin's police cruiser, reached the turnoff to the town of Kayenta. A hotel sat off the highway, the familiar tour bus parked in the back lot.

The miles from Baby Rocks to Kayenta had gone quickly. Justin Blue Eyes traveled faster than the tour bus, and there'd been no sign of the Chevy truck. For a while, as she followed behind Justin's police SUV, she'd tried to come up with some kind of explanation for all that had happened, unable to reconcile the chaos with her carefully regulated life.

The orange soda and the sandwich, which she ate on the way to Kayenta, helped to calm the shakes, and she saved the other can of soda for later. Now, as she left the highway and turned into the hotel parking lot, she regarded the singular events from a distance, as if Tolliver's attack had happened to someone else—easy enough to believe if not for her throbbing face.

She lowered her own window as Justin pulled up and put his window down, but he didn't speak for moment, his eyes traveling over her face.

"I've got to report in for patrol duty," he said. "The station is closed by now, so I'll meet you in the hotel cafe. Give me fifteen minutes... order coffee, whatever else you want."

He paused. "I'll dig up some aspirin and an ice pack at the station." She nodded and his cruiser moved away.

She parked in the front lot, grabbed her wallet and car keys and headed inside.

The lobby was deserted except for the desk clerk, and she looked around, uneasy at being alone.

"Can I help you?" the clerk asked, not looking up from his newspaper on the counter.

"Where is everybody?" she asked.

"Fire dance," he said, turning a page. "Put on for the tourists every week. The cafe is open if you want something."

"I'll be back in a minute," she said, and followed the hallway to a restroom.

She needed to get a room for the night, a place to lie down and recover from the lassitude, both physical and mental, that had to be a kind of shock. She'd talk to Justin, hear what he had to say about Vangie, and then collapse into bed and not decide anything more until tomorrow morning.

She turned on the water faucet and let the water run as cold as it would get, thinking she should have asked the clerk for aspirin as she scooped water onto her face.

Her wrists were sore, beginning to bruise, and it took a moment to remember why, her face having claimed all her attention.

She patted her face dry and looked in the mirror.

No wonder Justin had stared.

Her mouth was swollen around a bloody cut on her lower lip, and a bruise darkened her jaw on one side of her face. She rested her forehead against the cool glass of the mirror.

"Okay," she said to her reflection. "You'll live. I'll talk to Justin first and then it's straight into a room." She used her fingers to comb out her tangled hair and pull it back again into the elastic band. She had changed into a clean shirt in Tonalea, and with the red cap on her head, she convinced herself she looked presentable.

She nodded at the desk clerk as she passed again through the lobby, who looked up this time.

"I will need a room, please," she said.

The clerk's eyes traveled over her face with a look of amazement, but he took her credit card, checked her in and handed her a room key before he spoke.

"Are you...okay?" he asked, and Marin ran her palms self-consciously down her jeans.

"I'm good," she said. "A police sergeant is meeting me here in the cafe, but I'd like to take my things to my room first. Could you tell him I'll won't be long if he shows up and I'm not back? His name is Blue Eyes."

"Oh sure," the clerk said. "Everybody on the rez knows Sergeant Blue Eyes. I'll pass along the message."

"I'll grab my bag from the car, be just a minute," she said.

Outside, the wind was blowing a fine skiff of sand across the highway, and rain clouds were stacking in the eastern sky. Lewis George was right, the fat, purple-bottomed clouds definitely meant rain, and she turned to admire the western sky as well, bright with the golden glow of sunset.

No sign of Justin yet, and holding the car door open with her foot, she leaned in and reset the car alarm, checked to see all the windows were closed for the coming rain, and reached into the back seat for her duffel bag.

"No cops here now," said a rough voice behind her, and a hand gripped her upper arm.

Tolliver.

A visceral reflex of pure adrenaline shot into her bloodstream, the fight-or-flight response surging so strongly her legs trembled with the need to run.

"Sergeant Blue Eyes is coming," she said. "He'll be here any minute."

"I don't think you can count on your policeman friend," Tolliver said. "Not after the message you left."

"Message?" Marin asked, looking at the blinking ignition light. She'd stuffed the car keys in her pocket. If she could get her arm free...

Tolliver tightened his grip and showed her the phone, *her* phone, in his hand, tossing it and her wallet in the front seat.

"The one you sent saying you're sorry, but you've had a change of heart, have decided you will go home after all."

"He won't believe it," she said, turning to face him, sure neither man had been close enough to hear the rest of her conversation with Justin.

"He'll believe it," Tolliver said.

He pointed down the road, toward a shed that was likely a winter bus shelter, and Marin saw the Chevy truck idling behind it.

"He'll see my car..." she started.

"It won't be here," Tolliver finished, and jerked her away from the car door.

She went to her knees, falling at eye level with the soda she'd bought at Baby Rocks, still in the backseat where she'd tossed it, lying on top of her green field jacket.

"I'll need my coat," she stammered, her heart pounding so hard she barely heard her own words.

"A coat?" Tolliver sounded incredulous. "In this heat?"

"It's cold here at night," she said. "And it's going to rain."

"You won't need it," he said, gripping her hair beneath the red cap and pulling her halfway up when she didn't stand. "I'll be here to keep you warm."

"Please," Marin said, twisting away. "My jacket's right here in the back."

Tolliver hesitated. "It might not be a bad idea to get all your things out of the car," he said, and pushed her as she reached into the back seat, releasing her arm to shove a rough hand up her shirt and hold her against his body, his breathing fast and shallow.

Not giving herself time to think, Marin grabbed the warm soda can, gave it a shake, and pushed back into Tolliver hard enough to throw him off-balance for the instant she needed to turn and flip the soda tab.

A spray of warm soda shot out directly into Tolliver's face, and Marin shoved him away and dropped the can, threw herself into the car, and slammed the door, punching the door-lock mechanism with her left hand and pushing the ignition button with her right.

Nothing happened.

Her heart stopped for one full second before she remembered she had to step on the brake and the clutch before the car would start, and she slammed a hand against the reset button and tried it again as Tolliver swore and beat a fist on the window.

The engine caught this time, belts revving as she yanked the car into gear.

"Don't die, don't die," she prayed, letting out the clutch with the gas pedal still floored, and she almost hit the hotel's electronic signpost when the car shot forward, tires squealing.

She wrenched the wheel around and skidded sideways onto the shoulder of the highway, catching a glimpse of Tolliver in her mirror before she lost sight of him in the cloud of dust ballooning behind her.

She straightened the car out and jerked her shirt down, knowing if the Chevy caught up with her this time, it wouldn't be to play road tag.

Her hands on the wheel began to shake.

"Think!" she commanded, but all she could think of was how quickly the Chevy could catch up with her and what would happen if they forced her off the road.

No Justin Blue Eyes to come to her rescue now.

She had turned east instinctively, away from the glare of sunset and toward town—and the police station—but Justin had said the station was closed. If she took the turn into town, she'd be among closed and empty businesses and headed straight into the vast expanse of Monument Valley.

No good. She needed people, lights, and activity.

Already she could see headlights in her rearview mirror which had to mean Tolliver; it was too soon for Justin to know she had left the hotel.

She resettled the red cap on her head and again commanded her brain to think.

She needed to circle back so Justin would find her. Surely the hotel clerk would tell him she'd suddenly disappeared after taking a room. Justin wouldn't believe any message Tolliver might send...or so she hoped.

She clenched the wheel to stop her hands shaking and aimed the red car down the highway, her foot hard on the gas pedal.

Driving straight down the highway like this was crazy. She'd seen the big Chevy sitting at the hotel idling, ready to give chase. The little sports car was fast, she knew that from this afternoon, but faster than the truck behind her?

The next police station would be in Shiprock, a hundred miles away, too far for her to chance outrunning Tolliver. This highway branched north and south, near Mexican Water, onto U.S. Highway 191, a major artery through Arizona, but Mexican Water was at least another forty miles away.

She'd never make it before Tolliver caught her.

At least her previous lassitude had vanished. She felt jittery, limbs trembling and heart pounding, but a grim determination had taken hold, too, what Edison had called her 'damn the torpedoes' mentality, meaning her tendency to forge ahead without regard for the consequences—something she'd called tenacity and he'd called stubbornness.

She and Edison Washburn had spent a lot of time driving the roads around the reservation during high school. It was a way to be alone together and a typical pastime. Now she just needed to calm down, orient herself, and find the landmarks she once had known so well. There were homesteads and small communities off the highways. She could lose herself in the maze of roads, both dirt and paved, that crisscrossed the reservation.

Near Dennehotso School, just ahead, there was such a maze cutting across to Rock Point and circling around toward Chilchinbito. She could get back to Kayenta and Justin that way. Even if those roads had been paved in the past fifteen years, the maze of interconnecting roads were largely unknown to non-locals. Tolliver and Cecil would go on to Mexican Water and turn south on Highway 191 searching for her—*if* they didn't see her turn off the highway.

She'd worry about that later.

For now, it was a plan, and she needed a plan.

Before finishing the thought, she again saw headlights in the rearview mirror and glanced at the speedometer. It was holding steady at 100 mph but Dennehotso was coming up fast; she'd have to slow down for the turnoff. She felt a flutter of hope as she turned onto the remembered dirt road. She drove a short way before again speeding up, her eyes on the rearview mirror, trying not to raise too much dust, and she almost hit a group of horses crossing the road.

The car skidded as she yanked the wheel to one side, the undercarriage scraping across rocks, and a boy of ten or eleven years, with an older Diné man, stopped and looked at the red sports car as if she had dropped from the evening sky. The horses, four or five shaggy ponies, took advantage of the distraction to spread out, pulling at clumps of bear grass while Marin tried to restart the car.

Hands sweaty on the wheel and gritty from the settling dust, she forced herself to wait before trying a second time, her frustration close to panic.

The man and boy moved on across the road, the boy bunching the ponies again and aiming them toward a dirt track to the east, the man shaking his head as he followed.

Marin called to them from the window. "Is this the road to Rock Point?"

The man said something in Navajo she didn't hear, and the boy looked over at Marin and walked back.

"My grandfather says yes," the boy answered, smiling, "if you can fly."

The boy helped push her car back onto the road, telling her he was out of school for summer vacation, and that yes, this was the road to Rock Point if she headed east—but it would be rough going for such a car.

Marin offered the wrapped sweet roll from Baby Rocks and the remaining can of Justin's orange soda as thanks, and the boy patted the hood of the car—'a sweet *chidi*'—and had her promise she'd give him a ride when she saw him at school in Rock Point.

The engine started when she tried again, and Marin sat for a minute, watching the boy run to catch up with his grandfather, recalling a life of interconnected paths and relationships, one where you were confident you'd see the same people again.

Rainclouds were layered along the eastern horizon as she followed a dry wash toward the east, and she thought again of Lewis George as she bumped along the ruts...he'd enjoy this ride.

She kept up the speed of the car as best she could on the rough track. It was not yet full dark, and the dust billowed behind her—she might as well shoot off a flare to advertise her whereabouts, but there was no help for it.

The track rejoined the highway at Rock Point, passing through the few buildings in town before the dirt roads led back into the maze, but she saw no sign of the Chevy truck, or anyone else. She'd passed the community school, the turnoff back to the west and Justin just ahead, when headlights flared in her rearview mirror.

Tolliver.

He and Cecil must have parked behind the community school and waited for her.

The Chevy truck pulled up behind her, and Marin no longer cared why the two pursued her. The reason didn't matter. Escape was all that mattered now.

She flipped off her headlights and pressed the gas pedal, racing down the highway toward Round Rock fifteen miles ahead, knowing she was back where she'd started—on a highway where she could be forced off the road before she could reach a town of any size.

The truck had fallen back—the headlights smaller in the mirror—but she had no doubt they knew she had to stay on this highway toward Lukachukai or take the branching highway to Many Farms.

Either way, the police departments in Kayenta or Chinle were too far away to be of help.

There was another cutoff nearby, and it lay dead ahead. She saw the sign, made the decision, and swerved, the car fishtailing onto a dirt track leading east to Los Gigantes Buttes.

She'd been here often—the Buttes were a well-known attraction—but the road to the Buttes was not part of any maze she knew about. It led only a short way past the Buttes and circled back to the highway. Still, she could hope Tolliver would miss the turnoff, and she could escape behind them.

The ground grew steeper as she neared the flat-topped buttes, the monoliths rising against the dark sky, the road either rocky or covered in deep sand. She passed the buttes and continued on, aware the track would end soon, and looked for somewhere she could hide the car while she waited to see if she had been followed. A jagged lava formation, a ridge jutting up from the ground to the north, caught her attention but to get to it she'd have to leave the track. It was full dark now, if she encountered a hidden wash or even a shallow ravine, the low-set car wouldn't make it.

She decided abruptly and swung north anyway, making for the ridge as directly as she could. There were no lights behind her, but she knew they'd be coming, almost as if they were tracking her... and she thought of her phone. At the hotel, Tolliver had been holding her phone.

She glanced at her phone lying in the passenger seat, picked it up and turned it off, knowing it was too late, and she stopped the car, put her head on the steering wheel.

All of her running, her maneuvering done for nothing. She could imagine Tolliver laughing, could imagine how entertaining he'd found it to check her at every move. He didn't have to chase her, he could block her escape until she gave up, until she stopped running, stopped fighting...if she gave up.

The low-set car scraped over the rough ground and jolted over rocks, wallowing in the deep sand as Marin pressed toward the lava ridge. Several times the wheels spun uselessly or the car high-centered on a rock, and she jerked the transmission in and out of reverse, rocking the chassis and gunning the engine until the tires caught again and she gained a few more yards. For a moment she envisioned the reaction of the man at the rental agency at this untoward treatment of the car, and she smiled grimly. Voiding the insurance was the least of her problems.

The lava ridge loomed close at last—tall rock slabs like leaning dominoes thrusting from the ground. Such lava ridges were common, and she drove as near to them as she could, managing to maneuver the car a short way between two slabs before she killed the engine.

Instantly the desert pressed in, the dust slowly dissipating, the silence making it easy to hear the sound of another engine coming along the bumpy track.

Tolliver.

She opened the door, first disengaging the overhead light, and got out, looking for a place to hide. The tall serrated ridges towered over her head, seamless and impossible to climb, and the night offered no protection even though it was now full dark, for Tolliver could simply use his headlights to see where her tire tracks led.

There was nowhere to hide.

"Panic is your worst enemy," her father had said to her countless times over the years, giving up trying to keep her off horses and mesa tops, focusing instead on teaching her a few survival skills with rope knots, and making sure she always carried a pocketknife.

"Look for the obvious and use it," he'd said.

She took a deep breath and looked around, the obvious not readily presenting itself, and she couldn't help wishing for the safe routines of her ordered life, wishing for Justin Blue Eyes to come to her aid, and even wishing for Bailey, her loyal companion now years gone.

More than anything, she wished she had never returned to this dangerous place.

CHAPTER FOURTEEN

THEN:

The Mesa

Marin looked down at Sheldon's huddled form, his leg twisted beneath him, and lifted her end of the blanket.

The girl was right, they had to get Sheldon to the split in the rocks.

Sheldon wasn't as heavy as Marin expected now they were on flat ground, but he was an awkward burden.

Bailey barked once and ran ahead, seeming glad to be moving again.

"I hope you know where you're going," Marin said to the girl's back.

"Better save your breath for carrying," the girl said.

"You're sure your uncle will be at the split?" Marin asked. "He'll wait for us?"

The girl nodded.

The mountains behind them turned a blue-black color as they walked, the coming night bringing out bats flying overhead in circles, diving down to snatch at insects, some darting toward the blanket and others swooping near Marin's face.

A full moon topped the eastern horizon, an enormous yellow ball, and she welcomed the light.

"Look," the girl said, and she pointed with her chin and mouth. "The rabbit is in the moon."

"What?" Marin asked.

It was growing harder and harder to lift Sheldon over the rocks and several times she had banged the blanket against a rocky ledge, feeling numb from her shoulders all the way down to her fingers.

"That's not a rabbit," she said, puffing with effort. "It's the man in the moon."

The girl shrugged and Marin could barely see the movement.

"Is it much farther?" Marin asked. If the girl didn't talk to her, she wasn't sure she could keep going. It was getting harder and harder to remember it was Sheldon inside this blanket. Sheldon, who needed her help and compassion.

The girl didn't answer, and Marin looked again at the moon, a floating, luminous ball in the night sky.

She flexed the fingers of her cold hands against the blanket to get the blood flowing.

"Why did you say it was a rabbit?" Marin asked.

The girl raised her chin toward the moon, pursing her mouth to point.

"It is a rabbit. See his ears at the top, and there," she said, making another motion with her chin, "is his body and tail."

"I don't see it," Marin said, grunting as she lifted Sheldon over a rock.

"He's leaning to one side," the girl said, and Marin turned her head sideways.

"I don't see a rabbit, I see a face," she said. "The man in the moon."

The sound of her voice must have startled something under the rocks for Marin heard a small skittering sound, and the girl paused and listened.

"When the moon is full, wild rabbits come out of their burrows to wait for dark and stare at the moon," the girl said. "They are easy prey for the eagles, who spot them from the air, even at a mile away. The eagle is my spirit guide...a brave and mighty hunter. The eagle has no predators; it has no fear."

"Eagles?" Marin said uneasily.

"They don't usually hunt at night," the girl said.

She laughed, and Marin wondered if the girl was talking out of nervousness. She'd noticed as the evening grew darker, the girl seemed less and less comfortable and more willing to talk. Talking about the moon and eagles was the most she had said since they had started out with Sheldon.

Marin didn't care. She was grateful, and she looked at the moon again.

It was hard to see a rabbit where she had always seen a face.

"If you say 'rabbit, rabbit, rabbit,' three times before saying anything else on the first day of the month, you'll have good luck all month," the girl said.

"Is that some kind of Navajo legend?" Marin asked. It was growing harder to talk and carry Sheldon at the same time, and she stumbled over hummocks of sage and stepped into cracks in the layered rock. Each time she tripped, she felt sure she would fall and not be able to get up.

"Nah," the girl said, and she looked around and grinned at Marin, who could faintly see the gleam of teeth. "I read it in a book," she said.

Marin grinned back and felt a quick pang of guilt. They were joking when Sheldon was hurt and cold.

She was certainly cold herself. The summer shirt she'd put on this morning wasn't much for warmth in this night air, and she worried about how cold Sheldon must be, even with the blanket around him.

"You'd think a desert would be warmer at night," she said, struggling along behind the girl, picking her way across the uneven rocks, around potholes and cedar roots that reached out to trip her. It was easier to see as the moon rose, bathing the land in silver, but Marin was grateful she was following and not leading. It must be harder in front, trying to choose a straight path to the rock split leading down the mesa, but the girl walked fast, skirting boulders and climbing over the rocky layers as if she knew the way by heart.

Marin stumbled on an uneven rock and dropped one side of the blanket; her numb fingers unable to keep their grip.

Sheldon rolled slightly, but mercifully he did not wake.

"I've got to stop for a minute," Marin gasped, and the girl stopped and put down her end of the blanket.

It was full dark now and the stars were bright overhead as Marin collapsed onto the nearest flat rock. Bailey, who'd been scouting ahead, trotted back and laid her head against Marin's knees, and the girl, too, came and sat beside Marin, sitting very close as if cold or afraid of the dark. It didn't matter which, for Marin welcomed her warmth.

She glanced over at the girl.

Long black hair hid her face, and she sat without moving, not seeming to be bothered by the cold even though she, like Marin, wore no jacket. Her left leg and arm were warm against Marin's right side, her scent a combination of burning wood and warm milk.

"I wish I knew your name," Marin said to her in a grateful burst that she was not out here alone.

"I guess I have lots of names," the girl answered in a voice pitched low, little more than a whisper, and Marin moved closer.

"I have clan names, names my friends call me, a name for school, a name my mother uses, and a name that is secret," the girl said.

"But you must have one *real* name," Marin said, and she whispered, too, not knowing why, and she wondered about a secret name. Why would a name be secret, and she opened her mouth to ask, but the girl continued.

"All of my names are *real*," she said. "I have names that say the clan I was born for and the clan to which I was born. I have names that say where I live and what my family does."

"But what name is on your birth certificate?" Marin asked. "What name do you put on your school papers? And what do you mean by clan?"

The girl shrugged, the small movement, their whispers, all swallowed in the night, a ringing silence wrapping them close.

Marin had never thought of the night as alive, but the dark had a waiting quality to it, a listening watchfulness the same as in the rock tunnel this morning. She had the crazy sensation that she was being watched, and she thrust her hand into Bailey's warm ruff.

She thought of wolves, of bears, and the thing Sheldon had said about skinwalkers and evil ghosts—something that had sounded silly to her before but no longer seemed so, on this mesa and on this night.

She opened her mouth to speak to the girl, and then closed it again. Maybe the girl was right, and it was not a good idea to speak of things that might be about in the dark.

A cold breeze brought the smell of pine from the mountains, and somewhere a fire burned. Marin could smell the woodsmoke.

It should be a gentle summer night, but the silence was too close, the darkness too black.

Even the moonlight was now cold and forbidding, and strange shadows moved among the rocks, shifting as clouds raced across the face of the moon, chased by the wind.

A coyote barked in the distance, and Bailey pricked up her ears, the night wind sifting through the dog's fur. A long strand of the girl's black hair blew across Marin's face, and as she reached to move it, the breeze and all the nighttime sounds suddenly stopped, completely ceased to be as if a heavy door had been slammed shut.

The silence was absolute, and Marin could no longer smell woodsmoke or the scent of mountain pine. The very air around her had been sucked away, and she was sealed in a vacuum of silence. An icy bead of sweat trickled down her neck and she could feel her heart hammering. She felt it but couldn't hear it, and she turned to the girl, puzzled, and saw her wide, scared eyes, and knew her own must look the same. She tightened her hand on Bailey, the dog's fangs showing in a snarl Marin could see but not hear, and she reached for the girl's hand.

A low sort of murmur began to build, a sound like that of running water or the roar of a distant crowd, a sound she didn't hear so much as feel, as if the night itself had acquired a voice.

Marin sat frozen as the sound grew louder, not daring to move and having difficulty breathing, straining her eyes and ears into the dark, not sure if the girl beside her was experiencing the same thing. She turned to ask, and the girl's eyes were closed, her lips moving as if she were praying, but Marin could hear nothing. Marin began to pray, too, saying the words, 'The Lord is my Shepherd,' over and over, unable to hear her own voice, unable to remember more of the psalm.

The low and steady sound grew louder, turning to pounding drums and a harsh chanting, and grotesque figures dancing around a blazing fire took shape before Marin's eyes—gnarled creatures barely recognizable as human beings with twisted limbs and hunched backs. Wolf heads with long snouts, sharp fangs, and pointed ears covered their heads, and they wore wolf pelts draped across their backs, the dangling forelegs with long claws jerking in frenzied rattles on naked chests.

The figures leaped toward the sky and down to touch the earth, outlined in flames of yellow and red, and the drumbeats pounded behind Marin's eyes in rhythm with the harsh chanting, the sound beating harder and harder in her head and chest until she couldn't breathe, couldn't think. She was close to blacking out when suddenly she was released from the vacuum, and the night sounds came flooding back. She could hear Bailey's snarls, could hear the girl whispering in a language Marin didn't understand.

She took deep breaths of cold air and found she was gripping the girl's hand with all the strength of terror as the normal nighttime sounds swirled around them, the sighing of the wind, her own beating heart. The hunched figures, the fire, the drums and chants, all of it was gone, all of it had disappeared into the night, and Bailey shook out her fur as a gust of wind lifted Marin's hair away from her neck.

Marin's eyes locked with the girl's.

"What *was* that?" Marin whispered.

"You saw it?" the girl whispered back, seeming surprised, her voice no louder than the stirring breeze.

"The fire? Those...dancers?" Marin said. "Of course I saw it. I heard it, too. So did Bailey." She paused, then whispered. "Were those the wolf-witches?"

The girl nodded and put her mouth close to Marin's ear. "*Yee naald-looshii*," she whispered, the word a mere breath. "Skinwalkers. We have to leave this place," she added, and bent and wrapped her hands around one end of Sheldon's blanket.

Never had Marin wanted so badly to run, as hard and as fast as she could to anywhere away from here, and the girl looked up.

"I can't do it," Marin whispered.

The girl didn't change position, just raised her head, waiting for Marin to pick up her end of the blanket, and shame washed over Marin in the face of the girl's courage. Still, it took everything she had to reach down and take the blanket.

Her hands felt like claws, stiff and cold, and she forced her numb fingers to grip, forced her legs to take the first shaky step and hold the blanket off the ground. She could see that the girl, too, was tired, could see it in the slump of her shoulders, could feel it as the blanket sagged closer to the ground, but the girl walked on, and Marin followed.

They took no more rests, for the mesa was now a sinister place, the ground an eerie wash of silver in the moonlight, the bushes and rocks deformed and menacing shapes. They were barely keeping Sheldon off the rocks, skimming the blanket across the layers of stone and low brush, and Marin concentrated on picking up one foot and then the other, making it into a cadence in her head, one foot up, one foot down, refusing to let herself think of the horror of those dancing figures...Sheldon's wolf-witches.

Marin prayed this nightmare would soon be over, prayed they were walking toward the split in the rock wall. They had twisted and turned so many times to avoid the breaks and the small gullies that Marin couldn't have said which way led to the cliff path. She thought she recognized the rock near the mesa edge that Sheldon had named Turtle Rock, but she wasn't sure, for it looked as if the head of the turtle had fallen away, and she shivered at how close she and Sheldon had stood to the edge, bouncing on the rock.

Bailey walked beside her, pressing so close that Marin tripped over the dog, spoke sharply and then called her back, afraid of losing her in the darkness, and suddenly Bailey stiffened and lifted her nose, growling deep in her throat and picking each foot off the ground with deliberate movements.

A finger of pure, icy fear touched Marin. Not again. She couldn't face seeing those creatures again.

The girl ahead stopped so abruptly that Marin stumbled, striking her knee on a rock slab, and she expelled her breath with a rush, barely able to keep from crying out.

"What is it?" Marin whispered, her mouth dry and her tongue thick, and she knew it didn't matter what it was, now she had stopped she wouldn't be able to go on.

The girl straightened. "My uncle!" she said, her voice high-pitched with the relief Marin herself felt.

A tall shape materialized beside her, and she cried out before realizing the man reaching out from the darkness was there to help lower the blanket to the ground, and the sudden release from Sheldon's weight made her stagger.

The man held a rope halter over one arm and Marin could feel more than see the bulk of the horse behind him.

Bailey circled both he and the horse warily.

"This man is my uncle," the girl said, her voice shaking.

No names again, and Marin nodded at the man who said something in Navajo to the girl.

"This girl is the daughter of a new teacher," the girl replied in English.

"How's the boy?" the man asked, also in English, his voice gruff.

"Badly hurt from his fall," the girl said. "We tried to hurry, but..."

Her voice trailed off, and Marin said nothing.

"There is a truck waiting," the man said, and he pointed with his chin toward the edge of the mesa. "I'll take him on the horse. You walk down behind."

The girl nodded and held the rope halter as her uncle bent to lift the limp Sheldon to the horse's back. The horse shifted nervously, and a sudden gust of wind swept across the folds of the blanket, making it flap, and the horse shied, jerking the halter from the girl's hands.

The girl's uncle, still holding Sheldon, stood rigid, staring at the uncovered face, and he quickly lowered the bundled form to the ground and stepped back.

The blanket fell away, and Marin saw Sheldon, his face chalky and white, his eyes open and glassy.

"No," she said softly. "Oh, no," and she knelt to feel for a pulse, to listen for his breath, but Sheldon lay cold and unmoving, the wind scattering sand across his face.

For a moment the only sound was that of the horse's hooves clattering off into the night, and Marin turned in confusion to the girl and her uncle.

"No," she said again.

The two of them, girl and man, stood immobile for a moment, the girl staring down at the blanket, and she licked her lips but didn't speak.

The man jerked his head at the girl and said in a rough voice, "He is dead."

"No," Marin said.

She pulled the blanket across Sheldon's face, looking up at the girl and her uncle. "He has a broken leg. We have to get the horse back..."

The girl took Marin's arm, pulling her away from Sheldon's body and shaking her head.

"Sheldon's not dead!" Marin cried. "We've got to get him down the mesa, get him to a doctor," she said, pulling her arm from the girl's grip.

The girl threw herself in front of Marin. "Be quiet!" she said, her voice low and intense. "You must not speak his name!"

Bailey whined anxiously, pushing herself against Marin's legs, and when the girl reached again for Marin, Bailey planted all four legs and barked, the dog's upper lip curled, until the girl stepped away and turned to her uncle.

He spoke briefly in Navajo, then turned and walked off in the direction the horse had run.

Marin fell to her knees beside Sheldon. "Where's he going?" she cried. "We can't leave Sheldon here." Her voice rose to a wail, and the girl knelt beside her as Bailey growled, her teeth still showing.

The girl spoke quietly, one eye on the dog. "If you speak his name, you will call his evil ghost to us," she said in a low voice.

Marin put her face in her hands, her tears hot on her cold fingers. "Sheldon's not a ghost!" she sobbed.

The girl placed a hand on Marin's shoulder, and Bailey growled. "He won't be left here," the girl said, her voice coaxing. "Come down with me."

"I won't leave him," Marin cried.

"Come down with me," the girl said again. "Your people are there, waiting...your father, others from the school, his aunt and uncle. They've come for him, come for you. My uncle is going to tell them."

Marin didn't move, didn't answer.

"You can't help him," the girl said. "We need to leave now. We need to go to our families."

"Go then," Marin said in a choked voice. "I'll stay here alone."

The girl stood, walked away a few paces, and came back. "I won't wait for you," she said.

Marin looked up. "I made him jump," she said, sobbing, her arm around Bailey. "We shouldn't have moved him."

The girl was silent, and Marin pulled her shirt tighter at the neck. She couldn't understand how this had happened. Only this morning she and Sheldon had set off for the mesa, carefree and careless. How could she tell her father, how could she tell Sheldon's aunt and uncle, tell anyone, what she had done?

She couldn't.

"Come with me," the girl said again, and this time she took Marin's hand. "We don't want to get too far behind my uncle," she said. "You know it's not good to stay here, your father will be worried."

She pulled Marin to her feet, and this time Marin didn't resist, but she bent and pulled the edges of the blanket tightly around Sheldon, covering his face.

Together she and the girl turned away, Bailey following close, and they reached the split rock cleft, a darker gash among dark shadows.

It was pitch black inside the narrow passageway, and the girl placed Marin's hand against one rough wall.

"To guide you," she whispered, and she started down the steep trail, Marin and Bailey behind her.

The girl's uncle must have caught the horse, for Marin heard the occasional click of hooves ahead as she stumbled through the deep sand feeling her way with one hand trailing along the wall. The darkness was so complete only the girl's breathing and Bailey's nose against the back of Marin's legs told her she wasn't alone.

She lost track of time, trudging in the sand through the solid blackness, tired and numb, moving forward without thinking until she ran into the girl, stopped in the trail.

"Look up," the girl said, her voice low. "Look up."

A thousand stars and more glittered overhead in the narrow band of sky above the rock cleft, making a shimmering pathway in the dark night, the shining pinpoints of light suddenly blurred by Marin's tears.

From close beside her, the girl spoke, her words no more than a breath.

"My name is Vangie...Vangie Tso," she said, and she continued down the trail, leaving Marin to follow in the dark as best she could.

CHAPTER FIFTEEN

▲▲▲

T he wheels of the big Chevy truck came to a sliding halt beside the small sports car, churning sand and scattering rocks, and Bud Tolliver stepped out before the vehicle came to a full stop, a flashlight in his hand.

He spoke to Cecil as he slammed the truck door.

"She's got to be close by," he said. "Probably hiding in the rocks."

He leaned into the driver's window of Marin's car.

"Keys are gone," he said and reached to flip open the glove box. "She must have her wallet and phone on her. She's hiding alright."

"Or running," Cecil said.

Tolliver swore and started for the rocks a few yards away, and Marin lay unmoving in her hiding place, trying to silence the sound of her own breathing.

"Get the truck lights on those rocks, Cecil."

"Bud, listen. We've got what we wanted. She's off the main roads, she's alone, there's nobody out here to help her. There's no way she can make it back to the highway with us watching the road. Let's let it go until daylight."

"Let it go?" Bud turned and spat into the sand. "You listen to me. If she isn't caught, it won't be just *my* job on the line."

He gestured toward the slabs of layered rocks and the mountains beyond. "If MacPherson gets out here and finds she's missing..."

"MacPherson's not out here yet, Bud," Cecil said. "We'll watch the road. If she runs, we'll find her easy enough. If she's hiding, a night out here, alone, will be good for her, make her easier to deal with when Mac does get here."

"We've got to find her now," Bud insisted, and he turned to Cecil. "And you're wrong about MacPherson," he said. "He was in Tuba City asking questions today. Don't forget that Land Rover of his can go anywhere this truck can. He knows by now we didn't 'encourage' her enough to go back home. Who do you think he'll blame for that?"

"Look around, Bud. Where's she gonna go? She can't drive in this sand. We're miles from anywhere and our instructions," he paused and repeated the words, "our *instructions* were to keep her out of Shiprock."

"Maybe my instructions were more explicit than yours," Bud said. "I'm in charge here, not you."

"Nothing was said about hurting her," Cecil insisted.

Tolliver laughed. "Who's going to hurt her? We're just going to hold on to her for a while."

"Is that what was going on today, Bud? You were just holding on to her? You got us mixed up with the Navajo Police, and I know that wasn't part of either of our instructions!"

Bud took a quick step toward Cecil and pushed him against the door of the truck. "I need your help, Cecil, but not so much that I couldn't do without it," he said. "If you'd been better at intercepting that damn letter in the first place, we wouldn't be here now."

"Why are we here, Bud?"

"What's that supposed to mean?" Tolliver demanded.

"Maybe it means I know more than you think about what's going on, about why you don't want MacPherson out here," Cecil said in a careful voice. "Maybe I want more than just a pat on the back if I agree to go along."

Tolliver released his hold and both men moved out of the headlights. The truck door slammed, and Tolliver spoke.

"Take this flashlight and circle around these rocks from the left," Tolliver said. "I'll go to the right. If we're lucky, we'll catch her between us."

The desert stillness reclaimed the night as the two men moved away, the jerky flashlight beams swallowed in the darkness. An occasional streak of lightning flashed from cloud to cloud over the mountains but there was no rain yet, and the only sound for a long while was that of the night wind sighing across the land.

Marin didn't move, her heartbeat loud in her ears, and she strained to hear, unable now to see the men from her hiding place or to tell where they were.

It was a good thing she'd looked through the car manual earlier, for the rear seat of the car was made to fold down for extended cargo space, and she'd pushed the release mechanism just enough to free the seat from its upright position, creating a crack to see through. The space was barely big enough for her to hide, and it felt as if she had been in here for hours. She ached to move and had to force her body into continued stillness, crammed as she was behind the seat and in the trunk. It was hard to breathe normally, and she felt lightheaded, but that was probably due to pure fear and not a lack of oxygen.

She closed her eyes and prayed the two men would leave, prayed for the strength to stay motionless just a little longer, and she added a prayer that Tolliver wouldn't shine a flashlight into the back seat. She'd made sure the overhead light was out, but her hiding place could be seen if they used a flashlight.

Both her legs were threatening to cramp when she heard a faint sound she couldn't identify, a popping noise, like a cork popping out of a bottle. Another pop followed, exactly like the first, and though the sounds were muffled, they could almost be gunshots.

The possibility paralyzed her, and she strained to hear what was happening. For a moment, there was nothing, then she heard boots scraping on rock, and the door of the truck was opened and shut, its overhead light blinking on and quickly off again.

Suddenly Tolliver spoke from right above her head, his voice loud and angry, and she almost cried out as his fist slammed down on her trunk lid.

"I swear, if I find her now, Cecil, all bets are off, instructions or not!" he said.

He was talking to Cecil, but the relief she felt knowing Cecil was still alive was forgotten as her car door was wrenched open, and Tolliver reached in and fumbled around the back seat.

She flinched, shrinking into herself, trying to become invisible. If she moved or made a sound, he would find her.

"It's freezing out here..." Tolliver said, almost in her face. "I'll get her duffel bag and anything else in here...you finish under the hood."

He rummaged about in the back seat and Marin's heart, a part of her she couldn't force into stillness, hammered in her chest as the duffel bag was dragged out of the back seat.

A drop of sweat run across her nose and into one eye, but she didn't move, and she heard the car's hood slam shut a few minutes later.

"Make sure you got the coil pack," Tolliver barked from near the truck, and her heart sank at the loss of the car. "I don't want her going anywhere when she decides to come out of hiding. We'll come back at first light. With any luck, she'll freeze to death." He lifted his voice into a shout, and the hair rose on Marin's arms.

"We know you're out here, in the dark, on foot, alone. Alone!" he yelled louder. "You hear me? *Alone!*"

Marin heard him. His words echoed long after she heard the Chevy truck start up and drive away, but she remained still, shivering, afraid of a trap.

As the terror faded and the night settled back into silence, her fear was replaced by the agony of cramped muscles she could no longer ignore.

Rolling, she pushed herself into the rear seat, where she sat listening.

All remained quiet, the normal nighttime sounds of the desert around her, and gradually she began to believe she was alone.

It was cold, but she'd stuffed her jacket into the duffel bag Tolliver had taken, unable to fold herself into the small trunk space wearing the bulky jacket. She still wore the red cap, though, which would help.

She climbed over into the driver's seat, turning over the names she'd heard: Cecil, Bud Tolliver, MacPherson.

Keep her out of Shiprock, they'd said. Was the invitation the letter Cecil had failed to intercept? It made sense, then, that they'd searched her apartment for it, not realizing it had gone to her house. It was time she admitted to herself what she already knew, there was no class reunion, and the invitation was Vangie's plea to come to the courthouse.

Was Vangie in trouble with the law? It seemed unlikely, and Bud Tolliver and Cecil certainly weren't the police.

She was tempted to read the card again, but was afraid the overhead light would be seen. Light was visible for miles in the desert. Anyway, she knew the contents by heart, the date, the time, and the place. But none of that provided a reason. Was that why Justin had said they needed to talk?

She leaned her forehead against the steering wheel, her shivering not entirely due to the cold. Despite what Cecil had said, Robert Tolliver didn't only want to keep her from reaching Vangie, he wanted to kill her.

She had to think of more immediate matters, like getting through this night, and she sorted through her options, patting her pocket to make sure the phone was there, and she checked for service. Nothing, and she turned it off again. Justin might track down her number, but leaving her phone on meant Tolliver could track it as well.

Option one was the car. She couldn't fix the disabled engine, but she tried anyway to start the car.

Nothing.

Option two was going back to the highway and trying to hitch a ride, or find a door to knock on, but she'd be taking a chance on being spotted by Cecil and Tolliver. They'd said they intended to keep watch, and there was this MacPherson person to worry about, too, someone she wouldn't recognize.

Option three was to walk into the mountains. A difficult option maybe, but it could be done, and done in the dark, as there was no question about which direction to take. Tolliver and Cecil wouldn't expect her to do such a thing, and by the time they knew she had, she could be in the mountains, hitching a ride down the other side and calling Justin Blue Eyes for help. There were summer sheep camps in the mountains, with their grassy valleys and deep springs, and in early June she was more likely than not to stumble upon one.

It would be a long walk into the mountains, into a cold night wind and the rain it would bring. The moon might not be visible at all tonight, for no stars showed in the eastern sky where the rainclouds were banked.

She wasn't sure about trying this, but she had to...she couldn't chance staying here.

She got out of the car, checking to be sure the overhead light was out, and faced into the east wind, ready to start out. She stumbled over something on the ground. Her heart stopped, but her fingers recognized her duffel bag. Puzzled, as Tolliver said he'd taken it, she tugged open the zipper and gratefully pulled out her field jacket.

Something heavy was in one pocket, and it took no more than a second to realize what it was. Suddenly, walking into the mountains was no longer an option but a necessity.

She took the gun from the pocket and examined it by feel, identified the silencer attached to the barrel. So, it had been shots she'd heard.

Whether this MacPherson person found her first or the police did, she had the gun that killed Cecil, and Tolliver had made sure her fingerprints were on it; he'd known she would wear the jacket. Perhaps Tolliver was calling the police even now to report the missing Cecil.

The thought galvanized her into action.

She dressed in layers, adding another shirt and a pair of socks, put the cap on her head and tugged on the jacket, put her phone and wallet in a pocket, and left everything else in the car.

She took the gun.

It was slow going, walking cross-country in the dark, and she vowed never again to be without a flashlight. When she walked into a small juniper tree, she stopped, defeated, to wait for the moon to top the mountains. She sat against the tree trunk and wrapped her arms around her knees, hugging herself for warmth and singing quietly under her breath.

"...gazing at the moon 'till I lose my senses..." but the words reminded her of Vangie, and she let the song die away.

She pulled the jacket tighter, lonely and homesick, no family to miss her or wonder where she was...lost, cold, and alone.

Like the boys in the snow so long ago.

"Bad things can still happen, Vangie," she whispered now as she had then.

"And yet you believe?" Vangie had asked her later, and she'd had no answer.

Suddenly the moon appeared, floating up over the rainclouds until gradually the clumps of sage and the gnarled branches of the juniper were washed in its silver light. She could see to walk now, but she sat for a minute longer, staring at the moon as it rose higher, the rabbit clearly visible, tilted to one side.

She was like that rabbit, perpetually struggling to stand upright, trying to find an even surface in a curved world. Tonight, she was as vulnerable as any rabbit fearing the whoosh of wings or the pad of clawed feet.

She fingered the gun in her pocket.

Maybe not *quite* that vulnerable, and she stood, pulled the red cap down tight, and walked into the mountains.

CHAPTER SIXTEEN

THEN:
Boys in the Snow

It was a gloomy day in mid-December of Marin's eighth grade year, the last day of school before the holidays, and it was snowing, the bus so cold that Marin pulled her feet onto the seat and hugged her knees for warmth.

There were forty miles of road still to go, both pavement and dirt, before they'd get home, and beside her Vangie was passing the time by blowing on the cold windowpane and making frost.

Vangie had been absent from school for an entire week earlier in the month, and Marin had worried she was ill. When she did return, all she would tell Marin was that she had not been sick, but Marin had persisted with her questions on the bus rides home since then, determined to get Vangie to give in and tell her why she'd been gone.

"Did you know that Mr. Stanley keeps a diary?" Vangie asked now, and Marin let herself be distracted.

Mr. Stanley was a new teacher this year, from Boston. He smiled a lot and told them stories in his funny accent, and he asked Marin endless questions about life as a white girl on the reservation, living here in what he called the middle of nowhere.

"A diary? You saw it?" Marin asked, and Vangie nodded.

"He was writing in it after lunch. He left it on top of his desk."

"What did it say? Something about our singing, I bet."

Mr. Stanley had been in charge of the Christmas program this afternoon.

"'Sing through your mouth and not your nose,'" Marin said, imitating his accent, and Vangie laughed.

"No," Vangie said. "It was something about bringing Christmas— bringing Christmas to this 'godless cultural desert'," she quoted. "Why would he say we are a cultural desert? What *is* a cultural desert, anyway?"

"Maybe he means there aren't museums and stuff here like in Boston," Marin said, and she pulled her fingers out of her gloves to blow on them.

She wasn't surprised Mr. Stanley wrote about God in his diary. He talked about God in the lunchroom and at recess, and he asked Marin about religious practices on the reservation.

Vangie leaned her forehead against the frosted window, melting a big circle on the glass.

"Do you know all of the songs we were singing?" she asked Marin.

"Yeah, I've sung most of them in Christmas programs before we moved here."

Vangie blew on the circle and used one bare finger to draw eyes and a nose.

"What are chestnuts, anyway?" Vangie asked.

A younger boy behind Marin was throwing celebration spit wads and she turned to glare a warning at him. "I don't know. I think they grow in England or somewhere," she said.

The bus slowed for a stop and the doors flipped open, blasting cold wind across the floor. Looking through the window at the blowing snow, Marin could barely see the dirt road leading off the highway, or the truck waiting there for the four kids who got off.

She sighed.

It took such a long time to get home with all the stops the bus had to make, and there were a dozen more to go. Mr. Stanley was always complaining that he lived in the middle of nowhere.

He should ride the bus.

Vangie blew fresh frost onto the big face on the window and drew a turned-down mouth.

"He made Sammy and Martha stand next to each other for the program today," Vangie commented, adding pointed eyebrows to the face.

Marin, beginning to realize Vangie was going somewhere with this, watched her draw a stick figure with a rounded back below the big round face.

"So?" Marin said.

"They are brother and sister."

"So?" Marin said again, seeing little reason for Mr. Stanley to know the taboo against physical contact between a brother and sister.

"So…I guess he believes different stuff. Like you do," Vangie added.

"Different like what?" Marin asked.

"You know, the stuff in the Christmas songs, all that."

"Oh." Marin stuck her hands beneath her legs and leaned back, but the seat was stiff and cold, and she hunched forward again. "I don't believe in Santa Claus, if that's what you mean," Marin said. "Only little kids believe that."

"But the Baby Jesus, the Virgin Mary? You believe that?"

"You tell me where why you were out of school for a week, and I'll tell you about the Baby Jesus and Christmas," Marin said.

Vangie considered a moment. "It was because of the *chooyin*," she whispered, her hand covering her mouth as she spoke.

Marin didn't know the word, and she raised her eyebrows.

"My first menstrual period," Vangie whispered. "I was gone because of the Sing my family held," she said, pride in her voice. "It was four days long, and there were many people there. A very good Sing. I am a woman now."

Marin had not yet started having monthly periods and was not looking forward to it. She had certainly never heard of a celebration for beginning menstruation. The most she could hope for was that her father would not notice when the event occurred, a hope she thought entirely likely, as he seemed to live his life apart from hers anyway.

"Like a party?" Marin asked. "A party with lots of singing?"

"Sort of," Vangie agreed, frowning. "But the *haatali* does the sing-ing of the ritual. My mother made the largest corn cake I've ever seen, and all of it was eaten. That's how many people were there."

"And that's good?"

"Of course," Vangie said.

"Why?" Marin asked, not knowing the word *haatali* but not ask-ing. She was wishing her own mother was alive to do things like this with her.

"It means I will be a strong woman," Vangie replied, blowing on the window to make fresh frost.

"You already are," Marin said quietly.

It was the closest she'd come to speaking of the night on the mesa. It was something she and Vangie never discussed, even though they both knew that night—the night they saw the wolf-witches—was the beginning of their friendship.

"So, the Baby Jesus? The Virgin Mary?" Vangie asked. "You believe that?"

"Yes," Marin said.

"Then you are on the Jesus Road."

"What road?" Marin asked.

"You believe in Jesus and God," Vangie said. "Like in the White Man's Bible."

"I believe in God and Jesus," Marin said. "But I don't think there's more than one kind of Bible."

"But you believe Jesus is good, right?" Vangie said. "He is supposed to take care of you?"

"Well, yes," Marin said, growing uneasy with the turn in the con-versation. "You pray, ask Jesus to help you, ask God to take care of you."

"And does he?" Vangie asked, drawing a second hunched stick fig-ure beside the first.

"Yeah..." Marin said slowly, and the memory of the mesa stirred.

"But bad things can still happen? Even when you are good, and you walk in all the right ways?" Vangie asked, using her fingertips to press tiny dots over the heads of the stick figures so that they seemed to be walking through a snowstorm, bowed beneath a big, frowning face, and suddenly Marin knew what they were talking about.

The boys in the snow.

Three days before, Marin and Vangie had arrived home—early because blizzard conditions had been predicted—and in the school-yard there had been a dozen or more men and trucks. Saddled horses and wagon teams stood grouped around as well, despite the snow and a cold, driving wind.

Men and horses were huddled together, heads down and backs to the wind, and a heavily bundled Mr. Genelli, the school principal, was in the center of it all, pointing here and there and giving directions.

Vangie and Marin got off the bus, and Vangie tilted her chin toward Marin's father, who was putting a large thermos and a flash-light in the cab of his truck.

"We've got four or five search teams out—on horseback, on foot, on wheels—looking for them," Mr. Genelli was saying as Bailey came to greet Marin. "But with this blizzard blowing in, and in the dark..."

He scrubbed snow from his eyes and face with both gloved hands before he continued. "We'll be going out in shifts—no more than three hours at a time in this weather—we'll coordinate the search from the school cafeteria. We'll keep the food coming and the cof-fee hot until we find them," he said, and Marin heard a murmur of agreement as his words were repeated in both English and Navajo and passed around the group.

"Keep track of each other," Mr. Genelli added. "Don't go off in this blizzard alone."

What's going on?" Marin asked her father, holding Bailey back from exploring the wagons and annoying the horses.

"Two first grade boys are missing," her father said, his face grim beneath his sheepskin cap.

"Missing?" she said. "How can they be missing?"

"No one's seen them since the start of games and recreation before dinner...and that was an hour ago," her father said.

"We think they just walked off," Mr. Genelli said. "The blizzard may have caught them unawares." He moved away to speak to a team of searchers on horseback ready to set out, and Marin turned to Vangie.

"Where would they go?"

"Home," Vangie said, and Marin looked at her, surprised.

"Walking home? In a blizzard?" Marin asked.

Vangie shrugged, her eyes taking on the shuttered quality that often baffled Marin.

"But it's practically Christmas!" Marin said, refusing to let Vangie shut her out. "There's the dorm parties, the Christmas program, the presents..."

"Doesn't mean they aren't homesick," Vangie said.

The blizzard had lasted two days, with heavy snow and freezing temps, and the searchers found no trace of the missing boys, though the search parties continued in three-hour shifts day and night throughout the storm. Hundreds of volunteers had shown up at the school to take the continuous shifts, but after the first day there'd been little hope for the survival of the two young boys.

When the storm had lifted, the small bodies were found—huddled together beneath a snowbank and no more than a mile from the school.

The bus stopped and the door opened, the cold air again blasting across Marin's legs, and Vangie rubbed her hand abruptly against the window, erasing the stick figures and the giant's scowling face.

"Yes," Marin said, answering Vangie's last question. "Bad things can still happen," she added, but Vangie no longer seemed to be listening.

CHAPTER SEVENTEEN

▲▲▲

*H*aastiin Sanii, Old Man, knew there were no good ghosts. Witches and ghosts were evil beings, something to be avoided at all times, so coming across such a one, even a *Bilagáana* one, was reason enough to return to the hogan and start the day over.

His morning had begun well enough; he had risen in the predawn darkness and—judging sunrise from the light beneath the storm clouds toward the east—had sung the sacred "Prayer of Dawn," offering the corn pollen in all directions. The words of the Bluebird Song were in his mind as he began the day:

Just at daylight Bluebird calls.
The Bluebird has a voice.
His voice is melodious that flows in gladness.
Bluebird calls, Bluebird calls.

The dawn, when it came, was gray and overcast. He didn't really expect to hear Bluebird's call on this wet morning, and there was much to be done, extra work for him, since his daughter and grandson had left yesterday for a squaw dance near Many Farms.

They had taken his grandson's truck, would be gone for at least the three nights of the dance, probably longer, and *Haastiin Sanii* had agreed to care for his daughter's sheep as well as his own and his grandson's roping horse.

In the grayness of the cold morning, he shivered, and under his breath he sang another song as he went to release the sheep from their enclosure before seeing to his own morning routines. What is eaten before noon makes one fat, so it wouldn't hurt him to delay his own breakfast for a time.

A semi-circular corral made of juniper poles and brush stacked against the outcropping of a nearby bluff held the sheep and the four goats, and he lifted down the gate poles, keeping a careful eye out for any lightning struck trees from the storm the night before. His hand went to the turquoise beads braided into his hair. It had protected him from the evil of lightning for many years now.

The sheep were reluctant to move away from the warmth of the pen, but the goats and the dogs persuaded them that fresh grass awaited, and slowly, in the still falling drizzle, *Haastiin Sanii* walked with the herd down a sloping hillside and into a small valley. There was plenty of grass here to hold them for the morning and small freshlets of water from the rain, so he would wait until after his own morning meal to take the horse and move the flock farther down the valley. He left the dogs sprawled in the grass near the flock and went down the bluff to fetch his own water.

It was there, in the wash, his arms outstretched to scoop water from the small ground spring, that the ghost-woman fell into his arms.

"*Eyaah!!*" he gasped loudly, and he dropped the water bucket when the woman screamed and clutched at both his arms. *Haastiin Sanii* recoiled instantly from the unwanted contact and gave another involuntary cry.

The ghost-woman's face was as white as a death mask, her eyes wide and staring, and he quickly looked away to avoid bewitchment. In the gray dawn, he could see that her hair, too, was white—long and wet—as was her skin and the shroud she wore. A water-ghost, for she seemed to be soaked head to foot, the sleeves of her white shroud dripping water onto his arms and hands. He took a step back, away from her, but the woman fell against him, still gripping his arms, and she gasped out a strangled sound. He closed his eyes, certain that his death was near, but instead, the ghost relaxed her death-hold and spoke in a quavering, human-sounding voice.

"Who are you?" she asked, straightening away from him to retrieve a green jacket from the ground.

The ghost-woman spoke in English, and it surprised him—a *Bilagáana* ghost?

"I'm sorry I startled you," she said. "I was afraid you were someone else."

Haastiin Sanii took a closer look, careful to avoid looking directly into her eyes, and in the growing light he could see a little color in her face, could see her hair was not really white, but more a yellow, in the way of the *Bilagáana*. What he had taken for a shroud was a white shirt, long-sleeved and damp, and she carried a green jacket that didn't look much drier than her clothes. Perhaps she wasn't a ghost after all, for as the light of day continued to grow, she did not disappear.

Even if she wasn't a ghost, the woman's eyes were wide and staring, and he thought that maybe she was crazy. Only someone crazy would have been out here alone in the dark and the rain, and nighttime was when the *chindiis* walked and did their mischief. Crazy people must be treated with care, he knew, and the same for witches. It didn't help to make them angry.

He looked at the woman, considering.

She was trembling now, as if cold, but witches and crazy people both were known to be clever. The sooner he saw her off the better, and he jerked his chin toward the direction of the bluff and motioned the woman to follow. He would show her every hospitality and then gently nudge her on her way.

In camp, he seated her with care on a sheepskin beneath the *cha-haoh* he and his grandson had built of slender poles and brush. The brush shelter stood fifty yards or so away from the summer hogan and provided a shady workplace protected from the summer sun.

Haastiin Sanii didn't want to insult this ghost-witch woman, but neither did he want her to contaminate the interior of his hogan and so necessitate its destruction. Better to use the *chahaoh* and destroy it after she had gone. After all, another brush shelter could be easily built.

Haastiin Sanii squatted beside the firepit and pushed aside the ashes, finding the live coals underneath. He added a small piece of steel wool to coax a flame from them, and watched the woman from the corner of his eye as he blew on the coals, adding small sticks as the fire grew. She had not spoken again and sat shivering in her wet clothes after hanging the green canvas jacket over a branch to dry.

He fed sticks to the fire until he had a good-sized blaze going, then placed the coffee pot on the low iron grill before remembering he hadn't gotten the water from the spring after all. He shook the pot and rose to return to the spring, leaving the woman beside the fire.

She looked somewhat better when he eventually filled a cup with hot coffee, and there was also the frybread his daughter had left for him. He would make more later—he prided himself on his ability to cook—and for now give this woman what he had.

He pushed both the coffee and the frybread toward the woman, inviting her with a nod to take it, and tears came into her eyes as her lips and chin began to tremble.

Very much like a normal person, but it could be a ruse to cause him to relax his vigilance so she could blow corpse dust over him. He busied himself with the fire and wished fervently to be rid of this evil.

Marin knew she made this man very uncomfortable, and she thought she even knew why, considering where and how he had found her, but she didn't know how to relieve his fears without making things worse. Just sitting here beside the fire with a hot cup of coffee in her hands was enough to do, and the coffee was good—strong and sweet—she had forgotten the custom of boiling the coffee and the sugar together. The frybread was even better...it had been a long climb and she'd spent the night in the rain. She was thankful she had stumbled upon a road into the mountains the night before, and she had even slept a little beneath the overhang in the wash until the rain caused the trickle of water to grow into a stream that had reached her sleeping place.

"Thank you," Marin murmured to the old man. *"Ahéhee',"* she repeated, lifting the coffee cup.

"I'm Marin," she said. "Marin Sinclair. I need to get to a trading post...someplace to find help."

She was fairly sure this man understood English, for most of the dealings in livestock and pawn were done with Anglo traders at the trading posts, but she could also understand why he would be cautious concerning such an unexpected intruder.

Haastiin Sanii had indeed spent many hours in one trading post or another, smoking tobacco and watching the comings and goings about the place and had some of his more valuable silver and turquoise jewelry in pawn with various traders; it was safe there and the traders had kept it for several years now, knowing that he would redeem it when he needed it.

Old Man refilled the coffee cup for the woman and thought about the nearest trading post, thought about how he would surely need his jewelry soon, for if this witch woman did not take his life, the sing needed to cleanse him from this evil contact would be long and expensive.

He thought of the singers—the *hataali*—that he knew of and which of them would know the appropriate curing chants. One of the Ghostway chants might be needed, and it occurred to him that he might even need the Night Way chant, the *Yeibichai,* if this woman was insane. That ceremony would have to wait until after first frost when the snakes were in hibernation and before the first thunderstorm, when there was no danger from lightning.

The *Yeibichai* was a long and expensive ceremony, and he began planning appropriate places and times in his mind, lost in rumination, one dismal thought following another, as he waited for the woman to finish the meal.

Marin sat and held the cup of coffee and studied the man on the other side of the fire. His face was seamed and wrinkled, but it did not sag at the jaw line, and his frame was tall and spare beneath the loose shirt of red cotton he wore tied around the middle with a woven sash. He wore little jewelry, only a single strand of rough-cut turquoise around his neck and small silver loops in both earlobes. His gray hair was worn long, and there was a turquoise bead woven into a strand of hair near one temple.

Marin wondered at his age, figured him to be quite old.

She inched her feet and her jacket a little closer to the fire and ate more of the frybread, wishing the man would speak to her.

The rain had stopped, and the gentle dripping from the pine and cedar trees surrounding the small clearing were beginning to slow as well. Birds had ventured out and were giving voice to the morning, and Marin sat and listened while she took in the area around her.

A hogan was built higher up the slope, a blanket hanging across the eastern door, and there was an empty sheep pen tucked into a rocky cliff a short way from the hogan. A handsome bay horse wearing a rope halter stood near the cliff, sheltering under overhanging boards propped between a few corral poles and the cliff.

She looked around for the sheep she knew must be somewhere close by, and the dogs, but they weren't in sight. She didn't see any sort of vehicle either, or any other person besides the old man, watching her surreptitiously now that she had finished her meal.

She thought of Justin Blue Eyes, wondered where he was and if he had any idea what had happened to her. Had the hotel clerk talked to him? Had he found her abandoned car by now?

The old man cleared his throat suddenly, and she flinched, startled at the sound. She had almost decided he did not know English after all and was not going to speak—she knew he was anxious for her to go—but instead of speaking, the old man rose to his feet and walked toward the corral.

She stood as well, catching up her jacket, thinking the man meant for her to follow, but he made no sign, and she paused. The horse was cropping grass, watching the man with one eye and a cocked ear, but didn't attempt to move out of reach when the man grasped the rope halter and led the horse toward the hogan.

Passing Marin without word or look, the man left the horse outside the hogan and ducked under the blanket door, emerging a moment later with an ancient-looking saddle, a bridle, and a thick saddle blanket woven in red and black yarns.

Silently, the man began to saddle the horse, smoothing the blanket across the horse's back and throwing the saddle over, pulling the cinch tight. He put the bridle on last, removing the halter and settling the bit into the horse's mouth before reaching to adjust the braided straps over the ears. Finally, he led the horse across to Marin.

Without really looking at her, Old Man thrust the reins out and spoke for the first time.

"You go now," he said, and pursed his lips, pushing his mouth and chin toward the east.

"I can't take your horse," she protested.

"You go now," he said again.

Marin opened her mouth to object and slowly closed it again. She was being asked to leave, but the old man was giving her a way to get down the mountain, and she had no wish to bring trouble to him if Tolliver had somehow managed to follow her here.

She took the reins.

Haastiin Sanii grunted and stepped away toward the fire, and Marin tied her jacket to the saddle before mounting, surprised when the man returned and pushed the remainder of the frybread into her hands. With one hand on the bridle, he pointed the horse's head toward the pines beyond the corral.

"Over there," he said, and he pointed again with mouth and chin, "is a good way to the trading post."

The sun slid suddenly from behind the clouds, and Marin felt the quick, hot warmth on her damp hair and clothing. It felt good, and the horse twitched its ears back and forth as if pleased to be starting out. But for her fear of Tolliver, the day would be any ordinary summer day in the mountains, and a wave of depression swept over her.

Nothing to do but keep going, and she waited for any more words the man might offer, for he seemed to be listening and thinking carefully, but he said nothing, only slapped the horse on the rump and stepped away.

"You go now," he repeated, and the horse started off, walking slowly despite the slap, and Marin turned in the saddle.

"I'll leave the horse at the trading post," she said.

Behind her, *Haastiin Sanii* shrugged, feeling relief as he watched her ride away.

She was someone in a lot of trouble or someone bringing a lot of trouble, but he had done the best he could. His grandson would understand about the horse.

He looked down at the wide sash wrapped around his waist and fingered the gun he had found beside the spring, then looked down the trail and considered the woman on his grandson's horse. He wondered if she knew a flashflood was coming and if she knew enough to stay out of the canyon.

He shrugged again, figured a witch-woman would know and a crazy person wouldn't care.

CHAPTER EIGHTEEN

▲▲

THEN:
Edison

M arin had dated Edison Washburn, known as "Wishbone" to his friends, ever since Rita, a cousin of Edison's, passed her a tightly folded note one afternoon in Freshman English class.

Inside, printed in small block letters, was a single line: How about a movie? The note was signed with a tiny wishbone.

Back then, the only movie was the drive-in theater in Shiprock, open from May until cold weather, and it did a thriving business.

It was really more a place to visit with friends and talk than to watch a movie, a place to share information and find out what the who of what was going on—who was dating who and who was breaking up, who was pregnant and who the father might be—and such information was endlessly speculated on and gossiped about.

In general, nobody paid much attention to the movie showing on the big screen.

In four years of high school, the only time Marin remembered ever going to the drive-in to watch the movie was the night she and Edison went to see *Billy Jack*, and she remembered that night not so much for the movie as for the near riot it caused.

Billy Jack, the Vietnam vet who was half Diné, had taken a lot of abuse from a town full of Indian haters and bullies before he at last let loose with his trademark *hapkido* moves, and every movie-goer with a working automobile horn blasted out their approval when he did, joined by hundreds of fists hammering on vehicle fenders, doors, hoods, and roofs. A mighty roar of whistles and shouts rose from the patrons inside the concession stand, and even the guys hanging around in the dark smoking weed and drinking cheap wine hidden in paper bags cheered, their faces a ghostly blue in the smoky light filtering down from the projection room.

"Edison, it's just a movie," Marin shouted over the noise, and Edison looked at her as if he'd momentarily forgotten her existence, his hand jammed hard against his truck's horn.

"It's a movie!" she shouted again. "It isn't real. They're actors. It doesn't mean anything!"

"It means something right now," Edison yelled back.

The big outdoor screen went suddenly blank, and the manager announced through the metal speakers that unless there was quiet on the grounds, the movie would be stopped, and everyone would go home—without a refund. That only made things worse, and it was a while before things got quiet enough for the manager to resume the film.

When Billy Jack was arrested at the end of the movie, led away by the police after defending his girlfriend's honor, Marin doubted there was a patron—a Diné patron at any rate—in the entire lot who did not have a fist raised in solidarity with Billy Jack and his on-screen confederates in a silent but emphatic gesture of defiance.

"Billy Jack isn't real," she said again to Edison when the cheers at the movie's end finally died down. "He's an actor in a movie."

"He's a hero," Edison told her. "*Our* hero. We don't analyze it, we just enjoy the moment."

That was Edison, always dealing in the now. It was a trait she both despised and coveted.

It was at the drive-in movie that Edison gave her the red cap.

It was late August, and Edison was leaving in a week for his first semester at the university in Chicago, leaving the same week Marin and Vangie's senior year was to begin.

Marin was glad of the chance to be with Edison on what was looking like one of his last free nights. She wanted to talk about their relationship and come to some sort of understanding before he left, but from the moment they arrived, his truck was a way station for friends and well-wishers. The first picture was over and the second had started, and Marin was getting discouraged about ever talking to him alone.

"Edison," she started again in a sudden lull between visitors, but a tap on the window grabbed his attention.

"Hardy-boy!" Edison said with enthusiasm. "Get in here, man," and he scooted over toward Marin's side of the cab to let Frank slide in.

"Edison," Marin began uneasily. Frank usually meant trouble, and his brother, Joe, was never far from his twin.

"Hear you're off to some big city school in *Shit-cago*, Wishbone," Frank said, glancing over Edison's head and giving Marin a nod.

She wasn't popular with Edison's friends, and she knew it: one reason being she was Anglo, but the bigger reason was she made no secret of disliking their drinking parties.

"Yeah," Edison answered. "I leave in a few days."

"So, when's the send-off party?" Frank asked, and he waved a paper sack under Edison's nose. From the smell, Marin knew the bottle was already open.

"Now, I guess," Edison said, laughing, and Frank whooped in approval and yelled out the window.

"Wishbone's havin' a going-away party!"

Edison looked sideways at Marin as he took the bottle, shrugging at her expression and taking a long drink, and more guys appeared, urging Edison out and to the tailgate, and he pulled Marin with him. More bottles appeared, passed over and around her head, until finally she gave up, shouting to Edison through the noise that she was going to the concession stand.

No one seemed to notice when she left.

Outside the truck, she stood for a moment, adjusting to the dark, unable to see much besides the hump-backed sea of vehicles and the faint gleam of metal speakers. The nighttime air was chilly, and she shivered as she headed for the concession stand, wondering how long it would be before Edison came to find her and what kind of shape he would be in when he did. His drinking bothered her, and Edison seemed to be drinking more and more, excusing it by telling her he was leaving his friends behind for college and was just having some fun before he left.

There was a lot about Edison's behavior lately that baffled her.

He had secrets of self that he never shared, and he seemed to have a contempt for himself that he looked to her to contradict, only to heap scathing criticism on her when she did so. His habit of mocking her, though subtle, was confusing, sending mixed messages of both affection and dislike.

After four years of dating, he said he still wanted to be with her, and she wanted to be with him, but it was growing harder to endure his habitual sarcasm.

She reached the concessions building—a combination snack bar and projection room—breathing in the warm air and the smell of popcorn.

She didn't want anything to eat, mostly she was hoping Edison would be alone by the time she walked back, but she did need to visit the restroom and she started toward the back, almost bumping into a girl rounding the snack counter holding a cardboard tray of popcorn boxes and soft drinks.

"Sorry," the girl said automatically, then looked up and giggled.

"Oh, Marin, it's you," she said.

"Hi Sheryl," Marin said, moving to go around her, her mind still on Edison, but Sheryl stepped in front of her.

"If you wanna have some real fun, forget the movie," Sheryl said, breathing into Marin's face, and Marin wondered how much she'd had to drink.

Sheryl leaned close, unsteady on her feet and her blond curls brushing Marin's face as she pointed across the parking lot.

"See that car on the end of the last row? The one parked beyond the exit lights."

Except for the cars parked nearest the concession stand, Marin could see little in the darkness, but she obediently looked past Sheryl's finger and nodded.

"The action in the backseat of that car is a lot more entertaining than the movie. One guy in and another guy out!" Sheryl said, giggling as popcorn spilled from the cardboard tray.

"We haven't figured out who the girl is," Sheryl said with studied seriousness, "so we're watching to see which guys we recognize." She giggled again. "Wanna come over?" she asked.

"Maybe later," Marin said.

"If you change your mind, we're in Annie's car," Sheryl said, weaving a path to the door. "Only one row up from the action!"

Marin smiled, then continued to the back, entering the dimly lit and dingy restroom.

Edison's name stared out from the scrawled names and graffiti covering the stall door, and she looked closer at the words written in black marker, her face growing hot, as if the writer was witnessing her discomfort.

'Edison Washburn thinks he's too good to date Navajo girls...'

The second show was more than half over, and Marin picked her way back to Edison's truck through the dark humps of gravel and the mostly empty vehicles, turning quickly away from the ones which weren't. The evening, so full of excitement and possibility, had evaporated into a kind of shabbiness, doubly so as she heard sounds of retching and saw a dark shape vomiting onto the gravel.

"Edison?" she said, but it wasn't Edison who answered from the shadows and she quickly stepped aside, her head bent, hoping she didn't attract any unwanted attention at this late hour. After the first movie, it wasn't a good idea to be roaming around alone in the dark.

She reached the truck and slid into the front seat, grateful to find there was no one with Edison.

"Hey, you were gone long enough!" Edison said and reached across to pull her over to his side of the cab, twining his fingers in her long hair, and studying her face in the light from the movie screen.

"What's wrong?" he asked, sliding down in the seat so that his head rested next to hers.

"You know what's wrong. The drinking. It worries me," she said.

"Everything worries you, Nightmare," he said, putting his arm around her shoulders, fingers still twined in her hair. "You need to lighten up. This will be our last date until I come home at Christmas." He tightened his arm, and she knew he meant to kiss her.

"But why, Edison?" she asked, pulling away. "Why do you drink?"

"To get drunk," he said.

"That's not funny," Marin said. She stared out the windshield, and Edison turned his face to hers without lifting his head.

"You're always so serious, Nightmare. It's hard not to tease you. Where's that 'damn the torpedoes and full steam ahead' attitude I love?"

"*You* are the one risking the torpedoes," she said. "Blowing your future out of the water, and for what?"

Edison pulled his arm from around her shoulders and put both hands behind his head. "I guess the drinking is just the *Indian* in me coming out," he said, and she widened her eyes so he wouldn't see her quick tears. Crying brought out the worst in Edison.

"Isn't that what you want to hear?" he said, his voice harsh. "I know it's what you *think*."

He leaned toward her, hands still behind his head, so close she could smell the liquor on his breath. "And you don't like that, do you? You'd like me to be as *non*-Indian as possible…the whiter the better. Right?"

"The same can be said for you," she shot back. "Aren't you the one who's too good to date Navajo girls?"

She knew as soon as the words left her mouth they were spiteful, but the whole night seemed tawdry now, tainted with cheap liquor and backseat sex. Edison was quiet for a time and the movie's dialog sputtered from the metal speaker. She looked toward the screen and had no idea what movie they were seeing...not that it mattered.

"Why do you date me, Edison?" she asked finally, her voice quiet.

He laughed. "Have you looked in a mirror lately?" he said and pulled her roughly to him, kissing her until she could taste the liquor as well as smell it.

Marin pushed him away; certain he knew what her question meant.

He let her go, breathing hard, and from experience she knew the best move on her part right now was silence. Edison had never hurt her, but he did scare her in certain moods. When he finally spoke, his voice was controlled and had taken on the familiar mocking tone.

"Maybe I date you because I need you to tell me what to do," he said. "Us *Indians* don't tell each other what to do, you know. It's one of things you White people do best."

He straightened in the seat when she remained silent, and suddenly he removed the red baseball cap he wore and turned it in his hands.

"I'm sorry," he said, and he leaned toward her and gently kissed her before putting the cap on her head. "Guess you better wear this while I'm gone. You can consider it your 'red badge of courage,' a reminder of what you've been through the past few years, dating me and all."

He gave the brim a tug and covered her eyes. "When I get back, we can trade the cap for a more suitable engagement symbol, like a ring."

"Edison—" Marin started, pushing the hat brim up, but he interrupted.

"I don't want to just date you, Mare," he said quietly. "I want to marry you."

He took her hand, and she didn't resist, surprised into silence but wary of stepping into one of Edison's mind traps.

"Will you marry me, Marin Sinclair?" he asked. "Until I can do more, will you take the cap as an engagement token?"

She twisted the soft red cap in her hands, not speaking as Edison lit a cigarette, inhaled and then slowly exhaled, and Marin knew she had waited too long to say anything.

"I can tell you're excited about the prospect," he said, and flipped the cigarette out the window.

"No, Edison, it's not that," she said quickly. "You know I love you...I *do*!" she said when he raised an eyebrow. "It's just...if you're serious, then we need to talk, decide things, you know, before you leave, before I leave, and I'm not sure we have time. I've told you I've applied for early enrollment in January at the state college in Flagstaff, so we need to talk—"

"What's to talk about?" Edison interrupted. "You white people, you love to talk and talk and talk. We're a perfect match. We belong together. We're a rhyme even—*Bilagáana-Bilasáana*," he said in a sing-song voice.

"Edison, stop," Marin cried, goaded into protesting. "Why do you do this? It isn't funny!"

"Maybe not, but it's true," he said. "*Bilasáana*, the red apple—the *smart* red apple, I should say—red on the outside and white on the inside. That's me in a nutshell...and you, well, you gotta admit you can't get much whiter than you, my blond *Bilagáana* nightmare," he said, reaching to caress Marin's hair. "A picture of you to show around *Shit-ca-go,*" he said, slurring the word, "and I'll fit right in."

"If you make it there!" Marin said, stung, and she pulled away.

She hated him in this kind of mood and she deliberately tried to find the words to hurt him as he had hurt her. "It requires *action* on your part and you aren't so good at that, are you? Watching and...and criticizing is much more your style. Your *Indian* style!"

"Ahhh," Edison said and laughed. "And now we come to tonight's main feature, the *Native American* argument." he said in imitation of a radio announcer's deep voice. "If you only had *half* of what I have—the scholarships, the paid tuition, any number of colleges begging me to grace them with my *Native American* presence."

He broke off, his voice bitter when he spoke again. "All my endless, amazing opportunities because I am *Native American.* "

Marin interrupted his self-pitying dialog. "And you don't even *care,*" she said hotly. "You don't even *care* that you have such opportunities, that you're *lucky* to have such chances."

She scooted upright and sat rigid in the seat. "You take it all for granted," she said. "The tribal scholarships, the colleges courting you, the choice of any career you want. Nobody is paying *my* way through college, and my grades are just as good as yours!"

"Yes, I have the temerity to take it for granted," Edison said. "*Temerity,* Mare. You wouldn't think a Navajo *jighaan* like me would know such a big English word, right?"

He turned to face her, his next words harsh, biting.

"Lucky old me. Want to trade places, Marin? Want to be the poor Indian getting the big scholarships from the kind-hearted White man? You tired of being Anglo, my little *Bilagáana* beauty?"

Marin shrank away. "Don't you believe in anything, Edison?" she asked, withdrawing from the argument and from him, weary. It was impossible to talk to Edison when he was in this mood.

He replied in the same weary way she herself felt. "Right now, it's about all I can do to try and believe in myself," he said quietly.

She heard the note of despair and turned toward him in sudden compassion, but inexplicably he began to laugh.

"Oh, Marin, you're so typical. Ready and willing to help the poor Indian, to *understand* the poor Indian, just as long as he stays a helpless failure and no real threat to your status quo. You remind me of every *Bilagáana* teacher I ever had, telling me how proud of me they were, what an *example* I was to my people, how *successful* I could be, while all the time they were setting me up to fail, were disappointed when I didn't."

Marin was speechless in the face of his bitterness and Edison shrugged.

"You'd better start learning to tell yourself the truth about the way things work in this world, Nightmare. At least be that honest with yourself."

"You've had too much to drink," Marin said.

"I haven't had enough," he contradicted mildly. "But then, *drinking's* what us Indians do best," he said, and he banged open his door, smashing it into the speaker pole with a force that belied the casual tone of his words.

"See you later, babe. I've got some more visiting to do," he flung at her as he slammed the door shut again, causing the speaker to hiss static at him as if it were alive.

"Really?" Marin said, angry now, and she pushed open her own door.

She turned and tossed the red cap carelessly onto the seat, and saw Edison's eyes watch the cap fall, but he made no move to retrieve it, didn't speak at all as he raised his eyes to her face.

"Is visiting one of your euphemisms for drinking?" Marin asked him. "*Euphemisms,* Edison. Do you know that big word, too?"

Edison didn't answer.

"Don't expect me to be here when you get back," she said as he walked away, his back stiff. "I've got some *visiting* of my own to do."

Edison stalked off, and Marin stood there beside the truck, at a loss to know where to go or what to do, only determined she wouldn't sit and wait for him to come back.

A wave of laughter reached her, high-pitched squeals coming from a car a few rows behind the truck, and she remembered the conversation with Sheryl at the concession stand—*the car near the exit lights*—and she walked across the hills of gravel toward the laughter.

Annie's car was easy enough to find; the beer cans alone, heaped in a small mountain by the passenger door, made it difficult to miss, and she tapped on the window before she changed her mind.

Sheryl opened the door, and more beer cans tumbled onto the gravel.

"Hey," Marin said, ducking her head inside.

The smell in the car, cigarette smoke and beer fumes, hit her in the face, but the giggling blond scooted across the front seat, her hand tugging Marin's wrist.

"Come on in," she gasped, and Marin let herself be pulled inside.

Annie and Sheryl were in the front seat, and there were four more girls in the back, all of them members of the 'in' set—not Marin's usual group—and all of them were twisted around, staring out the back windshield.

"You would not believe how many liquor bottles we've seen smuggled into that car," Sheryl said, inhaling from her cigarette as Marin squeezed into the front seat. "At first we were worried about, you know, date rape and all, but then we heard the girls inside the car laughing and we saw all the booze going in...I guess they know what they're doing."

Annie, behind the wheel, leaned forward, waving Sheryl's smoke away from her face with one hand and holding an unopened can of beer in the other.

"Hey, Marin," Annie said. "Here, have a beer. Sheryl, could you please blow smoke somewhere else?"

"Where?" Sheryl asked, and Marin jumped when Sheryl suddenly shrieked. "Kevin *Murray* just got into the back seat of that car! Can you believe it? Mr. Kevin I'm-so-f'in perfect *Murray!*"

Annie leaned forward, the can of beer extended, but Marin shook her head. "I'm driving," she said as a wave of laughter erupted from the girls in the back seat. "As are you," she added under her breath.

"What's that?" Annie said, but Marin shook her head.

In the mood Edison was in, he might not wait for her to come back, and she could have kicked herself for ever getting into Annie's car in the first place. She'd have to go back, and hope Edison hadn't left her to make her own way home. Angry or not, despite what she'd said, she couldn't let Edison get behind the wheel in the shape he was in.

She edged closer to the door, trying to make a somewhat graceful exit.

"When Kevin comes out, let's all be waiting for him!" Sheryl said, and Marin winced.

"Wanna bet on how long he stays in there?" Annie asked, again leaning across Sheryl. "We've been taking bets on every guy that goes in. Nickel a bet. Sheryl runs the timer."

A fresh series of high-pitched squeals erupted in the back seat, and Marin turned.

It was easy to see what the girls were watching.

Four or five guys she recognized from school stood around the back of the car parked one gravel-bump over, the glow of their cigarettes sporadically illuminating their faces. The boys stood close together, leaning against the car's trunk, not talking or jostling each other, not even looking at one another as they stood and smoked.

Marin watched them and knew with certainty that whatever was happening in the back seat of that car was happening with deliberate intent, for this wasn't just adolescent necking at a drive-in movie.

She remembered Sheryl's words about the liquor she'd seen go into the car, and for the first time she understood the meaning of the word prostitution as an act against oneself.

She didn't want any part of this.

She reached for the door handle, but Annie's voice stopped her. "The back door is opening," she said. "Time, Sheryl."

"Uh...two minutes, I guess?" Sheryl said, glancing at Liz in the back seat. Kevin and Liz had been a couple until recently.

"Who cares?" Liz said, shrugging.

"Come on, Liz," Sheryl said, giggling. "Let's all get out! Kevin will *die* when he knows you've been watching!"

The girls piled out onto the gravel, adopting various nonchalant poses on the back of Annie's car, and Marin edged away toward the front bumper, hoping to escape unnoticed.

"Surprised to see us, Kevin?" Sheryl called in her high-pitched voice, and her words were followed by shrieks of laughter and wet, kissing sounds from the girls as Kevin emerged.

The disheveled Kevin straightened his pants and smoothed his hair, not looking at anyone around Annie's car, and Marin felt like the worst kind of voyeur. She looked away, angry at the boys, angry at the girls, angry at herself for being here.

She stood, meaning to walk away, but a figure from a row ahead walked—no, marched—across the graveled humps and toward the car.

For an awful moment Marin thought that she and the girls milling around Annie's car were about to be confronted, but the figure marched past and moved purposely to the back door of the car where Kevin stood still fumbling with his clothes.

In one quick movement Kevin was shoved aside, the back door of the car was yanked open, and the overhead light blinked on. Loud voices and cursing rose from those inside, and Marin didn't catch all of what was said, but she recognized the figure who bent and reached into the back seat.

Vangie Tso.

The line of boys at the back bumper melted away like so much smoke, and Vangie put an arm around the waist of the girl in the backseat and pulled her out, limp and unresisting. Not speaking, Vangie straightened and turned back the way she'd come, moving slowly, the girl she supported dragging her feet through the gravel.

The girls around Annie's car were suddenly silent, and no one moved until Annie slid off the back fender and got into her car, shutting the door quietly. The others followed suit but Marin stood frozen in place at the bumper, convinced her burning face was visible even in the dark.

Vangie moved past without comment, the girl's head limp on her shoulder and bobbing gently with each step, but Marin knew Vangie too well to doubt she'd been recognized. She watched the slow progress through the gravel, unable to move until a loud burst of laughter exploded from inside Annie's car.

Scalded, as if the bumper had suddenly become hot to the touch, Marin pushed off the bumper and caught up with Vangie, taking the other arm of the inert girl and pulling it across her own shoulder. Vangie looked across at her, and Marin gave her a wry smile. Between them they pulled the girl through the gravel, her feet dragging and head hanging, her dark hair hiding her face.

The girl murmured something as they walked, and Marin smelled the bittersweet scent of wine on her breath.

"Is she hurt or just drunk?" Marin asked quietly.

"Does it matter?" Vangie said, a bite to her words.

They reached Vangie's car, and together they shifted the girl as gently as they could into the front seat, where she landed without making a sound, her head lolling and her hair falling back from her face.

"Rita," Marin breathed.

"Yeah," Vangie said as she straightened.

"Does Edison know?"

Vangie shrugged and shut the door. "He knows," she said after a moment.

"I don't understand," Marin said.

"Neither do I," Vangie replied, but she was looking at Marin.

"Vangie..." Marin began, wanting to explain her presence in Annie's car, wanting to explain how the busyness of high school crowded out so much and how she missed spending time with her as they once did, but Vangie spoke first.

"Edison's waiting for you," she said, walking around to the driver's door. "He said to tell you."

"Thanks," Marin answered, and she spoke the next words quickly to get them out before Vangie left. "We had a fight, Edison and me, and one thing led to another. It was a stupid place to be—Annie's car, I mean—and I'm sorry about it, about all of it. I'm sorry about us, sorry about Rita. I didn't know."

Vangie didn't respond, and Marin turned to go, wishing very much to be home.

"There's a lot of drinking in Edison's family," Vangie said suddenly.

"I didn't know," Marin said again, not sure why this information was being offered. To prove alcoholism ran in families? She knew that already.

Vangie seemed to realize what she was thinking and frowned. "It takes a long time," Vangie said, the words sounding like an explanation.

"A long time?" Marin repeated, still not understanding, and Vangie nodded.

"Generations, sometimes," she said. "...to change the pattern."

"To stop drinking?" Marin said, and Vangie nodded.

"Their children will be better at it, and their children, and so on until the pattern is broken," Vangie said. "You understand?"

Marin nodded, thinking maybe she did understand a little.

"You're sure Edison wants the change?" Marin asked after a long pause.

Vangie smiled briefly, her teeth flashing. "He wants it," she said. "It takes a lot of strength, a lot of faith."

"Edison doesn't seem to have much faith in anything lately," Marin said.

"Use yours, then," Vangie answered.

Mine's not much better, Marin almost said, but she bit her lip.

Vangie interrupted her thoughts.

"I've got to get her home," she said, getting behind the wheel, and Marin remembered Rita's mumbled words.

"What did she say to you back there...?" she asked.

Vangie stared out the windshield and didn't immediately answer, starting the car and letting it idle a minute before she said quietly, "Báhádzidii..."

"Which means?" Marin asked, and Vangie sighed.

"A dangerous thing to do," Vangie said.

"Dangerous how?" Marin asked.

"Dangerous to your soul," Vangie said, and she put the car in gear and looked up at Marin from the open window.

"Guess it's not the eighth grade anymore, Nightmare," she said in a low voice, and Marin stepped away as the car began to move.

"Guess not," she whispered, and she stood watching until Vangie's taillights disappeared, the night somehow darker and pressing down with a sad heaviness.

The movie was over, the giant screen blank, and she stood for a while in the dark, leaning against the cold metal of a speaker, knowing she needed to find Edison and wondering what she would say to him when she did.

CHAPTER NINETEEN

▲▲

Marin dozed in the saddle, letting the sure-footed bay pick his own way down the mountain trail, the warmth of the sun and the pine-scented air, fresh from last night's rain, making sleep irresistible, even with the fear of another confrontation with Tolliver.

She wasn't aware she had fallen asleep until the chattering of squirrels woke her. The horse had wandered off the path and was pulling leaves from the nearby tree branches while the squirrels and several blue jays scolded.

"Stay awake, stay awake," she chided herself, guiding the horse back to the path and letting her legs dangle from the stirrups so as not to get too comfortable.

Fortunately, the horse hadn't wandered far from the trail, and she tried to keep herself alert by estimating how long it might take to get to the trading post, and what she'd do when she got there. Where there was a trading post there'd be phone service and people who could help her get in touch with Justin. After all, the hotel clerk had said everyone on the reservation knew Justin Blue Eyes.

The trail she rode slanted downhill, overlooking the deep canyon running through the heart of the mountain, and the occasional break in the trees afforded spectacular views of red rock cliffs falling away to the stream along the canyon floor. The trail would most likely intersect the canyon floor at some point and perhaps continue along the stream for a way before climbing out, but for how far? It wasn't a good idea to be in the canyon after so much rain in the high mountains.

An old board sign nailed to a pine tree caught her attention, the words painted unevenly in black letters.

Watch out for sheep, those that drive cars.

She smiled at the mental image, but the sign disturbed her, for the main road up the mountain must be close by or the sign wouldn't be there, and she was uneasily aware that Tolliver, in the Chevy truck, could be close by, as could MacPherson, in a...what had Tolliver said?

A Land Rover. MacPherson was driving a Land Rover.

The old man had said nothing about switching from the trail to the road, and he must be familiar with both.

The horse twitched a shoulder, slapping at flies and catching Marin's leg with his tail, and she moved her feet back into the stirrups, deciding to keep to the canyon trail and hope that the road didn't veer too close to it.

The trail dropped steeply as they wound toward the canyon floor, and the horse placed his feet carefully, head lowered, while Marin leaned back to redistribute her weight. When they reached a rocky ledge a few feet above the canyon floor, the horse bunched his hind-quarters and jumped, a flurry of sand and rocks tumbling down behind them.

The canyon was wide here, perhaps thirty feet from wall to wall, and the red cliffs towered so high overhead Marin could see no way out here as she'd hoped. She crossed the stream to see if there was any sort of crevice or fissure in the wall where the path continued, but there was nothing. The path must follow the canyon floor itself, but for how far?

She'd have to backtrack to the road or risk getting caught in a flashflood.

The horse stretched his neck to reach the water, and she loosened the reins, giving him his head to drink, standing in the stirrups to stretch her legs and get a better look. Far down the canyon, she could see lower bluffs, so more than likely the path resumed there.

Still...

She turned her attention back to the horse, ready to hurry him along and out of the canyon when she heard an engine, a vehicle on the road above.

The horse heard it as well, and he lifted his head, his muzzle dripping water, and Marin turned back to the trail and the rocky ledge as a black SUV roared around the embankment overhead, so close to the canyon edge that a shower of rocks and dirt rained down.

The horse reared, dancing on his back legs and refusing the short jump to the ledge. Twice she pulled his head around, but the horse refused, throwing his head until Marin lost her balance and twisted sideways onto one stirrup.

Instantly the horse snatched at the bit, gripping it between his teeth, head forward and down, crazed with the instinct to run.

There was nothing Marin could do but go with him, and she bent over the horse's neck and fed slack into the reins, hoping he'd release the bit so she could regain control. The sand on the canyon floor slowed the horse to a trot and then to a walk, and Marin dismounted and walked beside him, her hand on his shoulder to calm him.

The horse accepted the bit again easily enough after a minute or so of walking, and she remounted and looked around, unsure if she should go back or continue on. The walls were lower here, but she still saw no sign of a trail leading out.

She'd decided they should turn back when she heard the rumble from up canyon, the sound more a vibration than an actual sound, and she glanced up at the sky, hoping it was thunder as her hands tightened reflexively on the reins. The sound grew louder, like a train approaching in the distance, or a strong wind rushing through the pines, and with a sinking feeling she knew she'd been right to try and avoid the canyon floor.

In one movement, Marin twisted the reins around her hands and dug both heels into the horse's sides shouting "Hi! Hi!" and slapping the ends of the reins across his rump to try and outrun the wall of water coming behind.

The horse leaped forward so quickly she almost lost her seat, clearing the width of the stream in one lunge, while behind them the sound of crashing rocks and cracking tree branches filled the canyon as the flood hurtled its collection of debris ahead of the water.

She had to get out of the wash before the boulders and broken limbs reached them, and she looked for an escape route, fighting to keep the panicked horse in the firm sand beside the stream.

"Easy now," she crooned into his ear as they raced between the red blur of rock walls. "Don't fall, easy now." She bent low over the horse's neck, his hooves throwing mud up onto her back and shoulders as he pounded down the wash, and desperately she scanned the canyon walls, twisting her fingers into the horse's coarse mane to keep from falling herself.

A flash of color caught her eye, and she glanced up and again saw the black SUV speeding along the rim of the canyon overhead, the wheels still so close to the edge that showers of dirt cascaded down the rock walls.

A dark-haired man waved wildly from the window, sweeping one arm forward in a follow-me motion, and he yelled something down to her that she couldn't hear above the roar of the water and the colliding boulders. She wrenched her attention back to the horse, concentrating solely on staying on his back and keeping the horse on his feet.

The lower bluffs were around them now, no more than five or six feet high, but even if the driver above was urging her to a known exit, they were out of time.

The roar behind her was deafening—it could be only seconds now before impact—and though the horse was running all out, he could not outrace a flash flood. Without her he'd have a chance to jump. She reined him away from the center of the canyon and relaxed her grip, ready to jump for the wall and any handhold she could find.

The horse faltered in the heavier sand, going down on his front knees in a way Marin hadn't expected, and instead of jumping, she was catapulted from the saddle in a headlong somersault over the horse's head before the bay scrambled to his feet and ran on without her.

Marin had hit the ground hard and rolled, coming to her hands and knees, and she jumped for the wall, reaching for a small cedar tree extending from the bluff. She managed to grab a branch near the roots, and swinging her legs up, she wedged herself between the wall and the tree a second before the first of the roiling debris—rocks, branches, uprooted trees, and mud—swept beneath her, ahead of a solid wall of roaring water.

The width of the canyon kept her from the worst of it, but the wall of muddy water behind the debris hit her hard, crashing over her head and shoulders, the cedar tree only a tenuous anchor to the wall. A large rock struck her a glancing blow on her shoulder and grazed her head before it ricocheted back into the maelstrom, and suddenly her right hand would no longer grip the tree roots. Her feet slid down the wall, and she willed every muscle in her left arm to hold on.

She couldn't do it.

The current was too strong, the muddy water rising too fast and pinning her to the wall, her useless arm making it impossible to push off and swim. She suddenly gave up the fight and relaxed her hold on the tree root, her last clear thought a regret for the fate of the bay horse.

A sudden, wrenching pull on her left arm yanked her upward, the muscles painfully straining, and Marin looked up into the face of the dark-haired man from the SUV. He was on his stomach, shouting something she couldn't hear over the water's roar. She mouthed the word 'no' but he held her left arm tightly and reached for her right, scowling down at her.

"Your arm," she saw him mouth. "Give me your other arm!" but her right arm hung limp, deadened by the blow from the rock, and she couldn't get any purchase with her feet on the slick wall or make him understand why.

"I can't lift it," she yelled, but he didn't hear her over the water's roar.

"Help me!" he shouted into her face as the current began to win their tug of war, dragging her from his grip and propelling her legs downstream. "Pull up!" he ordered.

"I can't!" she gasped, twisting in his grip, the muscles of her shoulder screaming in protest. "Let me go!"

"Give me your other arm," he shouted, and she couldn't answer for the loose debris of sticks and mud slamming into her face and mouth. The water rose higher, and the man was unable to keep her head above it. Incredibly, instead of releasing her, he dropped into the water beside her, still holding her arm as the current dragged them both under and swept them into its swift center.

Marin broke the surface gasping, swallowing mouthfuls of muddy water, but her arm was still in his grip, and he surfaced beside her, water streaming from the dark hair into his eyes and mouth as he released her arm and grasped her about the waist, holding her and treading water against the violent push of the flood.

"Swim for the edge!" he shouted into her ear. "Kick your legs!"

He held on to her, and she floundered in the torrent, trying to kick but it was hard to keep her head above water, and her legs quickly became heavy and numb with cold. She felt his hand leave her waist and twist into her hair, and he turned her onto her back and pulled her chin up, his arm across her shoulders as he carried her along with him.

"Swim!" he commanded. "Kick!"

His hand tight in her hair, he pulled them both, swimming a one-handed stroke with his free arm through the waves of rolling mud and water. Gradually they were swept toward one side, away from the center of the current and moving toward a branch in the canyon. She could feel the strong scissoring of his legs alongside the feeble kicks of her own, and he struck out hard as they neared the branch, fighting to avoid being swept downstream and missing the smaller tributary.

"Almost there!" he shouted.

She barely cared anymore, and she began to fall in and out of awareness as he kicked doggedly for the narrow juncture ahead. Suddenly he pushed her upright and there was solid ground beneath her feet. He held onto her until she was able to stand and then wade through waist deep water in the smaller draw, still half carrying and half dragging her. The roar diminished behind them as they left the main canyon, and he released her waist but retained his hold on her upper arm as they waded downstream, the canyon gradually widening so that the force of the current and depth of the water began to decrease.

Ahead, a rock shelf extended from the canyon wall, and he lowered her to a sitting position on its edge, letting go of her at last while he remained standing in the water—hands on knees, head down—breathing heavily as mud and water streamed from his face and clothing.

"Your arm's hurt?" he asked after a minute, lifting his eyes, and she nodded.

"Rock," she managed.

"Lucky I was about," he said, and Marin thought of the black SUV and knew it was not luck at all.

"You almost got us killed..."

"Us?"

"The horse and me," she said. "You spooked him with your SUV.

"Land Rover, and you're welcome," he replied.

"You're MacPherson," she said.

"Cullen MacPherson," he agreed, hands still on his knees, talking over the rush of the water.

Her right arm hung uselessly, more numb than painful, and Marin knew she could neither run nor fight.

"Why didn't you just let me drown?" she asked, muddy water running from the ends of her hair. "It would have saved you the trouble of killing me."

"I don't want you dead," he said, sounding surprised.

"Which is more than you can say for your friends," she said, pushing back a dripping strand of hair. Edison's red cap was gone, and to her own ears her words sounded distant. She gripped the rock shelf beneath her fingers as dizziness swept over her.

"I lost my hat," she said sadly, and the world went black.

CHAPTER TWENTY

B efore Marin opened her eyes, she smelled the woodsmoke mingled with the smell of drying clothing, and she heard the crackle
of burning wood.

She was warm, inside a sleeping bag and relatively dry, but her
arms and her neck were stiff, painful.

She didn't move, waiting for the blanks to fill and tell her where
she was.

She had felt like this sometimes as a child, waking in a strange
place, not knowing for the first few moments where she was, but back
then the sensation was usually pleasant.

Not this time.

There had been the old man, the horse, the flashflood, and Cullen
MacPherson. She had no memory after that or of getting here…wher-
ever here was.

Nearby she heard quiet snoring, and she opened her eyes into
semi-darkness and turned. Bedsprings squeaked beneath her, and
the gentle snores stopped. A low growl took their place, and a dog
the size of a small bear materialized beside her head, his nose level
with her face. Marin froze, careful to make no eye contact the dog
could interpret as a challenge, and at last the big dog retreated,
returning to the center of the room to curl up near a fire burning in
a rusted iron woodstove.

Slowly she lifted her head, this time careful about the squeaking
bedsprings. She was in a bed pushed against a log wall, a bed complete

with the squeaky bedsprings and a sagging mattress, warm inside what must be MacPherson's sleeping bag.

She was in an old hogan.

The interior of the six-sided room smelled musty, but it was dry except for the puddle of rainwater near one caved-in wall, and the room was warm. A coffeepot was on the stove, and there was a wooden box holding a stack of foil trays pushed against another wall. A large backpack leaned against the wooden box.

The doorway of the room was across from her, a tarp of some kind partially covering the opening, and it was dark outside.

She must have slept for several hours.

Cautiously, trying to keep the bedsprings from squeaking, she pushed herself upright and exclaimed involuntarily at the unexpected pain.

The dog came to his feet, his growl a deep rumble in his chest, and Marin was eye to eye with him, afraid to move until suddenly the dog leaned forward and licked her across the face.

She yelped, surprised, and the tarp across the door was pulled aside.

Cullen MacPherson stood in the doorway, a much greater threat than the dog.

"I heard you cry out," he said. "Are you okay?"

She nodded and MacPherson stepped over the threshold and ordered the dog outside.

"What's his name?" Marin asked, more for something to say than any real curiosity. Slowly she sat up and pushed the sleeping bag aside.

"Bear," he answered as he filled a tin cup with coffee. "I can give you something for the pain," he offered, but Marin shook her head.

"It's alright," she said, and he regarded her without speaking.

"Better use this, then," MacPherson said, unscrewing the lid of a plastic bottle bearing a label that read 'sugar.' He poured a generous amount into the coffee, stirred it, and handed it to her.

"Sugar acts as a sedative," he said as she took a sip. "It'll help."

"You're the second person to tell me that in the last two days," she said. "Believe it or not, my life up till now didn't usually require sedation."

Taking her chin in his fingers he turned her face from side to side, not seeming to notice when she flinched at his touch.

"Nasty bruise," he commented. "Seems a bit soon to have bruised so quickly..."

"It's from yesterday...courtesy of your friend, Bud Tolliver," she couldn't resist saying, but her voice trembled.

"Did he say he was a friend of mine?" he asked mildly, examining her mouth and jaw.

"He mentioned your name," Marin said, determined not to show fear.

She pulled away and MacPherson released her.

"You're having one hell of a weekend," he said, taking several of the foil-wrapped trays from the stack. "RTE's," he said, and at her puzzled expression explained, "Ready-to-eat. You must be hungry."

"Rain stopped a while ago," he commented, putting the trays on the stove. "Sun even came out for a while before it got dark. You were out a long time."

"I didn't get much sleep last night, courtesy of..."

"Bud Tolliver," he finished. "I'm getting that."

They sat in silence as the trays heated, and the familiar sounds of a desert evening drifted through the tarp over the door. The sounds were soothing, although perhaps the hooting of an owl some distance away could be considered portentous. The smell of the food made her mouth water. Even her distrust of Cullen MacPherson wasn't enough to keep her from accepting the warm tray of...something. He could have let her drown, she reasoned, and antagonism wasn't in her best interest. She was tired and hurt and needed to rest.

"Nice place for a home," he said, adding sticks to the fire and settling in to his own meal. "Nice grassy bluff overlooking the stream."

Marin didn't comment, and he glanced over. "I wondered why no one lived here."

Marin continued eating but pushed her chin and mouth to indicate the collapsed wall.

MacPherson frowned.

It's a *chindii* hogan," she said, swallowing.

His expression stayed the same.

"The woman who lived in this hogan probably died here," she said. "It's dangerous to live where someone has died."

"Dangerous?"

"Evil spirits, ghosts. If you believe in that sort of thing."

"Why destroy only one wall?"

"North wall," she said, chewing. "It's collapsed so everyone will know not to live here. The broken wall lets the spirit escape to the north when someone dies—north being the direction of evil."

He refilled her cup. "You don't look Navajo," he commented, putting the pot back on the stove.

Surprised, she looked up. "Diné, and I'm not."

"You sound like you believe what you said about the spirits."

She shrugged, took another mouthful. "What is this, anyway?" she asked.

"Hash," he said. "MREs taste best when you're hungry."

"The Diné believe you should never speak the name of someone who is dead. You risk calling the evil spirit to you."

"Diné? You mean Navajos?"

"They call themselves Diné," Marin said. "It translates loosely as 'The People.' I gather you're not from around here."

"Did I say that?" he asked, and Marin gave him a look.

"You don't have to say it. Your clothes, your shoes, your wristwatch, your Land Rover—even your haircut says it for you. You're definitely city, and I'd guess from somewhere in the East."

He lifted an eyebrow but didn't speak, and they concentrated on eating.

"But if the person was a friend," he commented a few bites later, "or a loved one, you'd have no reason to fear their ghost."

"It's no longer them, and there are no friendly spirits," Marin replied. It means to do you harm."

"Such as?"

"Take over your body, your will." Marin said and she shivered.

"Scared?" he asked.

"No," she said, meeting his gaze. "Cold."

"Why did you say a woman lived here?" MacPherson asked after a few moments of silence, and Marin took a bite before she answered, noting that despite his casual attitude he was paying close attention. She would have to be careful what she said to this man.

"Did I say that?" she asked, imitating his own evasiveness, but he merely raised his eyebrows.

"It was just a guess," she said. "Most everything in here is on the woman's side of the hogan, and there's pieces of a broken loom under the bed."

She pointed to the door behind him.

"The door always faces the east. The north side is generally the woman's."

He smiled suddenly. "The direction of evil?" he asked.

"South side is generally the man's," Marin said.

"And the west?"

"Company," she said.

"It seems very... proscribed."

"How the first hogan was built is part of the Diné creation story. Its construction is described in the Blessingway sing and symbolizes the partnership of a man and a woman."

"Interesting..."

"Where are you from?" she asked.

"My people are from Scotland," he said, not quite answering her question.

"Um-hmm," she lifted the coffee cup. "Faeries and little people..."

"I think you have us mixed up with the Irish," he said, smiling. "You're Scottish, too, judging from your name."

She lowered the cup. "It's English," she said.

"Sinclair is a Scots name," he answered. "As is Marin."

It was the first time he had used her name, and she fell silent, no longer hungry, again mindful of where she was and why.

She put the empty tray to one side.

"Why don't we stop playacting?" she said. "You've given the victim a last meal, you don't have to trouble yourself with small talk as well. Go ahead and do what you're going to do, because I'm not running anymore."

A look of surprise crossed his face before he scowled.

"I have no intention of hurting you," he said, placing a few sticks on the fire. "Of course I know your name."

"Really? I don't remember telling you my name when you pulled me out of the water."

"You knew mine, and as I remember, you passed out before either of us said much of anything."

"Am I a prisoner?" she asked.

"No, and I'm not going to hurt you," he repeated. "I assume Tolliver did. Want to tell me what happened?"

"Nothing that you probably don't already know. I got the impression I was supposed to end up like Cecil."

"Cecil?" he asked sharply. "What about Cecil?"

Marin took a sip of coffee, trying to think as the scalding liquid burned from her throat down to her stomach, and she wished she hadn't mentioned Cecil at all. Mentally she measured the distance to the door.

"Bear wouldn't let you get far," MacPherson said, nodding toward the dog who had returned inside.

"*Shásh yáázh*," Marin said to the dog, who crossed to her and thumped his tail.

"I think Bear has taken a liking to you. What did you call him?"

"*Shásh yáázh*...it means 'bear cub'."

Marin didn't say more and after a pause MacPherson said, "I hope you're telling the truth. It matters."

"Why would I lie?"

"I have no idea," he answered. "I don't really know you. Are you saying Cecil is dead?"

"I think he might be," she said and watched his reaction, ready to move. "I think Tolliver might have killed him."

MacPherson sat back on his heels and stared into the fire, saying nothing, and Marin suddenly remembered the gun. No doubt it was in the muddy waters of the wash along with her jacket, her wallet, and her phone.

He made no move toward her, but she was apprehensive, and she looked closer at him—dark hair and eyes and a face that under other circumstances she would instinctively trust—and she thought of him jumping in the water after her, holding her head above the waves, refusing to let her quit.

She moved, causing the springs to squeak, and she tensed when MacPherson shifted his gaze from the fire to her, studying her face in the firelight, and she reminded herself that plenty of criminals were attractive.

"You don't seem to be in any hurry to tell me what all this is about," she said, thinking that every time he looked at her he seemed to be mentally sizing her up.

"You can relax," he said eventually. "I'm in no hurry to tell you because no matter what I say, it's going to make things worse."

"No worse than fighting off Tolliver," she said in a quiet voice. "He wanted to kill me... he still does. Anything you tell me has to be better than not knowing what's going on."

"Mind if I use that cup for a while?" he asked, and Marin handed it over.

"Why were you in my apartment?" she asked.

He filled the cup, took a sip, and narrowed his eyes at her through the steam. "You assume I was?"

She raised her eyebrows. "The invitation wasn't there," she added.

"I tried to prevent it getting to you. It would have made things a lot simpler."

She smiled. "Don't underestimate Vangie Tso," she said, mentally scoring a win on being right about the invitation.

"What else were you after?" she asked, "You searched the apartment."

"You want to know a person, you look at how they live—what they read, what they collect, what they save. I needed to know what you were like."

Marin's own eyes narrowed.

"And what did you find out?"

"You don't keep much for clues, but what I did find was interesting enough."

He paused, took a sip from the cup and met her eyes. "Othello," he said.

Marin looked away and a minute passed in silence.

"Why Othello, Marin?"

She made no reply.

"The destruction of the human soul through the destruction of faith," he said.

She turned her face away.

"'But there where I have garnered up my heart, where either I must live or bear no life...' You have that phrase underlined. Have you lost your faith, Marin?"

"It was my father's book," she said. "His favorite, and you had no right to be there."

"Feel free to change the subject," he said.

"Bad cop Tolliver, and now you, the good cop," she said. "Guess you should have gotten to me first. As it is, I have no reason to believe anything you say and certainly no reason to trust you."

"No need to explain anything to you, then," he said.

A sudden gust of wind swept through the doorway, sweeping rain and a flurry of sparks across the floor, and the black dog stood and shook.

MacPherson scraped the fire coals together with a stick, then he and the dog stepped outside.

They were gone only a moment before they returned and Marin gave a sudden cry that startled the horse MacPherson led, and the bay shied away, his head tossing.

"Easy there," MacPherson said, holding onto the bridle. "Guess you're surprised to see her again," he said to the horse. "She seems surprised to see you."

"I thought he'd drowned," she cried, crossing the room and stroking the horse's neck.

"He seems fine," MacPherson said. "I thought he should come in here. It's raining again, and he's had a rough day. I'll take him out again to graze after a while."

He led the horse to the broken wall, and Marin sat on the bed.

"I found him down by the wash," he said. "Just standing there like he didn't know where to go, the saddle hanging beneath his belly."

"With my jacket?" she asked.

"No. Is it important?"

"It had my wallet and my phone…"

"I was hoping to find someone to give us a ride out," MacPherson said, "but the horse was the only means of transport I found."

He looked across at Marin. "You'll have to tell me sometime how you came to have him. Last I heard, you were in a red sports car. What happened to it?"

"What happened to your Rover?" Marin asked in turn.

"Don't know," MacPherson said, carrying in the saddle and tilting it against the wall. "I walked all the way back to where we went into the water, but the Rover's gone."

"How can it just be gone?"

"I was hoping maybe you could tell me."

"How would I know? I was in the water, remember? Tolliver could have taken it, but he has the truck."

The horse stood quiet, resting its weight on three feet, head down, and MacPherson fed a few more sticks to the fire.

Marin watched the horse, the firelight flickering over his damp coat, and she felt a little better. The dog lifted his head and cocked his ears when Marin yawned, and her mouth was still open when MacPherson spoke.

"Tolliver and I work together," he said.

Marin snapped her mouth shut and sat up.

"Cecil, too," he said, standing beside the fire, hands clasped. "I started out as an engineer," he said. "Mining, electrical, industrial—over the years I've become what you might call a troubleshooter."

"Any reason you're telling me this?" she asked.

"Just hear me out, okay?"

She shrugged, and he went on.

"I'm a trouble-shooter—a negotiator if you will—for the company I work for. We're involved in land and mining deals, various arrangements with the Navajo and Hopi tribes regarding their mineral resources."

Most anyone who'd grown up on the reservation knew about mineral leases with off-reservation companies. Most of the leases had been entered into years ago, but she knew about them, everybody did, and most of what she knew was bad.

"Would I recognize the name of this company?" she asked.

"Probably," he said.

Marin scooted back until her back rested against the wall and regarded him.

"That's your business?" she asked. "Stealing resources?"

"*Dealing* for resources," he corrected.

"I know the coal mined from Black Mesa alone was supposedly worth over three hundred million dollars, and the Diné saw maybe six million dollars in royalties," she said. "I know a pipeline company was allowed to use reservation water in order to move the coal to the power plants, and the price per foot paid to the tribe for their water wasn't even close to the going price. I know there are many homes out here still without water wells, without electricity. Doesn't that seem a bit ironic to you?"

"The Navajo tribe, under questionable representation, sold a non-renewable resource for very little money in return," he agreed. "What you may not know is that the original treaty has been renegotiated since the sixties or seventies, which is the time period you're referring to. Things have changed since then."

"Renegotiated or not, the coal company dug up grazing lands and bulldozed hogans—and have never completed restitution."

"There was a federal law passed in 1977 requiring mining companies to restore the land for grazing," he said, and Marin laughed.

"Restoration that was never completed, unless you call piles of tailings from the old uranium mines restoration. The original lease stated the companies weren't responsible for 'land destroyed by the normal wear, tear, and depletion incident to mining'—the word 'normal,' of course, being open to interpretation."

MacPherson looked at her. "I'm impressed," he said.

"I grew up here," she said. "Everyone knows this stuff," she added, thinking of Edison, of Vangie and her involvement with reservation politics. She cleared her throat and stopped talking, irritated at herself. She'd do well to listen instead of giving this man free information.

"I can't deny what's happened in the past," MacPherson said. "I just ask that you realize much of it *is* in the past."

"What does any of this have to do with me?"

"What do you know about uranium mining?" he asked.

"Uranium mining?" she repeated, careful now about what she said, and MacPherson smiled.

"There are hundreds of uranium mines on the reservation," MacPherson said.

"Where are you going with this?" she asked. "The Navajo Nation has oil, gas, uranium, coal—and the uranium mines were mostly closed in the 1980s. You're saying Tolliver attacked me because of uranium mining?"

"There are shafts from those mines all over the reservation, including," he looked at Marin, "some in this mountain range where we are sitting."

"I know that."

"Do you know about the cancers?" he asked.

She looked up. "What?"

"Uranium miners dying from cancers related to radiation exposure." MacPherson paused and took a drink of coffee. "The company I work for still owns some of those uranium mines," he said, "closed or not."

He took a breath and Marin waited for the point of all this, knowing it was finally coming.

"Vangie Tso," he said. "She claims she's lost her uncle and her brother to cancers in the last five years."

"What?" Marin said. Justin had said Vangie's uncle was dead, but he hadn't said how.

"According to her, they both worked in our uranium mines," MacPherson said. "Vangie Tso has since filed multiple wrongful death suits, all against the company for which I—"

Marin finished the sentence. "—for which you work. You, Tolliver, and Cecil."

MacPherson nodded. "You seem surprised," he said. "I assumed you knew this."

"I had no idea," Marin said. "I haven't been back here in over ten years." She paused. "How could something like that happen? Isn't radiation exposure monitored? Don't miners wear badges or some kind of protective suits?"

"A lot of safety regulations regarding radiation weren't always enforced."

"Or weren't mentioned," Marin said. "The miners weren't told, were they? They weren't told about the danger."

"They've been compensated," he said. "The Radiation Exposure Compensation Act passed in 1990 paid up to one hundred thousand dollars to the miners who were exposed...or to their families."

"Compensated," Marin said. "If that's true, why is Vangie suing now?"

"She's suing the company," MacPherson said. "The hundred

thousand is from the Federal Government, and only her uncle qualified for that. The others she's representing didn't meet the government's radiation exposure standards, didn't provide the proper paperwork."

"Dying wasn't proof enough?" she said, and he held up a hand.

"There's more," he said quietly. "Vangie Tso has been diagnosed with lung cancer as well."

Marin caught her breath, then pressed a hand to her mouth.

"I'm sorry," MacPherson said. "We thought you knew. We thought that's why you were coming here, now."

"I hope you're telling the truth," she said finally, using his own words. "It matters."

MacPherson didn't answer, and for a long time the only sound in the room was the hiss of the fire. It was raining still, pattering softly on the roof, and Marin gathered the peaceful sound to her before she stood and walked to the door.

The black dog raised his head. "Down, Bear," MacPherson said. "Let her go."

Marin stepped over the dog and walked into the night.

The smell of wet cedar and sage was strong and she could hear the rush of the wash below, the water high.

She headed toward the sound, toward the tall cottonwoods faintly outlined against the cloudy sky. Raindrops pelted her as she walked, finding their way down her neck, and distant thunder still rumbled in the mountains. She breathed in the smell of the desert, the creosote pine and the faint smell of ozone, and thought of Vangie, but the expected tears did not come.

She'd forgotten how to mourn, worn thin so many times with so many deaths that there was no part of her left to mourn.

The cottonwoods took shape as she drew close, and she looked down on the wash. The sound of rushing water covered the other nighttime sounds, and she could see the faint gleam of the water and a small, round structure set back in the trees on the high bank.

A sweat house.

She made her way down to it and examined the forked poles covered over with brush and dried mud that had hardened years ago, saw the small entryway. A gust of wind brought a spray of raindrops down on her head from the cottonwoods and Marin whispered the song:

He put it down. He put it down.
First Man put down the sweat house.
He built it of valuable soft materials.
Everlasting and peaceful, he put it there. He put it there.

Everlasting and peaceful...and the tears started at last—tears for words that held no real meaning in her own life.

And in Vangie's life? Vangie who was dying?

Please come, Marin. I need to see you.

A movement in the darkness made her turn, and MacPherson stood there.

"Expecting ghosts?" he asked quietly.

"I know a few," she answered.

"What were you whispering?" he asked after a moment.

Marin gestured toward the sweathouse, forgetting he probably couldn't see the movement.

"The words to a song Edison told me once," she said.

"About this?" he asked. "What is this?"

"Sweat house," she answered. "The verses, there's a lot more of them, are part of the ritual—steaming rocks, rolling in sand, dousing yourself with water—until the entire song has been sung."

"It sounds almost like a religious ceremony," MacPherson said.

"Following the Beautiful Way keeps the universe in order," she said, listening to the cottonwood leaves dripping rain.

"I saw the photograph with the dog," he said. "Edison...and?"

Marin nodded, the mood of the sweat house still with her. "Edison and Bailey, my dog."

"What happened?" he asked. "You moved away. You couldn't reconcile your culture with his?"

"I could reconcile more than you might think," she said. "He married Vangie instead."

MacPherson cleared his throat. "I didn't know," he said.

"I thought you knew everything about me." She held out a hand and let the raindrops splash on her upturned palm. "You asked me before if I believed what I told you about spirits."

"Yes?" he said.

"Anyone who's ever lived here for any length of time could tell you of strange experiences...a sort of dissolving of the barriers between the past and the present. It tends to change how you think about things."

"It's happened to you?"

"Off and on since I was a kid. Oddly enough, it happened to Vangie, too. It brought us together," she said.

"Tell me?" he said.

Marin stared into the night and considered his request. She caught a faint whiff of wet fur and knew the dog was near, and she lifted a hand to twist a strand of hair around her fist.

"It's not something I talk about much," she said. "But it tends to happen when I'm in a place where a number of people have died—a battlefield, ruins—or places with an ancient history. I tend to know where I am, I just don't know *when* I am."

"Events which actually happened?"

"I think so," she said.

"Ghosts?"

"Maybe. I don't know."

A sudden spatter of raindrops blew from the tree leaves, and MacPherson put a hand to her cheek to stop the slide of a droplet. Surprised, Marin took a step back, becoming aware of him in relation to the here and now and not in the context of the past and the dreamlike mood that evoked.

MacPherson straightened and dropped his hand, and when he spoke, his voice was resigned.

"There's a bit more you need to know," he said.

"I've guessed some of it. Vangie was giving me a courthouse date in the invitation, wasn't she?"

A fresh spatter of rain began to fall, beginning softly then growing to a rapid cadence, and MacPherson rubbed a hand across his face.

"Vangie Tso has named you as a witness who can prove she, and the other claimants, are who they say they are, and that they were working for the company where and when she has indicated in the lawsuits."

"Surely there are records of employment," she said.

"I haven't seen any company records," he responded. "If there are any to see."

"Did you destroy them?" she asked, but he shook his head.

"We've had no reason to destroy anything. Vangie Tso hasn't produced birth certificates or other proofs of identity—no marriage licenses, no death certificates—until last week I wasn't convinced her suits had any validity to them."

Marin pulled the neck of her shirt tighter about her throat, and MacPherson continued.

"They could have worked at any or all of the mines around here. Now that the mines are closed and most of the companies are defunct, any remaining viable corporation is a convenient scapegoat just by virtue of still being in business."

He bent to pick up a cottonwood leaf and twirled it between his fingers. "Vangie Tso and the rest could have been exposed to radiation in any number of ways," he said and gestured with the leaf toward the unseen mountain ranges around them. "Like I said, there are hundreds of abandoned mine shafts in these mountains, tons of radioactive tailings," he said. "Abandoned mines have been used as sheep pens or storage rooms for hay and grain, mined rocks have been used for cement or home construction, sand from the tailings has filtered into rivers and streams. Any of those things could be a source of exposure."

He continued, but Marin wasn't listening. She was thinking of all the contamination seeping into the water and blowing in the sand. Like a deadly corn pollen, the poison had spread in all directions across Dinetah.

"When the dam collapsed at Church Rock nuclear site, almost a hundred million gallons of radioactive wastewater were released in that one incident," MacPherson was saying. "It's impossible to calculate the effects, present and future, of these incidents. It's not the fault of one company."

"Dying isn't so hard...it's the living that's hard," she murmured, thinking of Edison. He'd said that to her often enough.

"What's that?"

"Vangie is dying," Marin said. "Now I understand."

"I'm sorry," Mac said.

"And last week?" Marin asked. "You said something happened last week to change your mind about Vangie's claims?"

"The company found out about you," Mac said.

CHAPTER TWENTY-ONE

▲▲▲

THEN:
The Sing

Marin and Edison were sitting in a booth at a café in Shiprock, having coffee after a movie and before Edison drove her home, when a youngish man walked in and spotted Edison.

He walked over to their table.

Marin watched as the two brushed palms, the young man talking in a low voice while Edison nodded, and she knew she wasn't getting home any time soon. Edison said something and made a gesture with his mouth toward the door, and the man went outside.

"He needs a ride?" she asked, resigned.

"Yeah," Edison said. "Mind if we make a stop before heading to your house? It's on the way."

Marin was aware a stop could mean anywhere between here and Gallup, but she agreed, hoping she hadn't just said yes to hours of bumping over dirt roads in the dark.

Not that her father would mind or likely even notice, her comings and goings were largely her own business. She sometimes wondered if her father's lack of concern was due to his trust in her judgment or just a general lack of interest in her whereabouts.

Edison left a generous tip on the table for the waitress—when Edison had money, he was always free with it—and they walked out into the cool summer night.

"You'd think a desert would be warmer," she said, pulling her jacket closer.

"No vegetation to hold the warmth," Edison said absently, looking toward the small group of people waiting at his truck.

An older man, his white hair wrapped in a *tsiiyééł* beneath his cowboy hat, and a boy of maybe twelve or thirteen stood next to the truck beside the younger man from the café, and two women stood near the tailgate, one holding a blanket-bundled baby strapped into a cradleboard.

The younger man stepped forward as they approached, but no one spoke.

Edison dropped the tailgate and the two women climbed in the back, the woman with the cradleboard handing up the baby to the other before she climbed in herself, and both women settled near the cab.

Marin glared at Edison. He knew how she felt about this automatic relegation of women to the back, but Edison shrugged and said nothing.

There was a long pause when no one moved, and it took Marin a moment to realize why. When she did, she quickly turned to Edison in disbelief, but the boy was already climbing over the tailgate in response to something said by the older man, and he was up and in the back before Marin could say anything.

Edison nodded toward the driver's side of the truck and opened the door for Marin to get in. She climbed inside, wondering what the older man had said, and determined to find out later from Edison.

It was a tight fit with four adults up front, herself squeezed beside Edison, the younger man beside her and the older man by the door. She knew Edison didn't expect her to ride in the back—but did the women? They had asked for the ride, but she felt foolish, like she'd committed an error in etiquette.

Edison left the cafe parking lot and pulled onto the dark highway. There was little traffic and no stop signs, and they passed a few scattered houses at the edge of town showing lights from their windows, and then the desert night surrounded them, the road ahead visible only in short pieces caught by the truck's headlights.

Usually, she enjoyed this long ride home in the dark with Edison, enjoyed the odd juxtaposition of motion coupled with the vastness of the desert and the lack of reference to visible landmarks. It was as if they weren't moving at all, until the dark outline of Table Mesa would show in the distance and dispel the illusion.

Tonight was different.

Packed in tight next to Edison, she watched the sweep of the headlights when he left the highway for a dirt road leading toward the east.

"Where are we going?" she whispered, and Edison looked at her.

"Why are you whispering?" he said in his normal voice, and she glanced at the two men, who appeared not to hear.

"I'm not," she said, stung by the remark.

The truck bumped over a deep rut in the road, and she bounced against the man to her right, who said something in Navajo that made all three men laugh.

She stiffened.

"Relax," Edison said without turning his head.

She said nothing, but she was embarrassed, angry at Edison's attitude, and she gripped the seat beneath her with both hands to prevent herself bouncing again and stared straight ahead, determined to say nothing more.

Once or twice she looked over her shoulder at the women in the back, able to see only their scarves and their backs pressed against the glass. She couldn't see the younger boy or the cradleboard.

Eventually Edison turned into a packed dirt clearing, the headlights sweeping over a pole corral and two hogans, one with a truck parked nearby, and Edison stopped his truck in the clearing, leaving the motor running and switching the headlights to parking lights before he sat back.

No one moved.

Neither hogan showed any lights from within, but it was impossible for the occupants not to know someone had arrived. The loud barking of several dogs announced their presence, and one of the hogans had quite a few people in front of it—all in traditional dress—standing near a horse and wagon. They weren't talking and seemed to be waiting, looking toward the other hogan.

Long minutes passed and Marin shifted position slightly, looking at the truck's panel clock. At this rate she'd never get home, and she began bouncing her right foot silently up and down to stifle her impatience. Edison reached over and placed a hand on her knee, and she made a face at him, safe in the dark cab, but he only smiled and lightly squeezed her knee.

Finally, lamplight showed from within the hogan with the truck out front, and a man appeared. The two men beside her came to life and the cab's overhead light winked on when they opened the door, making her blink in the sudden bright light.

Edison stayed inside the cab with her, and the women climbed out of the back without assistance, handing over the cradleboard in reverse order from before, the boy jumping over the side. All of them stood together in a group before they moved toward the lighted hogan, and the young man who'd initially asked Edison for the ride said a few words to the man at the hogan door and came back, waiting as Edison lowered the window.

They spoke in Navajo for a moment, and Marin saw the man press something into Edison's hand before he, too, moved back toward the lighted hogan.

Edison waited until all of them were inside and the hogan door was shut before he raised his window and shoved the gearshift into reverse.

"What did he give you?" Marin asked.

"Gas money," Edison replied as he backed out of the clearing and onto the dirt road.

As they bounced along the way they had come, Marin was silent. It was a few minutes before she noticed Edison's smile in the dashboard lights.

"What's funny?" she asked.

"You," he said. "You haven't even noticed the headlights aren't on."

Marin smiled, though a little reluctantly. She was still smarting from his treatment of her on the way in, but driving without headlights was an old game with Edison—him driving and her protesting. She knew he did it now as a sort of peace offering and she accepted by falling in with the game, objecting as usual until he flipped on the lights.

They reached the highway with words once more established between them, and Marin felt free to ask questions as they resumed the trip home.

"Who were they, Edison?" she asked, and he shrugged.

"Oh, you know," he said. "Begay and Benally—Smith and Jones." On the reservation, the names Begay and Benally were as common as Smith and Jones elsewhere in the country.

"Why were all those others standing outside?" she asked. "Were they waiting until someone came to the door?"

Marin was familiar with the custom. It was only polite to give those within time to make ready for receiving company instead of barging in.

"I didn't see any others," Edison said.

"They were standing by a wagon in front of the second hogan—the ceremonial hogan—all of them dressed in traditional clothing. The men were wearing the loose pants with the tall moccasins," she said, and Edison shook his head.

"I didn't see any of that," he said.

"Really? Next to the horse and wagon...tall moccasins with silver conchos up the sides? Velveteen shirts and skirts? Even the children were in traditional dress."

Edison looked at her and frowned. "I know you're annoyed at giving them a ride tonight, but what's up with all this?" he asked, and Marin was suddenly quiet.

It was entirely possible Edison *hadn't* seen any of it.

"What did you see?" she asked.

"Two hogans, one with a truck parked out front—the one with the lights," he said, and looked down at her. "No wagon, no horse, no other people."

Marin changed the subject. Edison didn't know about Vangie and herself...the things from the past they sometimes saw, and the truth was it was disturbing to Marin. She didn't understand why she saw these things. Vangie took it more in stride, but neither of them talked much about it, just as they had never discussed the events that night on the mesa.

"You must have seen the truck parked in front of the family hogan, the one our riders went into. Why were they visiting so late at night?"

Edison drove for a while and didn't answer.

"Edison," she said again when a few miles had passed and he hadn't spoken.

His face when she looked at him, was serious, closed.

"Something was wrong, wasn't it?" she said, and he sighed.

"You won't leave it alone, will you?" he said. "You're relentless at times, like a dog with a bone, you know?"

He didn't say anymore, but he didn't have to. This, too, was an old argument between them, and she knew now why he was reluctant to say anything. Sometimes she wished lying was an option with Edison, and they rode in silence until the black outline of Table Mesa appeared.

Almost home.

As they drew even with the mesa, she spoke.

"I suppose the hospital in Shiprock was out of the question?" she said, and he sighed.

"I don't know. I didn't ask. The baby was sick, and they needed a ride," he answered flatly.

She recognized the defensive note in his voice, knew he didn't want to be pressed, but she went on anyway.

"Edison, we've gone over this—" she started patiently, but he broke in.

"I know," he said. "I've heard it all before. You're right, I'm wrong—
they're wrong. Do we have to talk about it?"

"It's just that the baby would be better off—" she said, and he interrupted again.

"In your opinion," he said. "But that's just it, isn't it? Your opinion
is the right one. With you, things are either completely right or completely wrong—black or white. No pun intended," he added, glancing
at her in the dim lights.

"I'm not trying to start a fight," she said, her own voice defensive.
"It's just that the hospital..."

"Stands to reason that if one way is right, the other way must be
wrong by default," he said, continuing as if she had not spoken. "Smart,
stupid. Anglo, Indian," he said, jabbing his finger back and forth
between them. "*Bilagáana, Diné.* Isn't that the picture?"

His hand dropped back to the steering wheel while Marin stared
straight ahead at the two tunnels of headlights in the darkness.

"Yeah, that's the picture, all right," Edison answered, not waiting
for her response, and with a sudden push of a knob, the headlights
went off.

"Edison!" she said, dismayed at his bitterness. "What is all this?
Are you fighting with me or with yourself? Turn on the headlights!
We're on the highway!"

He didn't slacken the truck's speed or turn on the headlights, and
they skimmed through the night, past the dark hulk of Table Mesa,
the truck only another black desert shadow.

"You think I don't know," Edison said after a few miles, "You
think I don't know that the baby might die? That the *ndishniih* in
that hogan won't be using the wonders of modern medicine to diag-
nose the sickness?"

Marin said nothing, and for a long time the only sound between
them was that of the tires humming along the highway.

"Edison...please turn on the lights."

"Living is just like driving in the dark, my *Bilagáana* Nightmare," he said. "The trick is to go very fast and not think about how messed up things are. It's not so hard to die, you know. Living is harder."

She made a small sound of protest.

"I know," he said. "Believe me...I know."

He reached down and flipped on the headlights before he looked over at her.

"Babies die in hospitals, too," he said.

CHAPTER TWENTY-TWO

M acPherson's words—*they found out about you*—echoed in the air,
and Marin heard them against the rush of water in the wash
and the soft patter of falling rain. She stood without moving until
MacPherson took her arm and turned her away from the cottonwoods
and toward the hogan.

"What do you mean, found out about me?" she asked. "Who am I to
them? Just another witness they don't have to believe." She pulled away,
a thought occurring to her. "Do *not* tell me this is some kind of racial
thing," she said, "my word against Vangie's," and he shook his head.

"It's more of a Winfield thing," he said.

"What?"

"Mark Winfield—you cared for him..."

"I *know* who he is," she said "What does Mark have to do with this?"

"Winfield," MacPherson said. "As in Winfield Industries. Ring
any bells?"

"Winfield Indus—you mean Mark's family? Their company?" she
asked.

"His father owns the company," he said.

"Okay, but I still don't see how I'm—"

"You've got connections to this case," MacPherson pointed out.

"Not really."

"How do you think it will look for the company when you testify for the opposition?" MacPherson asked. "You, who are intimately
involved with the Winfields...and privy to their dealings."

"I'm not privy to anything!" she said.

MacPherson stood still, studying her face, his eyes narrowed, and finally he sighed.

"You're getting wet," he said, taking her arm. "You need to be inside."

"I can walk," Marin said, pulling away, irritated.

Bear emerged from the darkness, blocking her way, and she turned to MacPherson, exasperated.

"He's just doing his job," MacPherson said. "Dogs are sensitive to voices."

The big dog whined but didn't move away.

"I know you're angry," MacPherson said. "Bear knows it, too."

"Shouldn't I be?" she asked, shrugging off his hand. "You've searched my apartment, looked at private medical records—which, by the way, is also illegal—a madman is intent on killing me, and God only knows what your company has done to *discourage* Vangie and the rest. And you're implying it's *my* fault."

They walked in silence for a few paces.

"*Are* you proof that Vangie Tso and her family worked in our uranium mines?" MacPherson asked.

Marin turned to him. "If I am," she said, "I'd be a fool to tell you. Cecil and Tolliver weren't able to get the job done, so they called out the big guns? I heard what they said about *you*."

"I'm here for damage control, nothing else," he said. "The police got involved, and the company thought the situation called for my intervention."

"Intervention?" she said and laughed. "The police were involved because Tolliver *assaulted* me! Justin—Sergeant Blue Eyes saved my life! Tolliver then tracked me halfway across the reservation to try and kill me again! I *walked up a mountain*, MacPherson," she said, close to shouting now, and he spoke sharply to Bear when the dog growled, but Marin barely noticed.

"I *walked all night* to get into these mountains, to escape Tolliver, only to find you here! It was your Rover that scared the horse!" Marin added for good measure before she turned away, breathing hard. "Okay," she said after a moment, trying for calm. "The horse bolting wasn't intentional on your part, but the rest still goes."

"Don't you think it's time we were candid with one another, Marin?" he said. "The company isn't playing games here. We're talking about the possible loss of millions of dollars...the loss of jobs, livelihoods, homes..."

"All the same things Vangie and the rest stand to lose or have already lost—and hey, let's not forget my *life*," she said.

"It doesn't make sense to kill you or even to hurt you," MacPherson insisted.

"You're the only one to say so—Tolliver certainly didn't, but then, he had other things on his mind," she said, her voice wavering and her eyes filling with tears.

MacPherson pulled her to his chest, touching her bruised cheek with a gentle finger when she stiffened.

"It's rain, not tears," she said, and he held her for a moment before he bent and gently kissed her.

"Was that to convince me you're one of the good guys?" she asked, surprised but not afraid.

"No," MacPherson said, his hands on her shoulders. "It was to convince me."

Lightning flashed suddenly, with a crack of thunder, and a fresh outpouring of rain pelted them as they climbed the slope to the hogan.

Marin stood beside the door for a moment, listening to the rain while MacPherson brought in more sticks for the fire and called Bear inside.

"*Nahaltin*," she murmured, and MacPherson turned. "It's raining," she translated.

"You speak Navajo?" he asked.

"Only a little," she answered and shivered.

"Take my jacket," he said, offering her the coat. "Your clothes are still damp, and you must be cold."

"I'm scared," she corrected. "It's hard to trust my feelings."

"Which feelings are those?" MacPherson asked her.

"Toward you."

"Good ones?" he asked.

"Maybe," she said. "If for no other reason than Tolliver wasn't anxious to have you around."

"I trust emotions only so far myself," he agreed, and he knelt to add the sticks to the fire.

Marin studied him in the firelight.

The brim of the hat hid his upper face, but she could see the deep lines from nose to mouth. He looked worried, tired.

"How did you find me today?" she asked suddenly.

"How did you come by the horse?" MacPherson asked in turn. "You never said."

Marin considered her answer.

"An old man at a sheep camp loaned him to me," she finally said. "I told him I'd leave the horse at the trading post."

"What trading post?" he asked.

"There's always a trading post. Just follow the roads. Your Rover may be there as well if somebody from around here found it."

"So, tomorrow we'll take our friend the horse and go find a trading post," he said.

"But what about Tolliver? He'll be looking for us."

"Did you see him kill Cecil?" MacPherson asked.

"I'm sorry if Cecil was a friend, Mac," she said.

He raised an eyebrow.

"Mac?" he asked, and Marin shrugged. "Have to call you something," she said.

"I didn't see him kill Cecil. I was hiding, if you recall, terrified I was going to be killed myself. I heard them arguing and I heard gunshots. At least, I thought I did—popping sounds."

She came and stood by the fire. "Later," she said, "when he left, I found he'd put the gun in my coat pocket. It had a silencer attached."

"A *gun?* Where is it?" Mac asked.

"I lost it in the flood." she said.

"You aren't sure about Cecil's death?"

"I heard Tolliver talking to him afterward, but I only heard his voice, not Cecil's. He could have been pretending, putting on a show for me."

"If he was, wouldn't that indicate he doesn't see you as a threat? I don't see him continuing to pursue you."

"You said yourself millions of dollars are at stake," Marin reminded him. "What's not to see?"

"You don't have a very high opinion of the company," he said. "Usually we don't have to resort to murder to get what we want."

"Just terrorism in general?" she asked sharply. "Breaking and entering? Attempted kidnapping? Assault?"

"Your landlord let me in," MacPherson said, ignoring her angry outburst. "If Cecil is dead, then I doubt it has anything to do with you."

"I'm a witness!" she said.

"You say you saw nothing," Mac countered.

"Tolliver may not know that. Why give me the gun if not to clear himself and incriminate me?"

"Without a body, the gun doesn't matter yet...and you've got neither," Mac said.

She held up a hand. "Okay," she said. "So, there's no body and no gun. You have no reason to believe that Tolliver wants me dead, no reason to believe any of this. But *you* weren't there."

"What Tolliver did to you was inexcusable, even to keep you from Vangie's court hearing, and he will be dealt with by the company, if not the law," Mac said.

He stood and brushed his hands on his pants. "It's late, and I know you're tired. Let's get some rest."

"But you haven't told me anything," she protested.

"What more do you want to know?"

"How about what happens now? Why does the company care about me?" Marin said. "You're mistaken if you think a few kisses mean I won't go to the police. I may have missed this court date, but it doesn't mean I'll miss the next one."

"There won't be a next one."

"Of course there will be a next one! You don't know Vangie. Her family, her people, this land... they're her life. She'll fight until the very end."

She stopped suddenly, realizing what she'd said, and MacPherson nodded.

"The end is pretty near," he said, gazing into the fire.

For a long while there was little to hear in the room other than the rain spattering on the roof and the hiss of the fire.

"How can you live in your world?" Marin asked.

She went to the horse standing against the far wall, bent and picked up the reins.

"I'm going now," she said. "I'm taking the horse and I'm going to Vangie."

"What about *your* world, Marin?" MacPherson asked, blocking her way. "I know what you do for a living, I just don't know why. What is it that has made you feel liable for the ills of the world, made you feel responsible..." He paused, studying her face.

"Not just responsible," he said. "You've convinced yourself you're *guilty* somehow, haven't you?"

Marin tried to push past him. "You know nothing about me!"

"I know you seem preoccupied with death and dying," MacPherson said, refusing to let her pass.

"You know *nothing* about me," she repeated.

"What is it you think you're guilty of?"

"Nothing!" Marin spat, and Bear stiffened and lifted his head.

"Do you think you're guilty because you're alive when others aren't?"

"Let me pass," she cried, trying to move around him.

"Do you think you somehow caused their deaths?" MacPherson asked. "Is this some kind of survivor's guilt?"

She pushed past him, and the horse stamped a foot, watching her, ears twitching.

"What is it you think you could have done?"

"There wasn't *anything* I could have done!"

"Done *when?* What are we talking about, anyway?" he said.

"We're not!" she cried, pushing him aside. "We're not talking! You know nothing about me!"

"Then talk to me!" MacPherson said fiercely, spinning her, his hands on her shoulders. "Because I want to know you!"

Marin struggled, but MacPherson held her close.

"How do I reach you?" he said. "It's not your fault people die, Marin."

He put a hand beneath her chin, and Marin felt her lips begin to tremble. "Those voices you hear in here, " Mac said, tapping her forehead gently, "those voices are wrong."

Unable to speak, she swallowed a sob and stood rigid, unyielding.

"Marin, Marin," MacPherson said, and he released her. "When was the last time you had any faith in your feelings?"

He paused, studying her face. "But it's not just that, is it? You've decided it's safer not to feel at all."

"I need to go to Vangie," she said, brushing tears from her face, her voice steady. "Surely you can see that."

"I can see that you're exhausted and upset, and I'm sorry for my part in it. Stay here tonight, rest, and I'll go down with you myself tomorrow."

He turned her toward the bed as he spoke and she went, too weary to argue.

"Where will you sleep?" she asked, sliding into the warmth of the sleeping bag.

"I won't," he said, and Marin was asleep before she could decipher his cryptic answer.

CHAPTER TWENTY-THREE

▲▲

THEN:
Christmas Break

I t was December and snow was falling, the highway slushy but not yet icy.

Edison was driving Marin home after spending the day with school friends eager to see him—home from Chicago for Christmas break—and Edison seemed to have fallen easily back into the high school trivia of basketball games and holiday plans. They had lunch with his friends, then did some Christmas shopping in the mall, where Edison had insisted on visiting jewelry stores to look at engagement rings.

She'd been looking forward to the long ride home and the chance to talk to him alone, but Edison was silent, the only sounds the swish of windshield wipers and the tires on wet pavement.

She'd said nothing more about her early acceptance to the university in Flagstaff, and he had yet to mention the letter she'd sent him at Thanksgiving about her decision to postpone their engagement until graduation.

"Edison," she said, trying to broach the subject now. "I *did* tell you I was accepted to early enrollment at the college in Flagstaff. I'm leaving next week for the January semester...Spring semester." She didn't mention her father's decision to retire, leaving his teaching position when the school year ended and moving them to Flagstaff permanently. She hadn't fully processed the surprise announcement herself.

"You mean you won't be here for graduation?" he said.

"I'll be here but I'm not walking...I'll still have my name called, and we can cheer for Vangie and Rita," she said. "I'm officially a graduate already."

"We were going to choose a wedding date..."

"We can be together then...you'll be back from school, right? Speaking of Chicago, you haven't said anything about how Thanksgiving went," she added. "Rita and Vangie were so excited about visiting you to check out the school, but I haven't had a chance to ask either of them the details."

Edison shrugged and didn't reply, and he reached down and switched off the headlights.

Marin sighed. "Turn on the headlights, Edison. You know I've never liked this...and it's snowing."

"Lighten up, Mare," he said. "Life is serious enough as it is."

She huffed an annoyed sound that turned to a choked scream when she saw the white forms huddled in the road ahead, the sheep barely visible in the falling snow.

Edison swore and the truck slid sideways as he braked, fighting to stay on the road. They hit the edge of the highway, plowing into deep slush before the truck shuddered to a stop.

Marin turned to Edison, angry words ready, but Edison wasn't moving—he was sitting with his head on his hands gripping the steering wheel.

Afraid, Marin touched his shoulder.

"Are you hurt?" she asked, but he shook his head without looking up.

"You?" he asked, his voice directed at the floorboard.

"I'm okay," she answered.

They sat in silence for a long time, the air inside the truck growing cold, their breath frosting the windows as the windshield wipers continued to swish back and forth.

"My life is a mess," he said finally, and Marin bent close to hear him.

"What's wrong?" she asked. "Is it school?"

Edison sat up, staring out the windshield. "My life is pointless," he said after a while. "I have no identity."

"Are you unhappy in Chicago?"

Edison shook his head. "It's just me. I can't go backward, and I can't seem to move forward. I feel like I'm in limbo—stuck between past traditions I can't use and a future I'm not sure I want anymore."

Marin touched his shoulder, but he didn't seem to notice. "You worked hard for this," she said.

"I did, but stuck like this I have no identity... I'm canceled out ," he said.

"Canceled?" Marin repeated, not knowing what to say, not understanding what he meant.

"An equal positive and a negative, Marin. They cancel each other out, equaling zero."

"Why can't both parts be positive?" Marin asked. "Make your own story work, like Vangie says. I can help..."

Edison sat back and looked at her. "You don't want anything to do with any of my parts, remember? I read your letter."

"I'm *not* saying no. You know I love you. It's just...I want to step back for a while. I want *both* of us to take some time to decide what we want—to decide which direction we're going. I want to finish a semester of college, as you have. Let's decide things between us in the Spring. We're young, there's no hurry."

"Okay, Mare," he said, holding up a hand. "I get it. I'd better get the sheep off the road."

He opened his door, and a gust of cold wind blew through the cab. Marin shivered, feeling the subject was far from resolved.

"Front tire is in pretty deep," he said restarting the truck after herding the sheep across the highway. "I'll have to push."

"Warm up first," Marin said, and Edison bent and held his hands near the heater.

"Edison, I didn't say no," she began again.

"Forget it," he said. "You're right, we should wait and talk about it in the Spring. "

206 ★ RABBIT MOON

"You know I'm not seeing anyone else," Marin said.

"Do I?" he asked, and Marin turned away so he wouldn't see her tears.

"I don't want to fight," she said, and paused, hearing something in his voice. "Are *you* seeing anyone else?"

Edison didn't answer, and she sat back in the seat, her world jerking to a full stop.

"You are," she said, her voice flat. "You've met someone at college."

He still didn't answer, turning his hands beneath the heater's warm air. Marin looked at his face and had an awful feeling.

"Is it serious?" she asked.

"Not in the way you think," he said.

"I'm asking for the way *you* think," Marin said, her eyes on the windshield wipers. Why couldn't life be like that...one sweep and everything cleared away, clean, without a trace.

"*You* said no when I asked you to marry me before I left," he said. "I thought you meant it."

"I *said* 'not yet'—there's a difference."

"This doesn't mean we can't be together, Marin. I *love* you. She doesn't expect me to..."

"What did you mean about it being serious but not in the way I think?" she asked.

"She's pregnant," Edison said into the floorboard, his head bent. "Maybe. *Maybe* pregnant."

Marin felt the words rather than heard them, the word 'pregnant' like a physical blow.

"We can work this out," Edison said when she didn't speak. "Let's wait and see."

"You didn't intend to tell me, did you?"

"I'm telling you now," he said. "This is partly on you. You said no...I *heard* 'no'."

"We're talking about you, not me," she said.

"I'm asking you to let this play out before you decide to *torpedo* us," he said, and Marin refused the smile she knew he wanted.

"You're the one who's torpedoed us. Your life's a mess, I get it. What about *our* life?" Marin said, her voice rising.

"I love you. Give me time, give *us* time, to make things work. I told you, she doesn't expect marriage or anything..."

"You think that makes it better? What about what I expect, Edison? You'll have a responsibility to her, to them if she's pregnant!"

"If she's not pregnant...if she wants nothing from me?" he asked. "What will your answer be then?"

Now was the time to tell him about the coming move to Flagstaff, the time to either end things or let it wait until she returned in the Spring.

"Let's decide things when we come back for graduation," she said, knowing it wasn't the answer he wanted, and Edison opened the door.

"I'd better push this *chidíí* out of the snow and get you home," he said, as if things were settled and Marin's world would simply begin to spin again, regaining its orbit as if nothing had happened.

CHAPTER TWENTY-FOUR

▲▲

T he sounds of MacPherson stirring woke Marin in the predawn
darkness and she lay in the warmth of the sleeping bag, hoping he wouldn't notice she was awake as she tried to analyze things
she'd been too tired to deal with the night before. In a few unguarded
moments she had let MacPherson come dangerously close, both emotionally and physically, a closeness that she now had to remedy.

She shifted position and groaned—the muscles in her neck and
shoulders seemed to have fused into one solid, aching lump, and it was
almost impossible to move her right shoulder.

MacPherson's face was suddenly over her own, peering down at
her in the darkness.

"Awake?" he asked, and she was glad he couldn't see her face as she
pushed herself upright.

"I'm awake."

MacPherson knelt before the fire to strike a match over the
small pile of kindling, and the flames caught quickly, the small pine
branches snapping and hissing.

He pushed the coffeepot close to the fire.

"Sore?" he asked.

"Yes," she admitted, swinging her legs to the floor with an effort.

"Well, your bruises look better," he said, digging into the backpack. "Here's something for the pain, if you feel you can trust me
enough to take it."

"I'll take it," she said grimly, pushing aside the sleeping bag and accepting the tablets. He watched as she swallowed.

"I've been thinking I should go down alone, Marin, come back with a vehicle. You don't look in good enough shape to be moving."

She shook her head and gingerly rotated her shoulder. "It'll be alright. I'm just stiff."

"Marin," he started, but she broke in.

"I'll walk down this mountain on my own if I have to, even if you take the horse and leave me."

MacPherson went to the fire, filled the cup with coffee, and brought it across to her. "Drink this," he said, standing over her as she swallowed. "Try to calm down and think about what I'm saying. You'd be safe here."

Marin took another quick sip. "I'm not your responsibility. Am I your prisoner?"

MacPherson raised his eyebrows. "What's bothering you? Besides the shoulder, I mean."

"Nothing," she muttered, straightening her shirt and running her fingers through her hair until MacPherson tossed a comb into her lap.

"Having second thoughts about trusting me?" he asked.

Marin shrugged, pulling her hair over her shoulder to use the comb. "I haven't had first thoughts yet."

"From what I've observed, you've convinced yourself you don't need anyone's help."

He paused, and she felt his eyes on her as she braided her hair into one long plait.

"But that only works so long," he said slowly. "I think you're beginning to see that."

"And I'm to understand you want to offer your help?" she said.

"Marin, a man's strongest instinct is to protect. Why would you think I'd act differently than my nature dictates?"

"I'm thinking that I don't really know much about your nature, one way or the other," she said, tossing the braid over her shoulder and bending to find shoes and socks.

"You must know a little," he said in a dry voice, and Marin promptly sat up.

"I said last night I didn't trust emotions," MacPherson said, watching as she pulled the edges of her shirt together, "not that I didn't have any."

He took the coffee cup and returned to the fire.

"Then protect me by taking me with you," Marin said quietly. "I don't want to stay here alone."

The sun topped the eastern horizon, and a thin beam of sunlight found its way into the doorway of the hogan, catching the smoke from the fire and creating a filmy light in the room.

"Your call," he said finally.

They ate a protein bar, then packed everything in his backpack, and MacPherson hefted the pack to a shoulder and moved to the door, pausing to lift his face to the sun.

"Nice," he commented.

Marin, scattering the ashes of the fire, looked over. "All traditional hogan doorways face the east to catch the morning sun."

She hesitated for a moment in the center of the room. "I almost hate to leave here," she said. "This place was a refuge."

"Even bewitched?" he asked.

"Maybe because of it," she replied. "Whatever ghosts are here seem old and peaceful."

MacPherson moved outside and whistled for Bear, and Marin took a last look around the room before she followed him out, watching as he saddled the horse and strapped the backpack on behind.

"I see you know something about horses," she commented, and he lifted his eyebrows. "The blanket," she said, indicating the gray wool blanket under the saddle. "I was wondering what we could use."

"I carry it with me. I find it comes in handy."

He caught up the reins in one hand. "You ride, I'll walk. We're going to be traveling uphill for a while, so it'll be slow going."

"Uphill?" Marin asked, grimacing as she mounted the horse, noting that he kept the reins. "We're not heading downhill?"

MacPherson looked up at her. "You're the one who said there were a lot of things I didn't mention last night," he said. "You can still stay here."

She shook her head, and he led off at a walk. Bear ran ahead, sniffing at tumbleweeds and exploring the undersides of rocks.

"You're quiet this morning," she commented. "Where are we going?"

"There's a mine nearby," he explained as they walked. "I need a few rock samples before I leave. It won't take too long."

Marin lifted her face to the warmth of the sun and breathed in the early morning air.

"I guess that explains why you've been camping in the hogan," she said. "I wondered why you were there."

He didn't comment, and they followed the edge of the wash uphill into the mountains.

The stream still ran fast and muddy, but not so high as the day before, and the tree leaves and green plants looked refreshed by the rain.

They walked in silence, the ground growing steeper, the horse moving easily with head up and ears relaxed, and the sun inched upward in the sky as the morning passed. MacPherson walked steadily, a dark patch of sweat beginning to spread across the back of his shirt, and eventually he paused, took off his hat and handed it up.

"You look like you burn easily," he said, but she hesitated.

"It's a hat," MacPherson said, "not a commitment."

"It's not that," she said, taking it. "It's just that I lost mine, during the flood."

"I remember. You seemed upset."

"Edison gave it to me, a long time ago. I'm sorry it's gone."

She put his hat on, settled it, then spoke again. "Do you mind if I walk awhile?"

"Suit yourself."

She dismounted and walked alongside MacPherson, pausing beside a piñon tree to take a cone and strip out the small nuts. She cracked and ate a few, savoring the taste, and passed a few to MacPherson who seemed surprised when he tasted them.

"Pine nuts," he said.

"Piñons," she corrected and laughed at his expression. "Where did you think they came from?" she asked.

"Restaurants," he said, and Marin laughed again.

"Sorry there's not more. It's not peak season yet," she said.

They walked on, Bear racing far ahead of them, reminding her of Bailey. She took off the hat and fanned herself, content to breathe in the cedar scented air.

"You seem to like this land," MacPherson said, watching her.

"I do," she said. "I told you last night."

"You're not Navajo...Diné," he said. "There must have been some prejudice living here."

Marin shrugged.

"I think there's probably a bit more to it than that," MacPherson said, watching her, and Marin put the hat back on her head and pulled the brim low.

"I guess that's a 'no comment,'" he said. "So, you were happy?"

"I never really thought about being happy," she answered. "I guess in a lot of ways I was on the outside because of who I was. But isn't that normal with any teenager?"

"Did you think it was normal?"

She considered a moment. "It was just the way things were."

She dropped the empty pinecone and MacPherson clicked his tongue at the horse, and Marin fell in behind him for a while, walking slowly and thinking of Vangie and Edison—and herself.

"You live here and so you think you understand," Vangie once told her when they were discussing college as Edison was preparing to go to Chicago. "For me, being a part of my culture is more than knowing the beliefs and following the teachings," Vangie had said. "It's who I am. I don't think about being Diné anymore than I think about being born a human-being and not a bird."

"Because you fit in here and don't have to think about it," Marin had answered dryly.

Vangie was thoughtful. "Being Diné is who I am without having to think about it," she'd said. "I won't be leaving the reservation."

She had hoped that Vangie would decide to come with her to college in Flagstaff. "Shouldn't you try other things, though? Other places?" she'd asked.

"Sure, I plan to visit all over—Rita and I are planning to visit Edison in Chicago—but this is my place to be who I am," Vangie had said, shrugging. "I know things change. I accept that. I mean, look at my grandmother, and my mother, how different their stories were from mine."

"Don't you want to change?" she'd asked, thinking of Edison.

"I want to choose," Vangie had said. "I want to choose what I keep from my grandmother's story and my mother's and choose what I accept from others who have different stories. Like you."

"How will you decide what to choose?" Marin asked.

"I will make a good choice for me."

"But how?" Marin had insisted. "You can't choose them all."

"Well, however I choose, it will be my own choice, and that isn't always true for everyone. I intend to make it for myself, and then later, my children will be allowed to make their choice for their story."

She'd touched Marin's hand lightly with two fingers.

"This place is not all of your story. You need to choose who you are, and this may not be the place for you to do it."

"But Edison and I have an understanding," Marin had protested.

"It's not about Edison. It's about you. Edison has chosen to divide himself against himself," Vangie had said. "*Baahadzidgo 'at'e.*"

Marin remembered the phrase. "Dangerous to your soul," she whispered now, and MacPherson turned.

"What?" he asked, and Marin walked a few steps before answering.

"Just thinking of something Vangie said."

The sun shone high in the sky as noon drew near, and the horse dozed as he walked, head down, eyes almost closed, bumping into Marin with his nose when she paused. The low, bushy growths of cedar and juniper had gradually given way to taller pines and there were spongy pine needles underfoot and branches to shield them from the direct rays of the sun, but it was hot, a true summer's day.

Marin stopped for a moment on the ridge they followed to look at the view of the desert floor below. Far to the north she could make out Shiprock peak and she pointed it out to MacPherson.

"Let's have a break," he said, indicating a taller than average juniper tree growing on the verge of the hillside, its branches wide and twisted and providing a large spread of shade.

MacPherson removed the pack from behind the saddle and loosened the horse's girth strap, dropping the reins to let the horse graze as he would, and Marin spread his jacket in the deepest part of the shade and sat down.

The view below stretched all the way to the eastern horizon, and Marin admired it as MacPherson knelt beside her to search around in the pack, coming up with two oranges.

"Do you know where you're going?" Marin asked, accepting an orange. "I thought you said this mine was close by."

"Did I say that?" MacPherson replied.

Marin considered for a moment. "Maybe I just thought you did," she said. "Actually, you don't give a straight answer to much of anything I ask."

Together they contemplated the landscape, Marin again directing his eyes to the large peak rising straight up toward the north. Purple shadows from the clouds passing between the sun and the land, played across the dry plains, moving in waves over the ground and sliding across the towering volcanic rock.

"It does look like a ship," MacPherson said. "One of those old sailing vessels."

"The Diné say Shiprock is a winged bird," Marin told him. "*Tse Bit'ai'*—the great bird who carried the People on his back from the far north—and was killed by the *Tsenahale*...monsters."

"Monsters?"

"Great winged monsters who preyed upon the people. Monster Slayer killed them with an arrow of lightning and changed their two young fledglings into the eagle and the owl."

MacPherson snapped his fingers and Bear came running across to him, the horse idly kicking out as the dog ran near his back hooves, and MacPherson rubbed Bear's ears and sent him off ahead of them.

"Where are you sending Bear? " Marin started, but MacPherson interrupted.

"Is your nickname really Nightmare?" he asked.

"How did you know that?" she asked.

"My first name is Cullen," he said.

"So you've said, but it doesn't suit you, somehow," Marin said.

"You haven't known me very long," he said. "Feel free to come up with another. You called me Mac last night...that'll do."

"Maybe," she said, frowning. "Mac is okay until something else comes to mind."

"I've been called worse," he said. "I hope your nickname isn't a reflection on your personality."

"No," she said. "It's a play on the sound of my name, but how did you know it?"

"Did you get it from Vangie?" MacPherson asked easily. "Were you dreaming about her last night?"

Marin snapped her head around.

"What do you mean?" she said. She didn't remember having the mesa dream...

"I mean," he said, peeling off a section of orange and biting it in half, "you seemed to be having a bad dream last night. Once or twice, you cried out."

Marin said nothing, staring at the blue sky and the fat white clouds dotted across the blue like rounded scoops of vanilla ice cream.

"You know," MacPherson said as he put another slice of orange in his mouth, "sometimes if you actually *talk* to another person, it can help."

Silent, Marin stared at her lap and thought about the things she kept in the box at the back of the closet at home, letters, an old diary. How much was in them?

Nothing about the dream—it was a recent problem and one she'd only discussed with Mark... and Dr. Lippmann.

"I was wrong," she said slowly, "about what I said last night. You do seem to know me. At least, you did a very thorough job of finding out things about me. Did you break into Dr. Lippmann's office, too?"

MacPherson didn't answer, and Marin ate a piece of her orange, watching the horse cropping grass nearby, close but not close enough for her to easily reach before MacPherson could stop her. A blue jay dropped gracefully to the ground near her, greedily eying the orange as he hopped closer, and Marin tossed a piece over, watching as the bird snatched it up and settled on one of the low cedar branches. She felt MacPherson's eyes on her and dipped her head to hide her face beneath the hat brim, startled when he reached over and tugged it completely over her eyes.

"No need to think of running, Marin," he said. "Can I hope that someday you'll trust me enough to talk to me, to tell me what this dream of yours is all about?"

His voice sounded light, but to her eyes his face looked grim and tired, and defiantly she pulled his hat from her head and tossed it in his lap.

"As much as I trust that you told the truth about not being my captor?" she answered. "Where did you send Bear?"

"He's just checking things out up ahead," he replied.

"Tolliver?"

"It's just a precaution, Marin, nothing more."

The blue jay swooped down and snagged another scrap of orange before flitting back to the cedar branches, and neither she nor MacPherson spoke for a while, listening to the chatter between the blue jay and a scolding squirrel. A cool breeze wafted beneath the juniper tree, and she lifted her braid to catch the coolness on her neck as Bear, tongue hanging, came trotting back and sat next to Marin, his large head pressed against her shoulder, the brown eyes gazing into hers.

MacPherson stood and walked over to the horse, scooping the reins from the ground and tightening the girth while the horse stamped and grunted his protest.

"Looks like you've made a conquest in Bear," MacPherson said. "He'll stay with you. I'm going to ride ahead for a ways. The mine opening can be hard to see. If you want, walk on, just head straight up. I'll be back soon."

He gathered the reins, re-tightened the girth on the bay, mounted, and looked down at her.

"Marin," he said, and she looked up. "If you ever do want to talk to me, about the dream or anything else, I meant what I said. I'll be here. I can be one of your strengths, if you'll allow it."

Marin started to speak, but he was riding away.

Bear shook himself and looked at her with a question on his doggy face, his mouth open and teeth showing as if he were smiling.

"Are you a friend or a jailer?" Marin asked him, and the dog barked once as Marin stood and shook out MacPherson's coat.

She felt vaguely guilty, as if she had been caught in a lie but that was ridiculous, she was under no obligation to talk to MacPherson about the mesa or anything else, and anyway, there seemed to be little he didn't already know without the benefit of her input. She shifted his coat to one arm, wishing she'd thought to tie it onto the saddle before MacPherson left, and she heard a crackle in one of the pockets. Hoping for another protein bar, she stuck her hand inside and pulled out a yellow square of paper, heavily creased, as if it had been handled a lot.

A telegram.

MacPherson's name was scrawled across the top in the space for recipient, and her eyes moved to the type-written lines beneath his name.

"Company gives go-ahead," she read. "Waste site feasibilities per your discretion."

The space marked *sender* had no name...only the U.S. Federal seal of an organization called the NRC, and she bent closer to look at it.

The Nuclear Regulatory Commission...

She flipped the telegram over, but nothing was on the other side, and she considered the brief line and what MacPherson had told her about his job. She refolded the telegram and stuffed it back inside his pocket.

Moving to a nearby boulder, she sat down to try and straighten out her racing thoughts.

Environmentally friendly projects, he'd said. What exactly had he said when they'd been talking about the mines?

I'm rather well-known for my efforts to negotiate projects that are friendly to the environment...

What a fool she was to have believed anything he had said. Cullen MacPherson was here on behalf of the government to check out sites for waste dumps—'waste site feasibilities'—and what better place to dump more waste, chemical or nuclear or both, than the abandoned mines scattered across the reservation, already contaminated with their heaps of radioactive tailings.

If MacPherson was telling the truth about Vangie having filed lawsuits, the legal proceedings, of which she herself must be a part, must be stalling any arrangements for the mine conversions into waste dumps.

She bit her lip. How clever MacPherson had been, how subtle after Tolliver's viciousness, convincing her there was nothing she could do to help Vangie's case, trying to persuade her that Vangie had little real proof regarding the lawsuits...until Marin had shown up.

No wonder they needed to get rid of her.

She shivered, though the summer air was hot and still.

But could Vangie's lawsuits make such a difference? Surely lawsuits regarding only a few of so many abandoned mines wouldn't affect any larger plans the company had to use them for dump sites.

Unless the adverse publicity was what they wanted to avoid.

Adverse publicity was something Vangie had always been very good at, and almost certainly the plan to use the mines as dump sites was being pushed through in secret, with MacPherson and his 'company' wanting to attract as little attention as possible to what they had planned. It wouldn't be the first time the tribal council had been manipulated into rubberstamping an agreement made with an outside company.

Or with the U.S. government.

The air was hot and still, and nothing moved except the heat waves shimmering from the rocks at the edge of her vision, and Marin stood and paced, clenching her fists, undecided on her best course of action.

A small lizard darted out of a crevice in the rock, its sides heaving and its mouth slightly open, and Marin knew she needed to make a decision and needed to do it now. She took a step forward, and a wet nose nudged her behind one knee.

It was Bear, tongue hanging, tail wagging, and he wasn't alone.

"Anything wrong?" MacPherson asked.

CHAPTER TWENTY-FIVE

▲▲▲

At the sound of MacPherson's voice, the small lizard vanished from the rock, and Marin steadied herself, stretching out a hand to Bear to scratch his ears before she turned to face the man behind her.

"You startled me," she said, "coming up behind me like that."

MacPherson stood near the boulder, hair dark and sweaty, shirt-sleeves rolled to his elbows and his eyes squinted against the bright sun. His face looked strained to Marin's eyes, and he lifted a hand and ran it over his mouth before indicating the rocky hillside behind him.

"One of the mine openings is there," he said. "Almost directly behind you."

"I don't see anything but rocks," Marin said, looking beyond his shoulder.

"There," he said, pointing. "See the dark spot against that rock? That's an air shaft."

Marin tried to keep her voice casual and her manner as easy as his own.

"Where's the horse?" she asked.

"I left him up there," he said, "and came back down for you."

"Why?" she asked, careful not to look directly into his face, as he was too good at reading her thoughts. "I thought you just wanted a few rock samples."

"I'll have to go in the mine to get them," he said, frowning, "I suddenly decided it's better if you go with me. I don't want to leave you out here alone...even with Bear here. Not with Tollever likely around."

"I'll be okay here," she said and seated herself on the rock. "I won't go anywhere."

MacPherson squatted in front of her, placing his hands on each side of her and studying her face. "What's happened?"

"I found out a bit more about you, that's all," she said, deciding there was no point in pretending.

"What is it you think you know now?"

"No, the problem is just the opposite," she said, shaking her head. "It seems I don't know anything at all."

His jacket lay nearby, and Marin glanced at it with a small thrust of her chin. "In your coat pocket," she said, and he ran his hands through the pockets and withdrew the telegram.

"I can explain this, Marin, but right now is not the time."

"Who are you?" she asked, looking into his face. "Is anything you've told me the truth?"

Bear came to stand beside them, and he turned his large head from Marin to MacPherson, listening, ears cocked.

"Trust is a fragile thing, Marin," MacPherson said gently. "We choose what we want to believe, and those choices make us who and what we are."

"I'm supposed to choose to trust you?" she asked.

"Depends on where your faith lies," MacPherson said. "Othello, remember?"

"Othello's faith was destroyed, and Desdemona ended up dead at his hands," she said and laughed.

"Something funny?" he asked.

"You searched my house, my records, my father's books. You must know my middle name is Desdemona."

"I didn't," he said.

"My father's favorite book," she said. "Am I going to end up dead, Cullen MacPherson? Like Desdemona? Are you going to kill me?"

Her voice broke, and MacPherson took both her hands, gripped them hard. "Othello allowed his faith to be destroyed by lies, he chose not to believe in Desdemona's faithfulness," MacPherson replied. "If I tell you that I believe, completely believe, what you've told me about Tolliver, about Cecil, will that help you to trust me now?"

"I can't suspend my own judgment, even for you."

Bear had moved away to explore a few small junipers, and he suddenly growled, going rigid, his nose in the air, and MacPherson stood.

"Is it Tolliver?" Marin asked.

"We need to go," he replied. "I'll explain more later."

He looked down at her. "Will you come with me? Suspend judgment for just a few more hours?"

"If it's a choice between you or Tolliver, I think you know my answer," she said, standing as well.

The sun stood mid-zenith and the air was close as they started the short climb up the hillside to the air shaft, and MacPherson walked quickly, Bear on his heels, Marin struggling to keep up with them both. The way was rock-strewn and so steep that she wondered how the horse had managed the climb. Dust rose beneath her feet and settled on the sweat on her arms and neck, and she pushed her hair away from her face, straining to see the air shaft.

"I thought the opening was close?" she panted from behind MacPherson, but he did not answer, and she spotted the horse.

MacPherson had left him tied to a juniper tree, unsaddled, and the horse lifted his head as they approached, curling his lips back from large teeth and nipping at the dog as Bear bounded across. MacPherson reached the tree and shouldered the backpack, leaving the saddle and blanket on the ground.

"You need the pack?" she asked, and he nodded.

"Come on," he said to Marin, and again started up the slope.

This time the climb was brief, a matter of a few yards before they stood beside a black hole almost flush to the ground with clumps of sagebrush partially covering it. Without MacPherson she doubted she would have seen the small opening, and she wondered if animals ever fell through it.

She leaned close and an icy current of stale air hit her face, and she recoiled. The black hole looked menacing, but MacPherson didn't seem bothered as he removed a coil of orange nylon rope from the pack and began to unwind it, knotting one end around a tree and placing smaller rocks and brush around to camouflage the bright orange color.

He lifted the backpack.

"I don't think I can go down there," Marin said.

"It's not a straight shot to the bottom," he answered. "There's a branch tunnel only a few yards down."

She shivered and he glanced up.

"Never been in a mine before?" he asked.

"Not this way. I was in a mining car. Why are you hiding the rope?"

"I don't want anyone who may be around to know we're in here," he answered. "Do you?"

"I'm not sure," Marin murmured, but he didn't seem to hear.

"Ever do any climbing?" he asked, strapping on the backpack.

"Up, not down," she said.

"About the same. Watch me."

Pulling a large flashlight out of the pack and shoving it into his waistband, MacPherson backed into the small opening, the orange rope around his waist and one leg dangling into the dark behind him as he rappelled down the shaft, and Marin shivered again.

Bear stretched his nose toward the chilled air and whined.

"I'm with you, Bear," Marin whispered.

A small circle of light appeared in the blackness below, and MacPherson called up, the sound hollow, echoing from the walls around him.

"Wrap the rope around your waist, hold it with one hand, and start down," he called up. "Brace your feet against the wall, and don't worry—I'll catch you."

"What about Bear?" she called back.

"He'll keep watch," MacPherson answered.

Marin picked up the rope, the nylon slick beneath her hands, and she looped it around her waist before backing into the opening as MacPherson had done, careful to avoid putting too much weight on her injured shoulder. Cautiously she inched one foot and then the other down the rock wall of the shaft, and was relieved to find MacPherson was right—the descent wasn't steep and slanted gently downward.

Cold air closed around her as she dropped beneath the rim of the opening, and she was soon engulfed in blackness. She turned her face upward, focusing on the outline of Bear's head centered in the light above her as she lowered herself, sliding her hands a few inches at a time along the rope.

Below her, MacPherson directed her movements.

"You're down," he said at last, the circle of light from his flashlight at her elbow as her feet touched the ground. "The shoulder okay?"

"I'm good," she said.

Their voices were strangely flat, bouncing off the rock walls encircling them, and Marin looked around as MacPherson played the light down an adjoining tunnel. The passageway was larger than she had expected, perhaps four feet across and the ceiling was high enough to walk upright, for her at any rate.

"This branch leads into one of the main tunnels," MacPherson told her, leading off down the passageway.

"Are there many tunnels?" she asked.

"This is one of the larger mines," he answered, feeding coils of a second orange rope behind him as he walked. The light moved with him, and Marin stayed close, but MacPherson seemed to feel no qualms about being in the pitch-black tunnel, walking rapidly as if he knew exactly where they were going.

She followed his steps as best she could, trying to avoid stepping on the rope trailing behind him and wishing, again, that she had her own flashlight.

The air grew stale, and Marin touched one of the rock walls as she passed. Never before had she been this far, this deep, into a mine, and she thought of Vangie, thought of her brothers and uncle working in such a dark and airless place. Only once or twice had she and Vangie ventured into the mine one long-ago summer and then only with Vangie's uncle as guide. He'd conducted them for a short way down the main entrance before turning off the tunnel lights to demonstrate the utter blackness and the feel of solid mountain around them.

The air grew colder as they walked, they must be going deeper, but it was hard to tell as the tunnel floor seemed level enough. Distance was hard to judge, and she pushed the button on her wristwatch to check the time. Only twenty minutes had gone by since they had entered the mine and Marin was surprised, she would have guessed an hour, at least, had passed.

Occasionally the tunnel they walked along intersected with smaller, branching passageways, and she could feel fresh blasts of chilled air each time they crossed in front of such an opening,

MacPherson chose to turn down some and pass by other tunnels as if he followed a blueprint of the mine, and she was glad he seemed to know exactly where they were going. He hadn't spoken since they'd started into the tunnels. Maybe he needed to concentrate to follow the map in his head—but niggling doubts about the wisdom of her decision to follow him began to surface. Placing her trust in him in the bright light of day seemed different than trusting him in this black, cold darkness, but again she assured herself it took a great deal of concentration to make all the right turns in this place.

Her fingers were growing numb, and she had begun to shiver almost continually when MacPherson's light suddenly stopped and moved about the walls, showing a large, roughly circular room with a high ceiling.

Heavy iron rails crossed the middle of the floor and dead-ended into a wall, dissecting the room into halves, and an old ore bucket, rusty and caked with lumps of gray dirt, lay on its side across the tracks. Several wooden boxes were stacked against the far wall, and Marin made out the words before MacPherson turned the light on her face.

"Why didn't you say you were cold?" he asked, handing her his jacket.

"Those boxes contain dynamite," she breathed, putting on his jacket.

"They're empty," he said, and he stuck the flashlight under one arm while he pulled the backpack from his shoulders and leaned it against the wall.

"Where are we?" she asked, the light playing across the opposite wall on a tall, closet-like structure made of wooden planks. Giant pulleys above it held loops of steel cable.

Marin stepped closer and felt MacPherson's hand close on her elbow.

"Careful," he said. "That's the elevator shaft. It goes straight down through all the levels."

"We're not going down there, are we?" Marin asked.

"No, of course not," he said, seating himself on a box, the flashlight in one hand and a length of orange rope in the other.

"Shouldn't there be a gate across that hole?" she asked. "For safety?"

He shrugged.

"Probably was, at one time. The room was usually lit up though, easy enough to see the shaft."

"Where's the elevator?" she asked.

"Below us somewhere." He patted the backpack.

"There's food in here if you're hungry," he said. "Candy bars and some fruit, the water canteen."

"No thanks," she said.

"It's pretty safe, really," he said, "as long as you stay away from that elevator shaft. There's a generator somewhere, but I haven't tried it to see if the elevator or the housing lights work."

"You mean this mine is still in use? You're sitting on boxes marked dynamite. You're sure they're empty, right?"

He nodded. "I came down a few days ago to check things out."

The air was stagnant, and Marin was cold even with Mac's jacket, and her lungs felt like they weren't filling properly. It was probably her imagination, but she couldn't shake the feeling.

*Cold and in the dark...*a faint memory stirred but she pushed it away.

"Whatever it is you have to do down here, I wish you'd do it quickly so we can leave. I hate being in the dark," she said.

"There's a flashlight in the pack," Mac continued as if she hadn't spoken, "but it has no batteries. They're in the pack, they're just not in the flashlight yet. You'll be able to find them easily enough."

A tiny frisson of fear caused her heart to jump beneath her breastbone.

"MacPherson," she began, and with no warning the flashlight clicked off.

"MacPherson!" she cried, her heart pounding, but the light was gone, and she was in darkness as solid as a black wall. She reached out for the place where he'd been sitting, but his voice came from somewhere across the room.

"I'm sorry Marin," he said. "Stay close to that pack. You'll find the flashlight and eventually you'll find the batteries to go with it."

"MacPherson," she whispered, shrinking against the wall.

His voice became sharp. "Marin, listen to me. I'm leaving the rope here, in this room. Do you understand?"

She didn't answer and she went to her knees, stunned.

"When you find the rope, follow it out," he said. "Do you understand? The rope will lead you out."

She didn't—couldn't—speak.

"Marin! Do you understand me?"

"Yes," she cried, aiming her words toward his voice. "I understand you! It was a good trick, wasn't it? All that talk about faith and trust, and I was stupid enough to believe it...so stupid." Even down to gaining her trust because of her love for dogs. "Congratulations," she said, her voice bitter. "You and Tolliver did your homework well, up to and including using Bear to gain my trust. Is he even yours?"

"Listen to me, Marin," MacPherson said, and his voice echoed from the walls.

"No. I'm finished listening to you."

"I need to know you're safe while I deal with Tolliver. He's up here,

Marin, on the mountain, and he has the Rover. I saw the tracks today when we left the hogan."

"You said he had no reason to kill me."

"You met me, which wasn't supposed to happen," Mac said. "Tolliver knows and will think I've told you what's going on in here."

Her knees were beginning to ache, and she eased herself down onto the dirt floor, careful to keep her back against the wall. "That's your explanation?" she asked. "You owe me more than that."

There was no answer from his side of the room, and the small rustling noises of his movements suddenly stopped. A sharp stab of panic made her voice shrill. "MacPherson!" she cried.

"I'm here," he answered, somewhere to her left.

"I think I have a right to know what this is about." she said, moving her hand along the wall toward his voice, but his sigh now came from across the room.

"A series of... negotiations...is scheduled to take place soon," he said, "and Tolliver needs those negotiations to happen without any interference from me, or just without me, period."

"Negotiations?" Marin asked. "About using the reservation mines as dump sites?"

"The nature of what I do is... somewhat sensitive," he answered.

"No doubt," Marin said. "Environmental espionage would be, I suppose." Another sigh came from across the room.

"Marin..."

"Who are you, MacPherson? I read the telegram in your pocket."

"We really don't have time for this," he said. "Try to trust me."

"I forgot about the most important character in Othello, didn't I?" she said. "The treacherous Iago..."

There was a long pause. "I'm a federal agent, Marin," MacPherson said, his disembodied voice coming from the darkness. "I'm with the Nuclear Regulatory Commission, as I'm sure you saw on the telegram. I'm a kind of trouble-shooter, like I told you, only I investigate criminal activities involving nuclear materials."

He paused. "Marin?" he asked. "Do you hear me? Answer me or I leave now."

She nodded before she remembered he could not see her. "Bombs," she said. " You help make bombs."

To her surprise he laughed. "No, the NRC oversees the operation of nuclear facilities. To quote the mandate, we're responsible for the 'possession, use, processing, transport, handling, and disposal of nuclear materials,' end quote."

"The disposal of nuclear waste," she repeated in a flat voice.

"Including its theft. I believe Bud is stealing uranium," he told her, and when she didn't answer, he spoke, his voice curt. "I'll talk, Marin, but only if I know you're where I left you. I need to hear you."

"But this mine is closed," she said quickly. "How can Tolliver be stealing uranium?"

"He's using tailings," MacPherson said. "In most of these mines, only the high-grade uranium ore was taken. He's taking the ore that was left, the low-grade stuff."

"What can he do with it?"

"Stockpile it," MacPherson said. "Sell it."

"Uranium isn't in short supply," she said. "Is it?"

"It's complicated, and we don't really have the time to discuss it at this moment."

"Give me the abbreviated version, then."

There was a brief silence. "Do you know what a breeder reactor is, Marin?"

"Your invasion of my privacy didn't find the physics degree?"

"A breeder is a nuclear fission reactor that produces as much or more fuel than it consumes," he said, ignoring her answer. "It works by converting U-238, which is low-grade uranium, into plutonium... the good stuff. A successful breeder reactor program can potentially eliminate the need to import fuels to produce electricity."

"If that's true, then why isn't the U.S. building these... these breeder reactors?" she asked.

"Public opposition to nuclear power plants, to name one, and an expensive price tag. Also, like you said—high-grade uranium isn't in short supply."

"So why use them?"

"Some countries figure that uranium ultimately *will* become scarce, and once the reactor has been built, the fuel cost difference alone will make the expense worthwhile. It's no secret that nuclear plants are a very inexpensive source of electricity, but in this country, we've become afraid of them."

"For good reason..."

"Nuclear energy is here to stay. We just have to learn to handle it safely. Unfortunately, electricity isn't the only use for plutonium."

"But why buy the—the low-grade stuff—from Tolliver?"

"Price," he said shortly. "The tailings are already mined and just sitting around waiting to be scooped up, so he can offer some very good prices to some very bad people."

"But he can't just transport tons of tailings from these mines without anyone noticing."

Her teeth were chattering, both as a reaction to the cold and the fear that MacPherson would leave her here in the dark, and it was hard to talk. Finding that flashlight was imperative, and she prayed he'd been telling the truth about it.

"He can if people believe he's cleaning up the mines for environmental purposes," MacPherson said. "It's a whole network. The collection, the handling, the transport. I've no doubt plenty of people will turn out to be involved, both in the government and in private companies."

"And one of those companies is Winfield Industries..." she said slowly.

"Yeah," he said. "There's been heavy equipment in this mine recently, the tailings are largely gone, and there's no clear record of where they went—I checked. Tolliver told the workers Winfield Industries was cleaning up—trying to get the lawsuits dropped."

"So, there are no lawsuits?" she asked.

"Oh, there are lawsuits alright. You were with Winfield's son for months. Who knows what he told you, what you found out?" Mac said.

"Mark was nothing like his father," she said. "He is... was... a good person, a gentle man. He and his father were estranged...for years."

"Tolliver targeted you, to find out if what you knew was damaging to their case, and I was sent to—" Mac started.

"—find out if what I knew was damaging to *your* case," Marin finished, and laughed. "Ironic, isn't it? You both want to keep me out of this for the same reason—so I won't testify—and neither one of you know what I would say. I guess simply asking isn't done in your line of work."

"Not with any degree of confidence, anyway. Somewhere along the line Tolliver decided it was easier to just kill you, Marin, and I've blown my cover by protecting you. I tried to prevent you from coming, but you got Vangie's invitation after all."

"Why kill Cecil?" she asked.

"Cecil could be bought, but he must have balked at murder—if he's really dead."

"Now that I know this, you don't have to leave me here."

"I need you to trust me for just a bit more," he said. "Can you do that?"

"It would be a lot easier if you weren't leaving me in the bottom of a mine!" she said.

His words reminded Marin that he had not yet told her about the telegram, and she thought of what he'd said regarding responsibility for the disposal of nuclear waste. Was she a fool to believe him a second time? Had this been his plan all along?

She opened her mouth to ask, but MacPherson spoke first.

"Just follow the rope," he said, the sound of his voice moving away. "By the time you find your way out, I'll be back with the police."

"Look what happened to Cecil," she said, her throat constricted. "What if Tolliver shoots you, too?"

"You're safe from Tolliver in here," he said. "When you get out, and you will, go for help with or without me. Tolliver wants me; he'll follow me down the mountain."

"Then why leave me here?!"

He didn't answer, and she listened, heard only a steady dripping from somewhere in the dark.

"MacPherson!" she shouted, hearing the hysteria in her voice. "Don't leave me here! I'm afraid of the dark!"

The seconds stretched into minutes, and she heard only her own harsh breathing, loud in the stillness.

"Go then," she shouted "I hope Tolliver *does* shoot you!"

Silence, her pounding heart loud in her ears.

"MacPherson?" she called. She heard the quaver in her voice and stopped speaking, holding her breath while the darkness, absolute and unyielding, enveloped her.

"I don't really hope Tolliver shoots you," she said, and to her own ears the words sounded wretched and afraid.

CHAPTER TWENTY-SIX

C ullen MacPherson sat, very still, on the back of the bay horse, exchanging silent stares with five pairs of dark and hostile eyes belonging to the five young men ranged around a water tank. Bear wasn't inclined to be friendly with them, either, and Mac ordered him down.

A rusty windmill stood beside a large, corrugated aluminum tank, and a random breeze ruffled the surface of the water and moved the windmill blades, the motion barely perceptible but for a low creaking sound. A dusty green pick-up truck, somewhat battered, was parked beside the windmill.

It had taken MacPherson, Bear, and the horse, almost three hours to get to where they now were, which seemed to him to be squarely in the middle of empty desert plain, as he'd left the foothills of the mountains behind him.

He had approached the five youths standing around the water tank to inquire about a trading post in the area, but once he had ridden closer, he had noticed the antenna on the roof of the truck and had asked instead if he might use the radio.

From the silence and the blank stares he was receiving now, he could have been speaking a foreign language, and for a moment he wondered if they spoke English, then realized how ridiculous that was.

Four of them looked to be barely beyond their teens, the fifth even younger, but the expressions currently on their faces were uniformly grim, and all of them were unsmiling as they watched his movements.

They were dressed similarly, in jeans and chambray shirts differing only in color, and all five wore cowboy hats and western-style boots.

One of the older youths, a few inches taller than the others, wore his black hair long and loose, and he had an eagle feather braided along one side and hanging at his jaw.

"Where'd you get the horse?" he asked, walking over and casually putting a hand on the stirrup.

He didn't look directly at MacPherson, his eyes focused on some point in the distance, and MacPherson sat without moving as the other four casually spread out around the horse on all sides, and Bear began to growl. The horse continued unconcerned with all of them, cropping the sparse grass with eyes partially closed and tail twitching, and MacPherson debated the pros and cons of dismounting. Deciding he was better off staying in the saddle, along with any advantage he might have from the greater height, he looked down and spoke carefully.

"This horse was loaned to a friend of mine," he said. "An old man in the mountains loaned him to her—a woman who needed help."

No one spoke or moved, and MacPherson felt a trickle of sweat roll from his neck and down the left side of his ribs. He had a brief vision of Marin, alone in the mine, and he held up a hand.

"Before we go any further, I need to tell you the woman is currently in an abandoned uranium mine up Cove wash. I'm hoping to keep her safe from a man named Tolliver trying to kill us. He took my Land Rover and I'm here looking for help. I'm telling you this so someone besides me knows she is there...just in case," he finished, looking into each of the five unsmiling faces.

A youth wearing black-rimmed glasses and a hat with a silver and turquoise hatband whistled and the horse went from placidly cropping grass one second to standing straight up on his back legs the next, and MacPherson was dumped backwards onto the ground.

Bear leaped forward, standing over MacPherson with his legs rigid and his lips pulled back in a snarl as the horse came back to all four feet, and the youth with the feather took the horse by the headgear.

He looked down at MacPherson. "It's his horse," he said, gesturing to the youth with the glasses and the silver hatband.

MacPherson had Bear stand down and he got to his feet, slapping dirt from his pants with his hat, and the youth who with the glasses ran his eyes from MacPherson's head all the way down to his hiking boots. There was a flicker in his dark eyes, and he turned and spoke to the others.

MacPherson didn't understand what he said, but the air around him changed as suddenly as if a thunderstorm had blown through and left behind freshly charged atmospheric ions.

Not understanding, but grateful for the change, MacPherson walked to the water tank and dunked his head under, then stood, dripping, for a minute as Bear drank. For whatever reason, he guessed he'd been temporarily cleared of being a horse thief.

"Neat trick," he said to the youth with the silver hat band. "My name is Cullen MacPherson, and I work for the U.S. government."

Instantly all five faces closed down again, and MacPherson pinched the bridge of his nose, sighing as he put his hat on. "Come on guys," he said. "I'm not the devil—I just need some help. I need to contact the police. I get your whole we-hate-the-government thing, but this is serious, and anyway, I'm not that guy. I'm the guy trying to save a few lives."

"You said there is a woman in the Cove mine?" the youth with the glasses asked, pointing with his mouth and chin toward the mountains MacPherson had just come down. He seemed to be the spokesman for the group and MacPherson recalled that he had been sitting in the driver's seat of the truck.

"Yeah, she's up there," MacPherson said, gesturing behind him, "Her name is Marin Sinclair, and she needs help."

"Marin Sinclair?" another youth said, the one MacPherson figured to be the youngest, maybe fifteen or so.

"You know her?" MacPherson asked.

"We know *of* her," the designated spokesman with the silver hatband said. "She's a friend of his mother."

MacPherson looked at the teen. "You're Vangie Tso's son?" he asked. "I didn't know she had a... Listen," he said, turning back to the group spokesman. "I need to use your radio to contact the police."

"No police up here, man," the youth with the braided feather commented.

"I need to use your radio," MacPherson repeated firmly. "There's a man, a killer, up here. His name is Tolliver..."

He paused, watching the unchanging expressions on the faces around him, and tried again. "He usually drives a blue Chevy truck, but right now he's probably driving a Rover," he said. "A new Land Rover, black. It's mine. Government plates. Maybe you've seen him?"

This time the result was a little more satisfying, and he saw an exchange of looks among the five.

"The man up at the mine," the hatband speaker said at last.

"You've seen him?" Mac asked.

"We're not around here much," he said, taking off the hat and adjusting his glasses. He looked pointedly at MacPherson's worn hiking boots.

"Seen his truck, though, and his tracks. Fancy boots," he said. "Not like yours," and MacPherson wondered exactly how he could know that by seeing only tracks. The tallest youth, the one with the feather braided in his hair, spoke up.

"He's into tracks," he said. "All kinds," he added, and he began to loosen the girth straps of the saddle, sliding it and the gray blanket from the horse's back while another pulled the bridle over the horse's ears and took the bit from his mouth, leaving the rope halter. They carried the saddle and blanket to the back of the pick-up truck, and three of the five youths piled into the back, the tall youth holding onto the bridle.

"You'd better come with us," the hatband spokesman said and started for the truck.

"What about the horse?" MacPherson asked.

"He'll be alright," he said, putting his hat on again. "Everybody knows he's Old Man's horse."

"I thought he was your horse," Mac said.

"He is. Haastiin Sanii is my grandfather."

At the door of the truck, MacPherson paused to order Bear into the back.

"I'm Cullen MacPherson," he tried again, and the three in the back looked down at their feet or off into the distance. There was a general shuffling of boots and a few throat clearings and the tall youth with the braid and feather spit over the far side of the truck.

The hatband spokesman was again the one to break the silence, and he walked to MacPherson and held out his right hand.

"Raymond Yazzie," he said, and MacPherson thrust his own hand out in return, prepared to shake, a little surprised when the youth only brushed the palm of his hand.

Raymond Yazzie pursed his mouth to indicate the three in the back. "Richard Benally," he said. "The guy next to him is Franklin Begay. We call them Smith and Jones. They're brothers," Raymond added, and the two nodded.

"Why do you call them...?" MacPherson started, and then let it go. They needed to hurry.

"That's Hanson Hoske with the feather in his braid," Raymond finished, and the youth with the eagle feather raised a quick hand to his hat brim and nodded.

"They call me Goat Roper," Hanson Hoske said solemnly, and Vangie's son rolled his eyes.

"And this is...?" MacPherson asked, looking at the boy.

"He's Garret," Raymond said. "Garret Washburn."

"And he goes by...?" MacPherson asked.

Raymond looked up at the sky and down again. "He goes by Garret," he said, shrugging.

"My dog," MacPherson said, and gestured to Bear. "He goes by Bear. He's friendly as long as he doesn't see you as a threat."

Silence fell, Raymond Yazzie waiting for a moment or two as if giving MacPherson the opportunity to say something more if he was going to, and when he didn't, Raymond walked around to the cab of the truck and climbed in behind the wheel.

Garret Washburn slid into the middle, and MacPherson took the passenger's side.

"I need to get in touch with a policeman by the name of Blue Eyes," MacPherson said as Raymond started the truck, revving the engine. "I've talked to him before, and he should remember me."

"Sergeant Blue Eyes," Raymond said, reaching up and settling his hat firmly in place.

"You know him?" MacPherson asked and Raymond dipped his chin in a quick nod. "Everybody on the reservation knows Sergeant Blue Eyes," he said, and he floored the gas pedal.

The truck wheels spit dust and small stones for a full ten seconds before Raymond Yazzie let out the clutch and sent them careening across the desert floor, barely missing the water tank or the horse, which reared and kicked out as they passed.

There were yells and shouts of encouragement from the three in back standing next to the cab, and MacPherson caught a glimpse in the side mirror of Hanson Hoske whirling the horse's bridle over his head.

"Where are we going?" MacPherson shouted as they bounced onto a rutted dirt track that apparently led back up the mountain. He put a hand out to grip the door frame as the right front wheel bucked over a large rock and came down hard, and Raymond geared down looked sideways at him.

"To the mine," he said, flicking his eyes over Garret and MacPherson and back to the road.

"Shouldn't we wait for the police?" MacPherson said.

"Yeah, we could do that, but the man in the fancy boots is at the mine," Raymond said.

"How do you know that?" MacPherson asked, alarmed.

"That's where your Rover is," Raymond said, and he geared up again and floored the gas pedal.

Dust as thick as smoke filled the interior of truck cab, and before MacPherson could speak again, there was a squawk of static and a stream of indistinguishable words from the radio on the dash. MacPherson couldn't make out anything intelligible, but Raymond responded readily, and several exchanges were made of which MacPherson recognized only the words *mine* and *gun* before Raymond signed off and replaced the mike.

MacPherson squeezed his eyes shut. He'd been sure Tolliver would stay away from the mine, but if Raymond Yazzie was right, he was up there even now.

Waiting for Raymond to give him the gist of the radio conversation, MacPherson finally decided he had no intention of doing so and asked impatiently, "Was that the police?"

Raymond nodded and said no more, concentrating on the rutted road.

"Sergeant Blue Eyes is coming?" MacPherson asked.

"He's coming," Raymond agreed.

MacPherson waited for more but nothing more was forthcoming.

"It'll take him hours to get up here," MacPherson said. "What are we supposed to do until then? Ask Tolliver to wait?"

"Won't be that long," Raymond said, maneuvering the truck around another rock.

"Why's that?" MacPherson asked, beginning to understand how Raymond's one-word-at-a-time conversations worked.

"He was already on his way."

"On the way to the mine?" Mac asked.

Raymond nodded.

"But why?" MacPherson asked.

"We called him earlier today," Raymond said.

"Why? MacPherson asked again.

Raymond shrugged. "To come get the gun," he said.

"Gun?" MacPherson asked, feeling he had somehow come in on the middle of the conversation.

"The gun my grandfather found," Raymond said patiently. He pursed his mouth toward the glove compartment, and MacPherson opened it.

A 9mm pistol lay in the glove box, a silencer attached to the barrel of the gun Marin said she'd found in her jacket pocket, the gun that may have killed Cecil.

"Your grandfather found this?" he asked, and Raymond nodded.

"Where?"

"Up at his sheep camp," Raymond said.

"Marin Sinclair left it there?"

They had left the foothills and were climbing, and Raymond geared the truck down without losing any noticeable speed as they jolted from side to side up the narrow road.

"She didn't exactly leave it," he said, and Garret snorted, the first sound he'd made. Marin must have dropped the gun at Old Man's camp without realizing it, and only thought she'd lost it in the flood.

"Raymond," MacPherson said. "Does Tolliver—the man up at the mine, the one with the fancy boots—does he know your grandfather found this gun?"

For the first time, Raymond looked worried as he met MacPherson's eyes.

"I don't know," he answered. "I guess he could have been watching the sheep camp before I picked the gun up this morning."

"We'd better hope he wasn't," MacPherson said grimly.

Raymond pressed his lips together and ground the gears down into first. "*He'd* better be the one hoping," Raymond said. "If he's hurt my grandfather."

Garret, riding in the middle, spoke up for the first time. "I told you she'd bring nothing but trouble."

"You mean Marin? Why do you say that?" MacPherson asked.

"It's what she does," Garret answered.

"You know her?"

Garret shrugged. "I know *of* her," he said.

"Well, she seems pretty serious about helping your mother," MacPherson said, stopping when he saw Raymond trying to catch his attention, shaking his head and frowning as he cut his eyes toward Garret.

For whatever reason, Garret wasn't a Marin Sinclair fan.

Another thought occurred to MacPherson. "Why is Sergeant Blue Eyes meeting you at the mine to get the gun?"

"He was already on his way up there."

"Because?"

"He got a call from some of the guys who'd been working up there that boxes of dynamite were being hauled into the mine lately," Raymond answered. "They wondered what was going on and called it in."

Raymond Yazzie looked over his glasses at MacPherson. "They said it was some guys in a blue Chevy truck," he said.

MacPherson took a deep breath. "Dynamite?" he managed. "Tolliver's been storing dynamite in the mine?"

"Yeah," Raymond answered. "Nobody's been working up there for a while now, and Sergeant Blue Eyes thinks something is going down."

"And I put her in there to protect her," MacPherson said, banging his fist against the door.

He turned to Raymond and spoke, his voice urgent. "We've got to go faster, Raymond. I'll explain on the way, but I think Tolliver is going to blow the mine."

▲▲▲

CHAPTER TWENTY-SEVEN

M arin wasn't sure how long she'd sat huddled against the wall, refusing to believe Mac had left her. She sat, alone in the dark, blind yet straining to see, the total blackness a physical, smothering weight she couldn't escape and couldn't force her mind to accept.

She touched her fingers to eyelids to check her eyes were open, knew she had to find that flashlight or go mad, and do it before something found her in the dark.

Groping for the pack, she fumbled with the knotted cords until a flap came free and loose items fell around her.

"No, no, no," she cried, patting the floor, praying she hadn't lost the flashlight.

Carefully she examined each item by feel before placing it back into an empty side pouch and tying it closed.

No flashlight.

She blew on her cold fingers and returned to the pack, resisting the urge to begin flinging items across the room.

The darkness felt increasingly threatening, closing tight around her in an uncomfortable way, the air stale and frigid, and a small doubt began to form in the back of her mind, but she shook it away. *There must be a flashlight.*

Mac wouldn't have left her in this darkness...

Except that he had.

A drop of water fell on her neck, and she jerked in surprise. Weren't the mines around here supposed to be dry? Another drop fell and she scooted away from the wall. Not too far, as she was mindful of becoming disoriented and there was the mine shaft. How close had it been?

The inside of the pack held clothing—denim, flannel—and the rolled sleeping bag, but no flashlight.

She sat back on her knees, defeated. She was so cold, but there was nothing to do but continue the search.

Grimly she began to untie cords and unzip every side pocket and every pouch, placing the articles on her lap one by one, the queasiness in her stomach growing, as if someone was in the room with her, watching her.

It was only because she couldn't see anything, she told herself, but she held her breath, listening. She heard water dripping and... something else? Someone breathing?

"There's no one here," she said out loud, forcing herself to return to the pack, examining each article by feel before returning it to a pocket and tying off each pocket with large loops to prevent her checking the same ones again.

At last she had gone through the entire pack.

No flashlight.

Reckless now, she pulled the pack toward her, no longer caring about any system or order, tearing into the first pouch her fingers found and ransacking it, tossing aside anything that was not the flashlight. If she emptied the pack completely, she would have to discover it.

If it was there...

Finally, the pack lay in her hands, empty and limp.

Disbelieving, Marin sank to the floor, holding the pack to her chest.

"Mac, how could you?" she whispered. She was sure he'd said the flashlight was in the pack.

If only she could see, and she again touched her eyes.

Edison had liked the dark, liked driving in the dark with no headlights, and he'd talked about the dark, too, but what exactly had he said, that last time they'd been together?

Had she been listening?

"I mustn't lose control," she whispered. "I take everything so seriously."

Edison had told her that so many times, told her she was too serious, told her she needed to lighten up. But he'd been wrong. She should have taken things *more* seriously, should have paid closer attention, and done it sooner, because then maybe things that had happened would not have happened.

Edison had not returned to college after Christmas, but she hadn't found out until that May, when she came home from her own first college semester in Flagstaff, planning to tell Edison she was ready to make their engagement official.

She'd been so excited to be back, eager to attend the high school graduation, eager to see and make future plans with Edison, eager to cheer when Vangie and Rita crossed the stage to receive their diplomas.

She huddled closer to the damp wall, unable to stop the past playing before her eyes like a film in a dark theater.

The gym had been crowded, noisy with children running up and down the bleachers, and she saw herself, sitting beside her father, about halfway up and in the middle bleacher section, feeling a bit left out, but glad her father had decided to come, even if it was only to hear her name called...

She didn't see Edison anywhere, and the band settled into place ready to play the entrance march—the first time since eighth grade that Marin hadn't played for a graduation.

The graduates lined up outside the gym doors, and she saw Rita in her white gown, first in line as her last name was Atcity. Marin waved and blew her a kiss, and Rita waved back.

The audience stood as the graduates slowly filed in, and she finally spotted Edison. He was standing in the rows of folding chairs on the gym floor, in the area reserved for family members.

Vangie stepped into view toward the end of the line, walking slowly down the aisle wearing the mortarboard with its red tassel and the white graduation gown which did little to conceal her advanced pregnancy. Edison stepped into the aisle as Vangie neared, and he gave her a long-stemmed red rose and a kiss, his hand lightly resting on the rounded bulge beneath her robe as Vangie smiled and accepted the rose, then continued up the aisle.

Marin stood frozen, her hand lifted to wave, and the rest of the ceremony passed in a blur.

She didn't tell her father anything, and she didn't hear her name called, pleading a headache as soon as the ceremony was over, and they left without attending the potluck reception readied in the school cafeteria.

Only Frannie Blue Eyes, Justin's sister, saw her go, and she took Marin's hand and squeezed, her eyes full of sympathy.

The move to Flagstaff was completed that weekend.

Vangie had sent a card with a picture of baby Garret Washburn late that summer, but other than cards at birthdays and Christmas, Marin hadn't written or visited, using college first, and then her father's illness as an excuse.

A brief letter from Vangie had arrived in February, telling her of Edison's suicide. He'd left no note, no reason explaining why he'd chosen to leave Vangie and his six-month-old son, but Marin thought she knew, thought he had tried to tell her that cold winter day during Christmas break, thought, sadly, that the two parts of Edison really had canceled him out.

A cold drop of water dripped onto her neck, bringing Marin back to the reality of the dark mine, and she wrapped her arms tighter and shifted position. It was hard to think of Edison, but harder not to in this place where the cold was seeping into her very bones, and fear was breaking down her ability to repress the past.

In mindless agitation she tapped both feet up and down to generate some heat and unexpectedly encountered something soft and firm near one foot. Without much real curiosity, she patted the floor until she touched the rounded bulk of the sleeping bag.

She hadn't thought to use the bag for warmth, and she pulled it toward her, worrying the draw-cord knots loose with numb fingers. The bag was tied tight and it took time to get it free, but its thick folds finally fell into her lap.

She felt an immediate comfort, easing the creeping fear.

"He said he'd come back," she whispered, getting into the bag and fumbling with the zipper. "Edison said he'd..."

No, no...it was MacPherson who had said he'd come back.

She maneuvered her feet and legs inside the bag, twisting to pull the material up around her waist, and something hard bumped against one knee.

She sat very still, then shifted her leg again.

The hard something again bumped her knee.

Moving carefully, she put her hand into the bag, inching her fingers down as if the precious object inside would jump away if startled.

"Please, God," she whispered and withdrew the flashlight slowly, cradling it between her cold hands and holding it gratefully to her face, the metal cold and smooth on her cheek.

It was a full minute before she remembered there were no batteries, and she'd found none among the articles inside the pack.

The disappointment was staggering, a stunning blow which pushed the air from her lungs like a hand slammed into her chest, and an anger so intense it robbed her of coherent thought swept through her, a murderous urge to smash the metal cylinder against the rock wall.

She couldn't think, couldn't breathe, and she hurled the flashlight across the room, heard the metal casing bouncing across the floor.

"I can't fix everything!" she shouted. "You can't expect me to fix everything!" she cried into the darkness.

"It's not fair! Do you hear me, God? I did my best! I tried so hard. I did my best, and it wasn't good enough!"

She pressed both hands against the wet rock, hot tears spilling down her face.

"I prayed so hard...I trusted you, and...it didn't *matter.*"

"I won't trust *you* again!" she shouted, daring God to contradict her, but all was silent save for the dripping water and her own sobs.

She didn't know how long it was before she opened her eyes— shivering, cold—opened her eyes and saw the gleam of rocks and a rivulet of water snaking its way down a crevice and across the floor.

She whirled and saw the flashlight a few feet away, the metal cylinder turning in a slow circle, the beam gently rocking.

"There's no such thing as darkness," she heard her father say as clearly as if he stood beside her. "Darkness only exists as the absence of light."

She slid down the wall and let the tears fall, staring at the beautiful, unexpected gift of light, as beautiful as the stars in the night sky so long ago.

"Look up," Vangie had said. "Look up...."

She heard Vangie's voice, felt Bailey's wet nose, heard the click of horse's hooves on the rocks, and she saw Sheldon, wrapped in a wool blanket and so, so still.

"Sheldon," she whispered.

As if his name had opened a locked door, the memories flooded in.

The rattlesnake, the ruins, the mesa...Sheldon.

"The mesa," she whispered. "Oh God... we were on the mesa."

The day had held such exhilaration, such freedom, and she'd been exultant, heady from the heat and the sun and the triumph of the climb.

She saw Sheldon's face, serious as he etched his initials into the rocks, felt again the surprise of seeing Vangie smiling down from the rock cleft, and there was Bailey, racing ahead on the rocks.

The memories flooded in, and she didn't try to stop them—she remembered the full moon, the horror of the wolf-witches, the cold dark—and Vangie, so brave and strong, whispering her name to Marin in the dark tunnel...

And she remembered Sheldon's death.

She took a breath, the flashlight a bright circle in the darkness, and something inside her loosened.

"Sheldon," Marin whispered. "I would give anything, even now, to change what I did."

Other memories crowded in—her father reading aloud to her and smiling over his glasses; Sheldon telling ghost stories with wide eyes or racing her to the trading post; Edison laughing while Bailey chased him around the yard. She thought of Mark, scowling over a game of chess or teasing her about her love life, and she suddenly remembered her mother, combing out Marin's hair and telling her stories about her life, her history, her people.

Clumsily, on her hands and knees, Marin crawled to the flashlight.

"You lied about the batteries, Mac," she said.

She crawled back and pulled the sleeping bag around her, holding the flashlight to her chest and playing the beam across the rock ceiling. She was so tired, as if she had been fighting a very hard battle for a very long time.

She raised a hand to her wet face, thinking about MacPherson's words of protection and faith and what he had said about choice... about choosing what, or whom, to trust.

"Some things are worth your trust," her father had once said. "Some people are, too, you just have to find them."

She'd believed in her father's love, had chosen to trust despite not understanding him, because she knew him, knew he wouldn't lie to her. Perhaps it wasn't God who had broken faith with her—perhaps she'd done it herself, refusing to trust unless she could understand the why.

"It's hard to trust," she whispered, "when I don't understand why."

Oddly enough, the thought gave her a sort of peace. How long had it been since she had felt this mixture of hope and possibility, an expectation her life would hold joy?

"Mark, I think this must be what you meant by...faith," she said out loud, surprised at hearing the word echo around the room. Faith, in anything, had been missing in her life for a long time, and this seemed a strange place to find such a thing.

Feeling a sudden energy, she was galvanized into action and kicked her way out of the sleeping bag, playing the beam of light across the floor, looking for the rope.

Articles of clothing and various items from the backpack lay scattered across the floor, and she worked the light in measured segments toward the opposite side of the room until she saw the orange rope, stretching across the floor and down a narrow tunnel.

Holding the light steady, she bent to pick it up, but the rope resisted her pull, and she traced its length backwards, discovering it was tied to one of the elevator's wooden beams. To follow it Marin needed it in her hand.

The rope was wet, and after several minutes of struggling with wet knots, her fingers numb with cold, she remembered the hunting knife in the backpack. She searched with the flashlight until she found it, and she knelt beside the open shaft, careful to stay back from the edge.

The blade was sharp, the rope gave way easily, and she sat back for a moment, putting the knife in her coat pocket as she added gloves to her mental list of things to carry with her in the future.

The flashlight suddenly began to tremble and the wooden housing of the elevator shaft shuddered as a distant generator came to life with a groaning roar, the vibrations hard enough to to roll the flashlight toward the shaft. She caught it before it fell and scooted back as the rumble filled the air, the sound coming directly up the gaping shaft.

A string of small yellow lights abruptly flashed to life around the top of the wooden structure, and Marin started as if physically shocked by the tiny electric bulbs. She got to her feet, able to see now as well as feel the shaking housing surrounding the shaft.

The noise shifted in quality, a metallic creaking added to the generator's roar...the squeal of rusty pulleys and stretching steel cable.

The elevator was moving.

CHAPTER TWENTY-EIGHT

▲▲

T he elevator rose slowly in the wake of squealing cables and the generator's roar, the floor vibrating, and the small string of lights quivering in anticipation. Any second now the elevator would arrive— the elevator and Tolliver.

It could be MacPherson, but there was a part of her which knew beyond a doubt it would be Tolliver, and dread prodded her frozen mind, urging her to hide.

Holding the flashlight, she ducked into the passageway leading from the room, the dim glow from the yellow housing lights allowing her to navigate the narrow tunnel for the first twenty feet or so, but after that the tunnel curved into darkness, and she fumbled for the flashlight switch.

She needed the rope, would have to go back for it.

The heavy creaking stopped, the ensuing silence more ominous than the noise, and she paused to listen, trying to remember all the twists and turns MacPherson had taken to get here.

Impossible.

She moved the light rapidly around the walls—she was standing in the middle of three intersecting tunnels with no idea which tunnel to take or which she had just left. A passageway ran straight before her, but the two others split slightly behind her, one to the right and the other to the left. She backtracked and quickly looked down each passageway but didn't see the rope. With rising panic, she scanned the floor ahead and behind—the rope was bright orange, she *had* to see it.

Nothing.

A scraping noise came from behind her, and she froze, killing the flashlight beam with a flick of her thumb. There was no place to hide unless she moved deeper into one of the three passageways but moving without the rope meant she'd risk getting lost in the maze of tunnels. She turned toward the noise, barely daring to breathe, careful about brushing the tunnel walls and revealing her presence, hoping that Tolliver—for Mac would have called to her—would stay where he was.

She crouched where she stood, holding herself in absolute stillness.

She could see Tolliver in the light from the elevator housing, moving in and out of her line of sight, pushing boxes across the floor, and after a few minutes, he walked toward the intersecting tunnels.

"Marin?" he called, and she felt not even a flicker of surprise. She'd known, really, since the first sound of the elevator that it would be Tolliver, his presence here in this place as inevitable as fate itself.

She shivered convulsively, trying to still her breathing as Tolliver called down the tunnel.

"I know it's you Marin, love," he said conversationally. "MacPherson always did have a way with women. He's left you here, hasn't he?"

Carefully, inch by inch, Marin crab-walked down the nearest tunnel, no longer caring which branch she took or where it led, her heart pounding as Tolliver dragged several more boxes along the first few feet of the tunnel behind her before he paused to flick on a large electric lantern...and caught her fully in the light.

Marin stood, keeping the wall at her back, willing to lose herself in the depths of the mine to escape this man as he moved to the center of the three intersecting tunnels, the lantern bringing the rock walls into sharp relief.

She stood still, gripping the flashlight as he bent and put the lantern on the floor, its strong beam lighting the tunnel.

She would have to strike out using her left arm, her right weak from her injury, and she waited until Tolliver came close before she lunged, slamming the metal flashlight across his face with the strength of desperation.

The metal cylinder connected, hard, with his jaw but not hard enough to make him fall, and the blow knocked the flashlight from her hand. She turned to run, her half-circle spin sending her long braid flying out behind her.

In one rapid motion, Tolliver caught her braid and yanked her backwards, catching Marin up short, her neck snapping back and up, and he grabbed her chin with his other hand, pulling her to his chest.

"I'll take that gun now, Marin," he said. "I know you must have it."

The pain in her neck was unbearable, the muscles and ligaments stretched beyond their limit, and she clawed at his hand on her chin, pushing into him to relieve the pressure, but the hand in her braid only tightened in response, his blue eyes staring directly down into hers. She tried to turn her head away, but he made another twisting turn, laughing when she cried out.

"Game over, sweetheart," he said, his voice thick. "I *want* that gun," he hissed into her face.

"It's...my pocket," she choked, putting her left hand into her pocket and tightening her fingers around the hilt of the hunting knife. She pushed harder into him, willing him to maintain eye contact, to realize nothing but the power of his own victory, her life depending on getting the knife clear without him knowing.

He shrugged without loosening his hold.

"Ah, well, doesn't matter. Better to just end it quick. Too bad I'm in a hurry," he added, gripping her chin roughly, and Marin tensed, feeling the muscles in his arm bunch for the jerk that would snap her neck.

"Goodbye, sweetheart," Tolliver said, "it's been fun," and Marin pulled the knife free and lashed back and up with a vicious swipe. Without pausing, she made a second swipe at her braid, as near to her scalp as she dared.

Tolliver released her so suddenly she fell to the tunnel floor but she was moving almost before she hit the ground, scrambling away on hands and knees until she managed to get to her feet and run, the flashlight left behind.

"My arm!" Tolliver screamed. "I'll *kill* you!" he shouted, and she chanced a look back. Tolliver stood in the passageway, the lantern spotlighting the scene as if he were an actor onstage, a dark stream of blood running down his forearm and Marin's long braid hanging from his fingers.

The image burned into her mind's eye, Marin ran as Tolliver's hysterical curses followed her down the tunnel. Tears streamed down her face as she lurched from wall to wall in the dark, but she didn't stop until a low rock outcropping knocked her to the ground.

Stunned, she lay there, breathing hard.

Tolliver had a lantern and could find her. She had to get up, had to keep going and find somewhere to hide.

In the near distance she again heard the unmistakable sound of the elevator, creaking and groaning, and she prayed Tolliver was on it, that he was leaving and not coming after her.

She stretched out her hand, feeling for the wall, blindly trying to regain her orientation, but there was nothing. She stretched out her other hand and a rock wall met her fingers, and she pushed herself to her knees. If she could make it back to the elevator room, maybe she could use the elevator as well...but she needed to get there before the small electric lights went out. Which way had she come? Sound was distorted here, a hollow echoing, and she turned toward what she hoped was the direction of the sound. On hands and knees, she crawled cautiously along the floor of the tunnel, sweeping one hand in front of her and brushing the wall with the other, afraid to lose contact.

She hadn't gone far when her hand encountered something in her path, some sort of bundle, the material coarse beneath her fingers, like a tarp or a piece of canvas.

She patted on and around it, thinking it was the pack and feeling for cords and pockets as she pulled it toward her.

The bundle was heavy—not an empty pack—and her searching hands found a fold in the material, and she turned the flap back. A cold roughness met her fingers, spiked, like the bristles of a hairbrush, and puzzled, she moved her hand up, running her fingers around a rim of hard, squared ridges...

Marin screamed, unable to stop herself if a hundred Tollivers had been nearby, and she shoved herself away from the wrapped body, scrambling backwards, touching the dead man's face in her panic and screaming again.

Back and back she pushed herself along the tunnel, mindless of any direction but away, until she encountered the rock wall, the rough stone scraping her back. She curled herself into a ball, no longer thinking, her heartbeat thudding, her breath rasping, and she whimpered when a whuffling, breathy something slammed into her back and shoulders and forced her face down on the rock floor.

Sharp pain raked across her neck and back, and a rough hand grabbed her coat collar and thrust a glaring light in her face. Frantic, she twisted to get her arms out of the coat, thrashing and kicking as she was hauled to her feet.

"Marin!" MacPherson's voice shouted so close to her face she could feel his breath. "It's me, Marin. It's Mac. Look at me." His hands patted her hair, her head, her shoulders and body, but she couldn't seem to stop screaming, the hysteria full-blown and uncontrollable.

Get off her, Bear! Get down!" Mac was shouting, and he wrapped both arms around her and held her tightly.

"It's me, Marin. It's me, it's Mac," he repeated over and over, until her struggles slowed and the cloud of hysteria began to clear.

"Where are you hurt? You're bleeding," Mac said, and he touched her neck, her face, her hair. "Where are you hurt?" he repeated.

"It's Tolliver's blood," she managed and started to shake. Pointing at the canvas bundle, she added. "That's Cecil, I think."

Bear stood beside the body, legs stiff, delicately sniffing at the folds of rough canvas until MacPherson called him off and held the lantern high.

"Yeah, that's him," Mac said, and he stooped to cover Cecil's face. "We'll have to walk out of here," he said to Marin. "But it'll be fast this time—we're going right out the front door. You think you can manage?"

She nodded. She'd crawl on her hands and knees to get out of this place if she had to, but it took too much effort to tell him so.

"Hold on to me, then," MacPherson said, and he placed one of her hands on the back of his shirt and pressed a flashlight into her other hand.

"Need this?" he asked, switching it on.

"Probably for the rest of my life..." she said.

Crouching slightly to allow for the low ceiling, Mac commanded Bear to follow and started down the passageway, Marin stumbling along behind and leaning into Bear when her knees wobbled, but she was on her way out of here, the flashlight mostly shining on her feet, but comforting all the same.

They emerged into the elevator room after a quick walk down the tunnel, the short distance not lost on Marin, and MacPherson circled the light around the walls and floor, picking out the chaos of items from the pack and the drag marks left by the heavy boxes.

She told Mac what she'd seen—Tolliver moving boxes across the floor—and Mac looked at the boxes stacked against the wall while Bear roamed around the room, sniffing.

"It's dynamite, isn't it?" Marin said. "Not so old after all."

A dark patch on the floor caught the flashlight beam, and Mac straightened and turned to Marin, running his hand down her hair. "Your neck is bleeding," he said, showing her his fingers. "So is the side of your face."

"Most of that blood is Tolliver's," she said again. "I cut him, cut my braid to get free...I maybe got a little close to my scalp."

Her voice rose, the panic again close, and MacPherson touched her mouth.

"He's not here, Marin," he said. "We saw him leaving...in my Rover."

Bear began to bark, and Mac knelt, picked up a small box. "The dynamite isn't much use to Tolliver without these," Mac said, holding up the box. "Detonators. Guess he decided to cut and run when he knew we were here."

Mac kicked the orange rope lying on the floor. "If I had known he was down here, that he left Cecil down here..." He broke off. "Let's get you out of here."

They walked for a while in silence. Cecil's body wasn't something she wanted to talk about.

"Why did Tolliver come back?" she said. "Was it for me?"

"No," MacPherson answered. "He meant to dynamite the mine, blow up the evidence, including Cecil's body. Your being in here must have scared him."

"He didn't act scared," she said, and Mac looked back. "You're sure he can't still blow us up? From a distance?" she asked, working to keep up with Mac on her shaky legs.

"Can't set off dynamite without the detonators. Bear found them all," Mac said.

"He found me, too," she said, reaching down to rub the dog's short ears.

"Yep... he went straight to you. I could barely keep up. I thought he'd bring the ceiling down on top of us with all the commotion he made."

She ruffled Bear's fur, recalling the claws scraping her back and shivered. "I thought I was being attacked," she said.

"I did notice," MacPherson answered, his voice dry.

"I get Bear finding me," she said, "but how'd he find detonators?"

"Sniffed them out," MacPherson said. "Bear is certified EDC...that's explosives detection canine. We work together, partners, huh Bear?"

Bear heard his name and gave a short bark.

"Good dog," she said.

"The police are on their way," MacPherson said. "Tolliver won't get far."

The air felt warmer the higher they climbed, and Marin welcomed the warmth as she thought about what he'd said.

"Did Tolliver leave the Chevy truck here?" she asked hopefully, but MacPherson shook his head. "If I had to guess, I'd say Tolliver lost his truck in the flashflood."

He looked back. "But don't worry," he said. "We've got a ride."

Marin was feeling better as she walked, the air easier to breathe, but her knees still trembled, and Bear's nose continually nudged her to pick up her pace. At least she could stop her teeth from chattering by clenching them together and she did so.

The light began to increase, more a change in the quality of the darkness than any real light source, and the tunnel became wide enough for vehicles, the roof high overhead. Iron rails were set along the tunnel floor and a huge generator stood beside an ore car, a liquid puddle of what smelled like gasoline on the floor. They passed the elevator shaft, the platform where Tolliver must have left it, and she shivered with remembered terror.

Fresh air touched her face, and MacPherson flicked off his flashlight when several figures appeared in the semi-dusk at the mine entrance. Hands reached out for her and she gasped and pulled back, grabbing Bear's collar.

"Friends," Mac said and took her arm.

She stepped outside, the early evening air warm and incredibly sweet, and stood for a moment in the mine's opening, adjusting to the light and studying the young men grouped around her.

They didn't look like police.

For a long moment no one spoke, and Marin lifted a self-conscious hand to her face as a youth with a feather in his hair looked Marin over from head to foot.

"*Yeenii*," he said with emphasis.

"What?" Mac said.

"Which one of you was screaming?" a youth in glasses asked.

In the fading light Marin saw her grimy hands and what remained of her once-white shirt, and she touched her choppy hair. The whole side of her face and neck felt crusty, stiff with dried blood, and she glanced at MacPherson.

"You do look pretty scary," he said.

"That's what he just said," Marin smiled, indicating the youth with the feather, and without warning her knees buckled.

Mac gripped her elbows and eased her down against the wall, and the youth in glasses disappeared for a moment and returned with a can of orange soda.

"Drink this," the youth said. "The sugar will help," he added, giving MacPherson a worried look when Marin laughed.

Thirsty, she took a swallow of the warm soda, and looked at the five of them.

Definitely not the police.

MacPherson urged her to take another drink, then he stood and spoke to the others.

"Sergeant Blue Eyes?" he asked, and one of the five shook his head and indicated the road below them.

MacPherson looked worried when he came and knelt beside her.

"Where's the police?" she asked. "Is Justin coming?"

"Hopefully on their way here," he said. "These guys are my ride. It's a good thing they were here. When Tolliver saw them, he took my Rover and ran."

"*Ahéhee',*" she said, and she tilted the soda can toward them in salute, including the one who stood leaning against the entrance rocks.

"Thank you, too, Edison," she murmured, and she was startled when the boy straightened away from the rocks and glared at her.

"You know Garret?" Mac asked, and Marin shook her head. She'd thought it was Edison standing there, hadn't thought he was real.

"Garret is Vangie's son," Mac added, and Marin smiled. She'd guessed that.

The youth with the feather was studying her, and he offered his hand. "I'm Hanson Hoske," he said, and she brushed her palm against his. "Glad you're okay," he added.

The youth in glasses cleared his throat, shifting from one foot to the other.

"Can you navigate?" MacPherson asked her. "We're in somewhat of a hurry and we can't leave you here."

"I can navigate," she said.

"This is Raymond Yazzie," Mac said. "He's the grandson of the old man who loaned you the horse."

"I've got to get to my grandfather," Raymond said.

"Is your grandfather in trouble?" she asked, but Raymond had turned down the trail beyond the mine entrance, and the others followed.

"What's wrong?" she asked MacPherson.

"Tolliver may think Raymond's grandfather has the gun. You dropped it when you were up there," he added, offering her a hand up.

"No," she said, taking his hand and standing. "Tolliver thought I had it."

"And now he likely knows you don't," MacPherson said, gripping the back of her shirt to steady her as they maneuvered their way down the steep trail. "Raymond's been talking to a Sergeant Blue Eyes over the radio, and there's a transmitter in the Rover. Tolliver could have heard."

"Is Justin coming?" she asked again, and Mac nodded.

"He's the Sergeant?" he asked, and she returned the nod.

"I contacted the Navajo Police when I got here," he said. "The Sergeant had already had a run-in with Tolliver."

"Yeah, I was there," she said.

In the twilight, Marin had a clear view of the road winding down the steep mountainside and beyond that to the desert below. She couldn't see much of the uphill road, the one leading into the mountains where they'd been, but what she could see was empty. There was no dust, and it looked as if no vehicles were going in either direction, up or down.

"Why didn't you drive the truck up to the mine entrance?" she panted as they walked, her hand on Bear's ruff, afraid her quivering muscles wouldn't hold her up much longer.

"Tolliver was up here," MacPherson answered, "He took off, like I said, probably when he saw us coming."

"You didn't go after him?" she asked.

"We came after you," MacPherson answered.

The five youths were waiting when they arrived, and no vehicle had ever looked better in Marin's eyes. She reached out a hand to touch the rear fender of the green truck, and Raymond turned to her with a faint smile of his own.

"*Shiłį́į́*," he said, his voice revealing the pride of ownership.

"What's that?" MacPherson asked.

"His horse," Marin said as Raymond got behind the wheel, and the other four jumped into the back.

The engine caught noisily, revving under Raymond's impatient foot, and MacPherson helped her in and got in on the passenger's side, ordering Bear into the back, the truck moving almost before Mac was seated.

Glad for the chance to sit, Marin collapsed into the seat.

It was almost dark now and she could see little other than the dim outlines of the rocks and trees as Raymond barreled up the mountain road, and she turned to look at the four youths in the back.

"You met Hanson Hoske," Mac said, talking over the noise of the engine. "Otherwise known as Goat Roper. The two next to him call themselves Smith and Jones, but their names are Franklin Begay and Richard Benally."

Marin laughed for a second time, and Raymond glanced over and smiled.

"You'll have to explain it to him," Raymond said.

"The teenager is Garret Washburn, Vangie's son," Mac added. "As you seem to know."

"Family resemblence," she said.

"We're all part of the Yazzie outfit," Raymond said, and she nodded, thrown against MacPherson as they jolted over a dip in the road. "Maternally. You met my grandfather up at his sheep camp," he added.

"And Vangie?" Marin asked.

"Second cousin," Raymond said.

Suddenly Hanson pounded on the rear window and pointed to the road ahead where a small cloud of dust was moving down the mountain toward them.

A tightness seized her chest when she saw the black vehicle.

Tolliver, driving Mac's Rover.

He was coming fast, driving downhill and directly toward them, with no headlights.

Raymond was also driving without lights, and Marin wondered if Tolliver could see them in the near dark, for he certainly showed no signs of slowing.

MacPherson shouted something, and Raymond flashed his lights on and off several times and leaned on the horn, but to no effect—the Rover continued coming straight at them.

"He sees us!" MacPherson yelled. "He just doesn't mean to stop!"

Hanson banged his fist on the roof of the cab, Marin thinking he was warning Raymond to stop or turn off the road, but Hanson began shouting out challenges as the Rover drew near. Franklin and Richard stood beside Hanson, also pounding on the roof, and beside them, his long hair blowing, Garret Washburn circled the horse bridle over his head and whooped war cries while Bear barked madly and ran from side to side.

Raymond shoved his arm out the window and yelled insults, his fist clenched, and the truck surged ahead with a fresh burst of speed, the horn blaring as Raymond barreled straight down the middle of the road toward Tolliver and the Rover.

Hanson Hoske yelled, "Custer had it coming!" just before Marin was thrown sideways into MacPherson when Raymond bounced over a large rock.

"Ram him!" MacPherson shouted, and Marin clutched his leg.

"Are you crazy!?" she said. "This isn't a game of chicken!"

"He needs that Rover!" Mac yelled. "He can't afford to wreck it!"

Marin braced for the coming impact but Raymond yanked the wheel to one side at the last second, spinning the truck in a complete circle and spraying the group in back with a shower of dust and rocks. A loud 'boom!' sounded and a large crater appeared in the road, the truck tilting heavily to one side before falling back to all four wheels.

The night was suddenly quiet.

No engine noise, no shouting, only dust sifting down and gently settling to the ground.

Marin raised her head, and beside her, Mac moved.

"You okay?" he asked.

"Was that dynamite?" she asked incredulously, and MacPherson nodded.

"Stay here," he said quietly, and he took a gun Marin recognized from the glove compartment and slid out the door. Raymond followed from the other side, and Marin peered out at the Rover sitting sideways in the road, almost close enough for her to touch its dusty side. The driver's door hung open, and MacPherson was searching through the lighted interior of the apparently empty vehicle.

It was full dark, the evening light gone, and it was difficult to see anything through the gloom and the settling dust, but she distinctly heard Bear growl just as she was gripped above the elbow and jerked from the truck cab.

CHAPTER TWENTY-NINE

▲▲▲

M arin fell to the ground beside the truck and looked up at Tolliver standing over her with a gun, his arm around Garret Washburn's neck.

"Stay down," Tolliver said. "The rest of you get out here where I can see you, or I'll kill the boy."

Marin got her feet under her and came to her knees, her injured shoulder throbbing, and Bear was suddenly there, fangs showing, the short ears flat against his head.

"Call him off MacPherson or I'll kill the kid and her, too," he said, his voice savage, and he stepped behind Marin, putting her between himself and Bear.

Bear took a stiff step, and Marin raised a hand, finding her voice through the paralyzing fear.

"No, Bear," she said. "Stay. Stay there. Good boy."

The dog stopped, hackles erect and quivering, and Tolliver backed toward the open door of the Rover, pulling Garret with him.

Raymond Yazzie suddenly materialized, the welt on his face visible even in the dark.

"You coyote! Let him go!" Raymond yelled, starting toward Tolliver, and the gun hammer clicked.

Raymond stopped mid-stride. "If you've hurt my grandfather," he said, "If you hurt Garret, I'll kill you."

"What are you talking about?" Tolliver snarled. "I don't even know who you are."

"Witnesses, Tolliver," MacPherson answered from behind Raymond. "Witnesses."

"Let him go, Tolliver," MacPherson said quietly. "It's over. Taking Garret won't help you."

"It'll keep his mother out of court," Tolliver said. "Her boy in exchange for dropping the lawsuits."

"She's dying, Tolliver," Mac said, and Marin drew in a sharp breath at a truth that still hurt.

Franklin, Richard, and Hanson positioned themselves around Raymond, all of them standing motionless and silent, and Marin looked up at MacPherson, then at Garret. Tolliver would kill them all without a second thought.

Mac frowned at her and shook his head. "No," he said. "No, Marin. Don't do it…"

She gave him a crooked smile and spoke to Tolliver.

"It's me you want," she said. "I'm the primary witness."

"I don't believe you," Tolliver said fiercely, pushing the gun under Garret's chin.

"Why do you think Vangie sent for me?" Marin said, "if she could make the case by herself?"

She saw her words register, and she got to her feet, her eyes on Garret, who stared back, his dark eyes unblinking.

"Tolliver," MacPherson said, holding out his hand to still the snarling Bear. "You know the police are on their way. It's over."

Tolliver shoved Garret to his knees and yanked Marin to him, his arm jammed under her chin so that she was looking straight up—into a sky of shining stars.

MacPherson spoke again. "Take me, Tolliver," he said quietly. "Hurting her won't help you any. You know Winfield would never go along with this."

Tolliver laughed. "It feels like it will help a lot. It's because of her, and you, that I'm not likely to get anything else from this."

Marin wasn't afraid, she wasn't even very concerned. She had known all along that Tolliver meant to kill her, and the fear she had initially felt was gone. Events had taken on a momentum of their own, a predetermined pathway that had never been under her control, and all she felt now was a desire to have it over and done.

"You'd go without me?" Mac asked, his eyes locked with Tolliver's, and Marin heard the rawness in his voice. She wanted to tell him it was okay, to tell him it was futile to fight the rhythms of this world. This was the way things were meant to be—Edison, Vangie, and now herself. Her life had come full circle, and she was onstage for the final scene...the scene to save Garret.

An ugly laugh came from Tolliver. "I admit that part's hard to take, MacPherson. You thinking you were so clever, pretending to be one of us, but there'll be another time to make things even with you. Winfield himself will make sure of it."

"No," MacPherson said. "It's over, Bud. Let it end here."

"Forget it," Tolliver said harshly. "I wouldn't let her go now." He held up his arm, wrapped in a bloody towel. "Not after this."

The gun Tolliver held was hard and cold, and he shoved it beneath Marin's chin and dragged her backward toward Mac's Rover.

MacPherson made an involuntary sound and took a step toward them, and Marin gagged as Tolliver's arm tightened across her throat.

"You'd better be able to drive this thing," Tolliver growled at her.

The door of the Rover pressed into the back of her legs and Tolliver lowered himself into the driver's side, pulling Marin down with his uninjured arm and pushing himself over and across to the passenger's side, never taking his arm away from her throat or lowering the gun.

Meekly, she collapsed into the driver's seat, and glanced up at MacPherson, only a few steps away and completely out of reach. He stood with his gaze fixed on her, and he held out his hands, palms up, in a curious kind of gesture, shaking his head slowly from side to side.

"Start it up," Tolliver ordered her tersely.

Raymond Yazzie spat into the dust and began to swear quietly, while Franklin, Richard, and Hanson stood protectively around Garret.

266 ★ RABBIT MOON

Tolliver leaned across Marin, the gun never leaving her throat.

"I'll drop her somewhere along the way, MacPherson," he said, "but I wouldn't count on finding her in quite the same pristine condition she's in now."

He laughed as Mac took a quick step forward, Bear trembling beside him.

"I can kill her now," Tolliver said sharply, and Mac stopped.

"Marin," MacPherson said, his voice urgent, and she could barely make out his face in the darkness. "Remember your strengths," he said, holding her eyes with his own. "We will find you."

"Get Garret to Vangie," she said, and at Tolliver's command, she started the Rover and put it in gear.

"MacPherson," Tolliver said through the open window as the Rover began to move. "There's a slim chance I might not kill her. But just so you'll know to keep yourself and any so-called police away," he said, and he leaned out and fired the gun.

"Drive!" Tolliver shouted, ramming the hot gun barrel into her cheek.

She floored the gas pedal and the Rover bounced into the dirt road. She could just make out Mac and the others—and she saw Bear, a dark heap on the ground.

Her hands clenched the wheel, and she whimpered, her foot lifting, but she pressed it down again at Tolliver's curse and the painful dig of the gun into her ribs.

Strengths, Mac had said, but what strengths? The only strengths she had were standing in the road behind her, but what did it matter?

Bailey was dead.

No, not Bailey...Bear. Bear was dead. Her *Shásh yáázh*.

She flinched when Tolliver reached across and turned off the headlights.

"We don't want anyone to know where we are, now do we?" he said, stroking the side of her face with the gun barrel, and Marin stared straight ahead.

Tolliver turned to look behind them.

"No lights following," he said with satisfaction, and returned his attention to her.

But Marin's mind was far away, driving in the dark with Edison, the road a lighter strip of darkness beneath a rising moon. She heard Edison's voice, could almost see him sitting beside her, and she turned her head to speak to him.

"Focus on the road!" Tolliver snapped, pinching her cheek and twisting.

"Marin," Edison was saying, "Lighten up. You worry too much. Always so serious. This truck will go over anything. You don't need the lights, you don't even need a road."

She shifted to a higher gear, the action pushing Tolliver away from her momentarily, and she listened to Edison's voice, knowing it was important to listen to him, important not to make mistakes.

"Living is just like driving in the dark," Edison was saying, and his words sounded familiar. "The trick is to go very fast and not worry about dying. Dying is easy. It's living that's hard."

Odd how his voice had turned into Mark's, and he was there with Marin now, Mark's voice intense.

"The mesa memory is in there somewhere," he was saying, and Marin struggled to hear him, Tolliver's voice and his hands rough.

"Watch for the turnoff," Tolliver said.

"I'm so sorry, Vangie," she said. "I'll get Garret back to you."

"Shut up," Tolliver said, and he squeezed her thigh, digging into her flesh until she cried out and the Rover swerved.

"Keep your hands on the wheel," Tolliver snarled.

Marin put her hands back on the wheel and stared at the barely perceptible track.

The road was narrow now, twisting down the steep mountainside between large boulders and alongside a ravine that fell sharply away to her right.

She drove faster and Edison again spoke.

"The trick is to go very fast," Edison said, but she was afraid to go any faster.

"Is there anything in this world you're *not* afraid of, Marin?"

Sheldon!

She turned her head to look for him and cried out when Tolliver jammed the gun, hard, into her ribs.

"I'm trying not to be afraid, Sheldon," she said, and pressed the gas pedal harder.

"Damn the torpedoes and full speed ahead!" Edison shouted.

"Did she jump or was she pushed?" Mark asked, his voice serious.

"The story is she jumped." Marin said to him. "She sacrificed herself for her family."

"Who the hell are you talking to?" Tolliver asked, and Marin spared him a glance.

"My strengths..." she said.

The land changed to pale silver as the full moon rose, gradations of shadowed grays in the moonlight filtering through the trees. The road branched ahead, one branch going higher into the mountains along the ravine's edge, and the other continuing downhill, and Marin swung the wheel onto the track angling up the ridge.

"What do you think you're doing?" Tolliver yelled, grabbing at the wheel.

Marin barely heard him, barely felt his vicious pinch, her eyes tearing as Tolliver twisted tender skin, but she held on to the wheel, listening to Mark, to Edison, to Sheldon.

"It's not so hard to die," Edison said again, and Mark had said the same. She believed them, and understood what she needed to do.

The Rover picked up momentum as they topped out on the ridge and the road leveled out before the steeper climb into the high mountains, the deep ravine still beside them as they bounced over rocks and across ruts.

"Slow down!" Tolliver shouted, his uninjured hand gripping the door, the gun held loosely, and Marin shifted into fourth.

Trees flashed by and brush tore at the undercarriage of the Rover, and she could see the gleam at the bottom of the ravine, the full moon reflected in the water below.

"I said *slow down*," Tolliver snarled, and he reached for the wheel with his injured left hand.

Marin knocked his arm away, and he screamed and hit her in the face with his good hand. Her head struck the window, but she barely felt it, and she kept the gas pedal pressed to the floorboard, as relentless as Edison had always told her she was.

"Of course, the snake was poisonous!" Sheldon was saying, his voice triumphant, "but I wasn't afraid!" he cried, dancing about on the ledge above the pool.

"I'm not afraid to jump, Marin!" he shouted, and above him an eagle screamed, wheeling high above the ravine, and she looked up.

"Fly! Fly to the rabbit in the moon!" the eagle screamed.

So familiar, so clear, and at last Marin understood perfectly.

She reached for the door handle with both hands, and the Rover swerved and tilted, the rear tires losing contact with the road and sliding over the edge of the ravine, the steering wheel loose and turning in half-circles.

Tolliver howled and lunged, and Marin threw herself against the door.

There was a brief glimpse of the moon and shining water, and she was hurtling along the ground, a tumbleweed tossed in a strong wind until she collided with something solid, something unyielding. Bright lights flared behind her eyes, and she lay without moving, looking up at the myriad of stars reeling through the sky in their nighttime orbit.

She felt no pain as she watched the moon top the mountains, round and full. She could see the rabbit, tilted slightly to one side as if struggling to stand upright.

"I jumped, Sheldon," she said just before the darkness claimed her. "I jumped."

▲▲

CHAPTER THIRTY

V oices spoke over Marin's head, but she didn't open her eyes, content to listen, almost able to make out the words if she cared to try. She didn't, and she let the words float away, letting herself drift with them.

"Nothing like being in the right place at the right time, " a voice said.

Lewis George.

"I'm here to keep you company on the way down the mountain," Lewis said.

"I remembered you, you know. The rodeo...in the stands," she said.

"Rest now. We'll talk more when you're awake. You and I have a few things to do yet."

"Are you a ghost?" she asked, and he chuckled.

"Something like that," he said.

Red and blue police lights flashed over her face the next time she opened her eyes, and Mac was hovering above her, his worried face turning red and blue by turns.

Other faces were there, too, and they leaned in.

"Is she conscious?" a voice asked, and she blinked, mildly interested in the answer.

"Her eyes are open," another replied.

"Hey there," MacPherson said, and another face appeared next to his, one she knew.

"This is Sergeant Blue Eyes," Mac said.

"J for *Jeeshóó'*," Marin murmured.

"Crackerjack," Justin said.

"You did remember," she said, smiling, and she closed her eyes again. She felt light, floating untethered, as if she were waking from a long sleep full of dreams and people and things she ought to remember before they receded out of her reach.

"The ambulance will be waiting for us at the bottom, and a crew is coming up in the morning to see if they can get down to your Rover... and to get to Tolliver," Justin said to Mac.

"Is there any chance he's alive?" Mac asked.

"Raymond says no," Justin answered. "He checked when we were bringing Marin up."

MacPherson nodded, his eyes on Marin as he spoke to Justin.

"Thank God we met you when we did," he said. "We wouldn't have known where she turned off the road, would have kept going if you hadn't been there."

"Sorry I didn't make it earlier. I ran into a muddy wash," Justin said.

"She doesn't seem to be bleeding badly anywhere," Mac said, "but it would be a miracle if there's no broken bones."

"We'll take her down in the SUV to meet the ambulance," Justin said. "I've given her something for the pain, but the ambulance guys say we'll need to keep her awake."

Marin listened, content to lie still and let things go on around her, and MacPherson's face bent over hers again.

"Hang on just a little while longer," he said. We have to get you down the mountain."

"Guys, let's get her in the SUV, hand her in to MacPherson," Justin said. "Raymond, Hanson, take the corners of the blanket. Franklin, Richard, take one side. Garret and I will take the other. On the count of three..."

Hands again reached for her in the darkness, their faces swimming in and out of focus, and she smiled into Lewis George's wrinkled face, waiting for her inside the SUV.

"My strengths," she murmured, and Lewis nodded.

They settled her full length across the rear seat, the red and blue police lights throwing their colored circles, and Mac gently lifted her head into his lap, taking her hand when she reached out.

She needed to talk to him, needed to tell him that she had to be with Vangie for as long as she could, had to work out a peace for herself here, but the words floated away in a growing fog.

"It's okay," MacPherson said. "Rest now...let the pain pills do their work."

Justin appeared with another blanket and tucked it around her.

"Guess this will put paid to any lawsuit testimony Vangie was counting on," Mac said.

"You mean my mom?" Garret said. "Mom doesn't need her to testify. The lawsuits were settled out of court."

Justin slammed the rear door and got into the front seat beside Garret, turning to look at Mac.

"Is that what you thought all this was about?" Justin asked. "The lawsuits?"

"I know it was," Mac said. "Vangie sent for her, arranged a meet at the courthouse."

"No," Justin said. "Winfield Industries settled...they paid out to all the plaintiffs."

"This is the first I've heard about it," Mac said.

"The son did it," Justin said. "Mark Winfield asked his father to approve the compensations. It was his son's last wish," he added. "The kid was dying."

"Mark," Marin murmured.

"I'll be..." Mac started. "Then what was all this about?" he asked, waving a hand to include Marin and the rest of them. "Why does Vangie want Marin here?"

"It's about me," Garret said. "Mom wants her to come and care for her, but I sure don't want her here. I'm sorry she bashed herself into a tree," he added, looking at Marin, who smiled. "I don't need a guardian," Garret finished. "I'm almost sixteen."

"What do you have against Marin?" Mac asked, and Garret glared.

"She killed my father," Garret said.

"That's enough," Justin said. "Edison was responsible for his own actions. Marin had nothing to do with it."

He looked over the seat at MacPherson. "I meant to talk to Marin about everything in Kayenta, but it didn't work out that way," he said.

"Garret can stay here with us," Raymond said, and Justin shook his head.

"You need to go on to your grandfather," he said. "Officer Mike is up there with him now, and he says he's fine, but I'll be back up later to see him myself, get a statement."

The police SUV roared into life, and Raymond turned toward his truck. "Later, *Jeeshóó'*," he said, and Justin waved him away.

"Go, check on your grandfather."

"What's it mean, anyway?" Mac asked.

"Family name. Don't ask," Justin said to Mac.

"Billy Jack forever!" Hanson called, and Franklin and Richard echoed the cry, their fists in the air.

There were five silhouettes, five fists held high and outlined in the headlights of Raymond's truck as Justin pulled away, and Marin smiled, glad Edison was still there.

Justin put his own arm out the window in acknowledgement. "Hold on to her," he said to Mac. "It's going to be a rough ride down."

MacPherson looked down at Marin and pulled her closer.

"Who's Billy Jack?" he asked.

THE END

ABOUT THE AUTHOR

▲▲▲

D rawing from her own life story in the Four Corners area of the Navajo Nation, author Jan Payne offers readers a journey into the heart of the American Southwest in a modern-day suspense series. Writing characters who navigate diverse cultural influences to explore the lines between the seen and the unseen, the modern and the traditional, the present and the past—she creates a world where the impossible becomes possible, and mythical legends may come to life.

Jan Payne is a member of Western Writers of America and Women Writing the West and currently lives in the Leech Lake area of Minnesota with her husband and their three big dogs. Visit her website at: jandpayne.com